Smith's
MONTHLY

*Every Month Original
Novels, Stories, and Articles*

USA Today Bestselling Writer
Dean Wesley Smith

TABLE OF CONTENTS

SHORT STORIES

FULL NOVEL

SERIAL NOVEL

NONFICTION

Smith's Monthly Issue #19

The Writings and Opinions of
Dean Wesley Smith

Introduction
CONSISTENT PRODUCTION

The question I get the most often now about *Smith's Monthly* is how do I do this month after month after month.

For 19 months now, give or take.

Honestly, when I stop and look at the fact that this has happened every month for 19 months, I wonder the same thing. But honestly, because it's fun, it hasn't been that hard.

And a couple factors make the production of this magazine even easier.

First off, at WMG Publishing, I have fantastic help.

These pages are copyedited by a wonderful woman named Judy. Thank you, Judy.

And the publisher of WMG Publishing, Allyson, makes sure this project gets out in quality form by doing all the electronic formatting herself and making sure it is loaded to all the sites. Thank you, Allyson.

I do the paper (and pdf file) formatting, but then Billy at WMG Publishing makes sure the subscribers get everything as soon as they can. Thanks, Billy.

So I have a team at WMG Publishing to help me. Every month. I doubt I could do this without them.

That is the first major factor that has allowed this magazine to continue for 19 months.

The second major factor is that every month my wife, writer Kristine Kathryn Rusch, reads the new novels that are in these pages and helps me fine tune them to be the best they can be. Thanks, Kris.

But the original question I know is asking about how I write this much.

And that is where the third major factor comes into play.

How do I write this much?

One word at a time, actually.

Thanks for the Support

Dean Wesley Smith

But the real answer to that can be found on my blog every day. I write about the process of my writing there and have been tracking it since this project started almost two years ago.

I also have some help out of my past in two ways.

I was raised reading in the 1950s and early 1960s. I love the novels of that period. And most modern readers don't realize that the novels up until the late 1980s were much shorter than they are today. Most novels (not all, but most) were around 50,000 words.

So when I started into writing my own novels without New York publishing contracts to force me to write longer, I naturally went back to writing novels in the 40,000 to 60,000 word range like the ones I read when growing up. That has helped and given me room in each issue for four or five short stories.

And here is where the second part of my past has come in to help. I have been writing short stories and publishing them for over 30 years. I have written a lot of short stories.

Most of those stories I am very proud of, but they have been buried in old anthologies or magazine pages and completely forgotten. So on months I didn't have time to write short stories, or was writing short stories for other markets, as I did this month, I have stories to put in these pages that are new to most readers.

That is one of the many things I love about this new world of publishing. Stories I wrote twenty-five years ago can now find a brand new audience.

But the most important factor in having this magazine make it 19 issues is you, the reader.

You bought this on a web site, picked it up in a bookstore, subscribed, or supported my blog efforts on Patreon. Readers, all of you, are the reason I am going on and this magazine will keep going into the future.

So thank you to all the wonderful staff at WMG Publishing for the support.

And thanks to Kris for being the best first reader any writer could ever ask for.

But most of all, thanks to all of you who keep buying these issues.

It is all very much appreciated. Now onward.

Dean Wesley Smith
April 18th, 2015
Lincoln City, Oregon

Coming Next Issue in Smith's Monthly

The Full Novel All in One Place
That was First Serialized in These Pages!

THE LIFE AND TIMES OF BUFFALO JIMMY

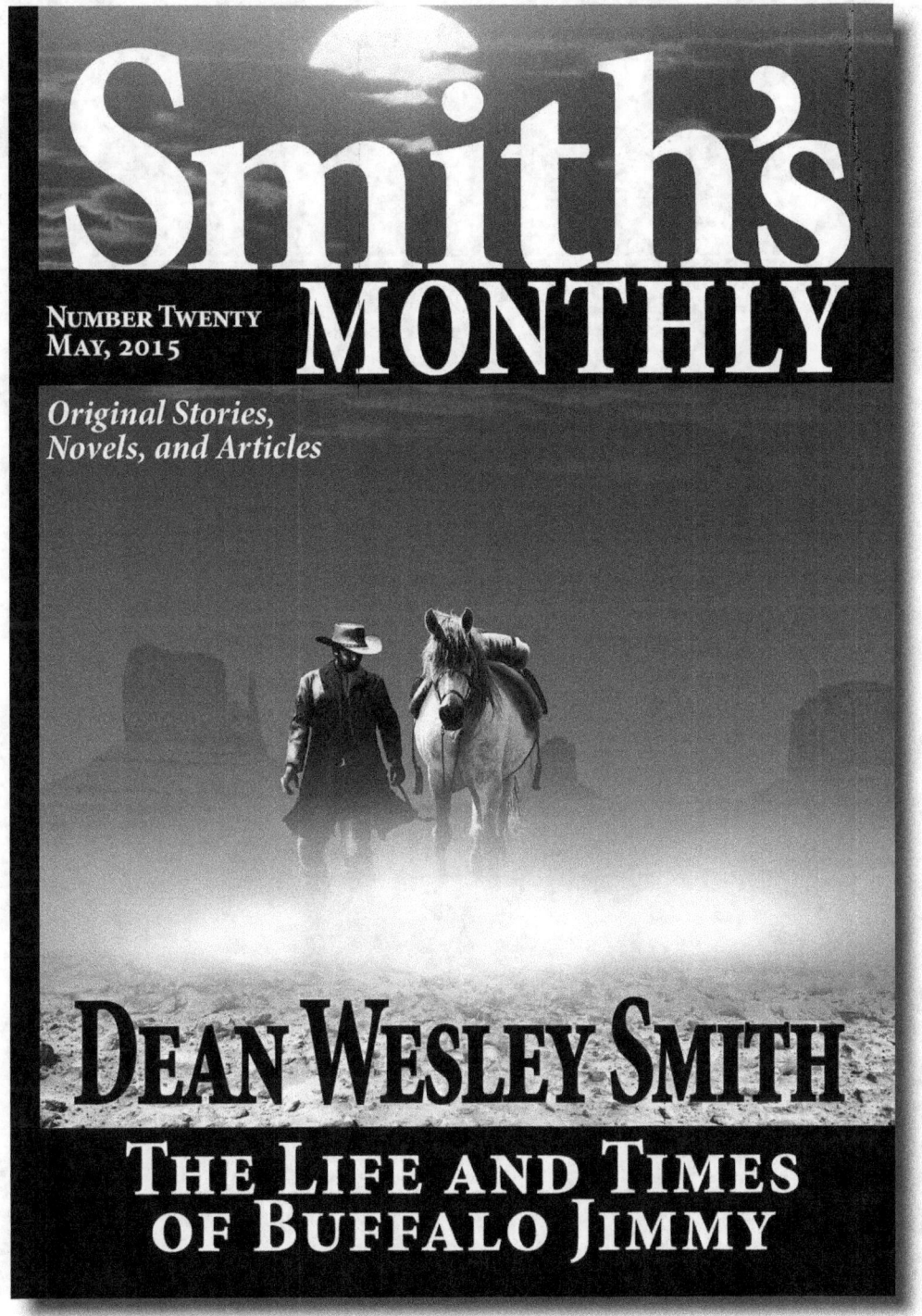

Smith's MONTHLY

NUMBER TWENTY
MAY, 2015

*Original Stories,
Novels, and Articles*

DEAN WESLEY SMITH

THE LIFE AND TIMES
OF BUFFALO JIMMY

USA TODAY BESTSELLING AUTHOR

DEAN WESLEY SMITH

THE
ATLANTIS FIFTY

A POKER BOY STORY

The desire to party often causes all sorts of problems. But Poker Boy never expected one of those problems to be frozen in time.

But being frozen inside a time bubble seems to be the least of the problems. They don't play poker in Atlantis.

First published in Fiction River.

THE ATLANTIS FIFTY
A Poker Boy Story

1

I GOT STUCK in an instant of time on Saturday afternoon at 12:37 and seven seconds, exactly.

Actually, I woke up stuck.

I knew something was very wrong the instant I woke up. Not only was my warning voice telling me something was wrong, but the sounds were gone from the Las Vegas Strip that normally filled the background of Patty's apartment like a faint sound of the ocean when you stay near the beach.

I could hear nothing.

Either I had gone deaf while sleeping, or something else was going on.

I tapped the bed stand with my alarm clock and heard the sound of my knuckle on the fine oak just fine.

Nope. Not deaf.

Patty wasn't in bed beside me, but I figured she hadn't been up long. We had both been up until after four in the morning last night, her working until three at the MGM Grand and me playing in a tournament in the poker room there.

And then we had enjoyed a wonderful half hour before sleeping.

That memory made me smile.

I strained to hear anything, at that point not thinking I was between moments in time. That usually takes me some focus to do and focus while I am sleeping is not one of my superpowers.

No sound.

My warning sense that something was very wrong was dinging in the back of my head like an annoying microwave timer that wouldn't shut off.

I rolled out of the big bed, shoving the thick tan comforter aside, and padded to the window across the soft brown carpet in my boxer shorts.

I pulled the blinds aside slightly and the night shade and after my eyes adjusted to the bright light, I knew instantly what the problem was.

There over Las Vegas, at about two thousand feet, was an airliner turning to make a final approach into the airport. Only it wasn't moving. It was just stuck there, as if someone had glued a decal to a phony blue-sky ceiling in a bedroom.

Now, don't get me wrong. I love my ability to step into a moment of time, out of the normal time flow. It's my second favorite superpower right behind being able to teleport. But unless I do the stepping between moments purposefully, or have another superhero or god put me in a time bubble, I didn't much like being out of whack with the real ticking of time.

I took a deep breath and imagined myself back in the normal flow of time. That's what I always did to drop a time bubble that I made.

Nothing.

Intense silence.

Not even the deep breath helped.

No wonder my alarm dinger was going off in the back of my head. Something was very wrong.

I headed for the bathroom. Patty Ledgerwood, aka Front Desk girl and my girlfriend, was in the shower, her head thrown back as water ran down her long brown hair.

Only the water wasn't actually running, more like glistening in sparkling droplets all over her as if someone had taken a still picture of her.

I can say without any chance of argument that she had a perfect body. And every detail, from her smooth skin to her deep brown eyes fit together.

Now I was no different than any other young man growing up. What stood frozen in front of me was any teenage boy's fantasy. A beautiful woman with a perfect body, naked in a shower, caught in a moment of sheer beauty, every perfect detail magnified by the wetness.

Even as a superhero, I wasn't immune to that, so for an instant after I opened the shower door, I stopped and stared.

Sometimes even emergencies can take a back seat to an opportunity of a lifetime.

So I stood there for a moment, just a moment, staring. Honest, it was only a moment.

And all I could do was ask myself how I had gotten so lucky as to have that woman in my life?

Finally I eased forward, feeling almost guilty, and touched her shoulder, bringing her into the time bubble with me.

The water around her ran off, but no more water came out of the faucet.

"Up for a rematch from last night?" she asked, turning to face me and giving me that smile that often made me forget everything around me.

And her being nude and wet like that was just damn near impossible for me to resist.

"In a little bit," I said, leaning forward and kissing her. "We have a problem I can't seem to get a handle on."

Her expression turned serious, and she turned to shut off the water. Then she realized it was no longer running, even though the faucet was turned on.

"Are we between moments in time?" she asked, looking at me.

Wow, another reason I loved this woman so much. She was scary smart. I nodded.

"How come?" she asked, quickly stepping past me and wrapping a blue bath towel around that fantastic body, making me slightly sad I had said anything.

"I woke up out of time," I said.

Back before I was a superhero, those were words I never would have imagined saying unless I was late for an appointment, or the start of a poker tournament.

"Can you clear us?"

I shook my head. "I don't think I did this one."

"Let's get some clothes on and call Stan," she said. "See if he has any idea what's happened."

"That's why I came to get you out of the shower," I said.

She laughed as she worked to dry off. "Sure it wasn't just to stare?"

"Well," I said as I headed back into the bedroom, "I did a little of that as well."

"Pervert," she shouted after me.

"Guilty and loving it," I shouted back.

I could hear her laugh as I worked to get dressed.

2

PATTY PUT ON her comfortable clothes, which were jeans and a white blouse. She pulled her hair back and didn't bother with any make-up. She looked fantastic and I told her so.

I also had on jeans, but wore a tee-shirt under my black leather jacket and fedora-like hat that served as my Poker Boy uniform. The hat and coat somehow helped me focus energy. I didn't need them inside the apartment, but in emergency situations like this, I felt better having them on.

When we were both completely dressed and had breakfast bars half eaten, we moved into the center of Patty's living room. I had tried a couple of times to drop back into the normal flow, without success.

And I had Patty stand across the room from me and I made myself concentrate on releasing her.

Nothing.

Around us the tan furniture and tan rug seemed completely normal. Everything seemed normal except the clock on the wall near the kitchen door was stopped.

So I was stuck between instants of time, and from what I could tell, I had brought Patty into the mess as well. But if I hadn't, she would have been really, really mad at me. I just never considered not including her these days in anything I did. We were so much stronger together than we were on our own.

"Stan, a little help?" I said at the ceiling. For some reason, every time I called out to my boss, the God of Poker, I shouted upwards. I was fairly certain he could hear me if I just said his name softly, but the old habit died hard.

Patty and I both stood there in her living room, waiting. Usually he appeared almost instantly, but after about five seconds I looked at Patty and shook my head.

"Laverne?" I shouted at the ceiling, hoping that Lady Luck herself would hear me.

Nothing.

We had no access to my team this time around.

"Let me see if I can jump us to my office and get out of this," I said.

Instantly I had alarm bells go off in the back of my head and Patty touched my arm and shook her head. "That feels wrong."

"I agree," I said, pushing back the alarm bells.

My little voice was telling me the problem was here and we needed to stay here and solve this. But it was really, really odd that my calling Stan or Laverne couldn't get out of this. They never had had troubles with coming into time bubbles before.

I went over to the window in the living room and looked at the frozen city below. The cars on The Strip were frozen in place, a couple of birds were stopped in midair a few floors below, and flags on the top of a building across the street hung at odd angles, clearly blown by a wind, but yet not moving.

I looked back at Patty who stood there staring at me.

"Do you have any idea how many gods or superheroes have the power to take a person between moments of time?" I asked, moving back over toward her.

She shook her head slowly as she thought, her long brown hair flopping around on her back as she did. "It's not many, I know that. And you are the only superhero that I know that has that power."

I wasn't sure what to think of that, but at the moment I didn't let myself dwell on it.

"Seems we have some spare time on our hands," I said, smiling at the worried look on her face and in her wonderful dark-brown eyes. "We might as well enjoy it."

The worried look turned to puzzlement.

I shrugged.

"We're trapped in a moment in time," I said. "Someone did this. It's either a widespread thing or a focused event and I'm betting on focused around the person who did it, since it takes some real power to hold a time bubble for very long that's very large. And to include us, it has to be pretty large, so I don't expect this to last that long."

She nodded. "Good point. Any way to know how far this bubble extends?"

I stopped and thought about that for a moment. In the past, when I held a time bubble, as I called them, keeping myself and others out of the flow of regular time, there was a limit. I once had a dog inside a time bubble and it couldn't get out, the edge of the bubble held it until I released the bubble.

I remember thinking that it would be a good and easy trap for anything wild, except that so far I hadn't learned how to project a bubble I wasn't inside of. And being trapped inside a time bubble with something wild hadn't really appealed to me, so I had tossed that idea out.

"I have a question," I said. "Was I supposed to be part of this bubble or just an accident?"

"If you are included only by accident, by bringing me in as well must be draining more energy," Patty said.

"Of whoever is doing this," I said.

"Let's go exploring and see if we can find the edge," I said, heading for the front door to her apartment.

Patty's apartment was on the seventeenth floor. Outside the corridor looked like a plush hotel hallway, with lamps scattered along the hallway and each door recessed into its own entryway.

The carpet was light blue and the walls painted off-white with hotel-like art that depicted nothing hung on the walls. Four elevators were near the center of the building.

No one was in the hall.

"What's going to happen when we find the edge of the bubble?" Patty asked.

"My gut sense is that it will be like walking into a wall," I said. "So walk slow and protect your face."

"Good to know," she said, laughing and shaking her head.

We slowly walked the entire length of the hallway with arms extended in front of us. We must have looked pretty silly, almost walking like movie zombies.

No edge to be found.

"That's an impressive-sized bubble," I said when we reached the other end of the hallway and stopped.

There were two floors above hers and we headed for the stairs to the left and slowly worked our way upward.

We made it all the way to the top floor without finding the edge to the time bubble.

"This is someone very powerful," I said to Patty as we stood outside the

USA Today *bestselling writer Dean Wesley Smith returns with a second novel to the world of* Dust and Kisses *from the first issue of* Smith's Monthly.

Together, Callie and Fisher work to discover the secrets of a galaxy that have been hidden in plain sight, even from the powerful humans who had rescued millions.

And in the process, they just might change everything.

Now Available
from all your favorite booksellers in trade paper and electronic editions.

stairway door in the upper hallway, the blue carpet making me feel more like standing on water than a floor. Here there were only four doors to the four expensive penthouses that filled this floor. I had no idea who lived on this floor, but my gut sense it was someone powerful and very rich in the local area.

The fear I was starting to feel suddenly twisted my stomach around the breakfast bar. I pushed it down and took a slow breath, getting my nerves under control.

"This might be generated mechanically," Patty said.

I looked around at the building and walls and windows and the lights on the walls. Damn she was smart and had the ability to see things I just flat missed.

"I think you might be right," I said. "This kind of field could be generated or amplified through the electrical system. So it would cover the entire building like a skin. A mechanical field might block calling out to Stan or Laverne because natural fields have never blocked me calling them before."

"Good thing we didn't try jumping out of here," she said.

"We'd have smashed right into the bubble wall," I said, glad our warning senses had stopped us. "That might have been painful or worse."

She nodded. "We still don't know why anyone would do this."

"I'm getting the sense that whoever did this is not after us," I said. "My warning bells are not going off, except when I suggested we jump to the office."

"Neither are mine," Patty said. "I bet that whoever did this didn't realize you were here and that the time field wouldn't get to you."

"I wonder why it didn't," I said.

"We'll ask Stan about that later," Patty said, smiling at what must have been my puzzled look. "Now we need to figure out who is doing this and why."

However, I had no idea how to find out that simple thing.

At that moment, the stairwell door at the other end of the hall rattled and stated to open.

"Freeze," I whispered to Patty and we both struck a pose we could hold that made us look like we were just two people frozen in time standing in the hallway.

It looked like we were going to find out who was doing this sooner, rather than later.

3

"THERE YOU ARE," Stan, the God of Poker, said as he came through the stairwell door and into the hall.

I released the breath I think I had been holding and relaxed.

Stan had on his normal button-down sweater and tan slacks. He could blend in anywhere and right now he seemed to almost blend in with the hallway as well, even though his colors seemed to clash with the blue carpet. It wouldn't surprise me if I looked away and looked back, he would be wearing blue slacks.

Right behind him was Screamer, dressed in jeans and a dress shirt with the sleeves rolled up. Screamer was a superhero who worked for the police. He got his name because he could put images in criminal's minds that made them scream in terror.

He was my height at about six foot and had intense dark eyes that seemed to see through things.

Through the door behind Screamer came Ben, a god in the library area and the oldest of our team. He was panting from climbing the stairs.

I had no idea how old Ben really was, but his old-fashioned suits and wrinkled face and hands made him look like a grandfather from a classic movie.

I was very, very glad to see them.

"Did you hear my call?" I asked as Patty and I stepped toward them.

"I did," Stan said. "But I couldn't jump into the building, so I stopped time for me and Ben and Screamer and we managed to merge fields with this time field down in the lobby."

"Twenty floors. Long climb," Ben said, still panting.

"So ever seen anything like this before?" I asked Stan. "Ever have anyone do a time bubble this large?"

He shook his head. "And neither has Laverne. It basically covers this entire building like a skin."

"More than likely run through the electrical system," I said.

Stan looked at me for a moment, clearly thinking, then nodded. "Possible."

"But why?" Patty said.

"I've been wondering the same thing," Screamer said.

"As have I," Ben said, still panting slightly.

"Anyone in a personal time bubble," Patty said, "can walk around just fine without generating something this large to take an entire building out of time. You would get the same effect with just a personal bubble."

That very problem had been bothering me as well. Clearly, if Stan and the rest entered down on the main floor and came up, the bubble holding this building was in the walls and covered the entire building. Patty was right, there was no reason to do that.

None.

Unless...

"Maybe doing something like this," I said, sort of sweeping my arms around me in a grand fashion, "in the walls or electrical wiring of a building, is the only way for whoever did this to generate a time bubble field."

"Mechanical only," Ben said, nodding. "Not a god power. Possible."

"Seen anything like this before?" Patty asked just a fraction of a second before I could.

"Crystals," Ben said, nodding. "In the old Atlantis days."

It always freaked me out a little when someone I knew as a regular person here in Las Vegas started talking about Atlantis. Not the casino, the actual continent and civilization that had actually existed and then had been destroyed. And more often than not, that person had actually been alive during the time of Atlantis.

Stan nodded. "I sort of remember hearing something like that from Laverne once."

"Do you remember who was doing it back then?" I asked Ben, then realized how stupid my question was. His memory was amazing and he could remember every detail and information in every book he had ever read.

"The God of Electricity," Ben said. "Actually, the real experiments in time and electrical powers were done by her assistant."

"Oh, no," Stan said, shaking his head.

Screamer and Patty and I just stared at my boss until Screamer finally said, "You want to fill us in on the problem?"

Ben nodded and took over from Stan, who for the God of Poker, looked suddenly very upset.

"Far before Atlantis, a giant by the name of Arges was the God of Lightning. He was a fan of Zeus and gave him the power to fire electrical bolts, which is why Zeus became known after centuries as being able to use lightning as a weapon."

I so wanted to ask about so much of this, because as I had discovered in my short years of being a superhero, the gods of mythology had often existed, and some of them still did. I had never heard if Zeus was still around, and had never had the courage to ask, to be honest.

Ben went on, with me saying nothing.

"When the gods and the giants managed to banish the Titans to the city that lies under Las Vegas, Arges was injured in the battle and he stepped down and gave his duties over to his daughter, who was a god. He died from his injuries before Atlantis came into being."

"Who was his daughter?" I asked.

Ben looked at me very puzzled, then said, "I need to spend some time with you getting you up to speed on the history of the gods, don't I?"

"I've been saying that," I said. "At least to myself."

"When this is over," Ben said, giving me that grandfather look he sometimes gave me, "we'll make the time."

"Laverne is Arges's daughter," Stan said. "Back in Atlantis, as Laverne was taking over more and more duties, she gave the duty of electricity to the Goddess Horae, a good friend of hers who also had control over planting and seasons and things like that."

"And a young man, a superhero of sorts," Ben said, "began work for Horae as Atlantis boomed. Over the centuries there, he got himself in and out of many troubles with his experiments with electricity and using it in different forms of travel and controlling time."

"What's his name?" Patty asked, again right before I could.

Ben shrugged. "Nothing worth pronouncing right now. Last I heard, in Atlantis, he went by Nicky."

"Still a superhero?" Screamer asked.

Ben nodded. "Last time I heard, still officially working for Horae, when or if she can ever track him down. He used to throw some wild parties, which is what caused part of his problems."

"And he could do things like this time bubble over the building?" I asked Ben.

"More than likely he could."

I didn't like the sounds of that. "When was the last time anyone saw him?"

Ben glanced at Stan, who only shrugged. "Atlantis," Ben said, "about sixty years before it was destroyed."

Okay, that silenced our little group standing in the blue and white plush hallway inside a giant time bubble.

For some reason my friends thought a guy who hadn't been seen in more thousands of years than I wanted to think about had done this to a modern apartment building here in Las Vegas.

I managed to not laugh. "I think we need another suspect."

And that also sent the entire group back into silence.

4

"THERE ARE NO other suspects," Screamer said after a moment of silence in the hallway.

I just didn't think a guy who hadn't been seen since Atlantis was the logical choice, so I changed the point of focus.

"How about we do a search of the entire building," I said. "See if we can find anyone moving."

Stan and Ben both nodded, so I sent Ben and Screamer to one apartment, Stan to another, and Patty and I would handle a third on this floor. Then we would check the last one and work our way down.

However, the search ended just about as quickly as it started.

As we neared the four doors to the four penthouses near the elevators, modern jazz dance music blared out over the hallway, almost vibrating one of the doors. The music seemed to be right out of the 1940s big band era.

Patty looked at me with a puzzled look and all I could do was shrug.

"That form of music was very popular in Atlantis," Ben said softly.

I just shook my head for a moment. Great, just great. Maybe this Nicky guy was inside.

I had no idea what I was walking into, but with Stan at my side and Patty and Ben and Screamer close behind, I used one of my superpowers to unlock the door and slowly eased it open, letting the intense loud music smack me in the face. It sounded like an entire band was just around the corner in the main area of the penthouse apartment.

And then, over the intense music, I caught the sound of laughing and talking.

Lots of laughing and lots of talking. Actually more like shouting, since that was all anyone could do over that amount of noise.

I eased around a corner of the entryway so I could see the huge main room of the penthouse and then just stood there, my mouth open, staring at about fifty people dancing, all dressed in brightly-colored robes and togas and all barefoot on the plush white carpet. The expensive white furniture had been pushed back to the sides to form the large dance floor.

The main room of the big apartment was completely full of people.

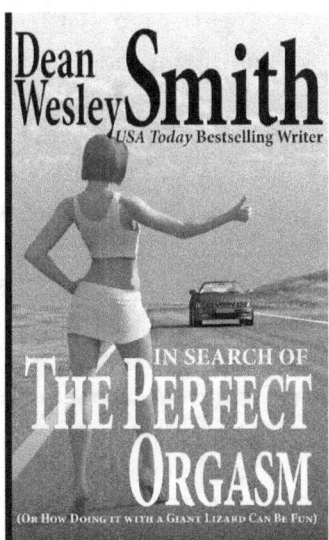

Everyone was young and all clearly having a great time.

I felt like I had walked into a college frat party. I hated drunken kids' parties when in college, thought them stupid beyond words and never went to a one, mostly because I never joined a fraternity or any other group for that matter.

I didn't much care for the party I was staring at either.

There were so many colors jumping up and down and swirling around, I almost got dizzy trying to watch it.

Suddenly, one of the dancers on the edge of the mob spotted us and smiled and broke away from his partner, a blonde with far too much long hair that seemed to function as a second robe and only allowed glimpses of her smiling face.

The guy coming toward us had long brown hair that looked like it was cut by putting a bowl over his head. He had on a brown robe that seemed a cross between a bathrobe and a toga.

He was smiling a huge smile that lit up his face and the smile reached his eyes. Beads of sweat had formed on his forehead from the dancing and I noticed the apartment had started to heat up.

None of my alarms were going off about him, so he wasn't a threat. At least I didn't think my alarms had sounded. Even inside my own head, I wasn't certain I would have heard them in this noise.

The music still pounded at me like a hammer and I could tell it was everything Patty could do to not cover her ears.

As the kid got closer, he went straight at Ben and gave him a hug.

"Uncle Ben," the kid shouted over the noise. "What are you doing here?"

Finally Stan couldn't take it any longer. He took us out of time, instantly silencing the music. I almost staggered at the relief.

"Thank you," Patty sighed softly.

Screamer just shook his head as if trying to clear it.

I didn't know it was possible to have a time bubble inside another time bubble, but it seemed it was. Thankfully.

My ears were ringing and even with that I could tell this guy wasn't a threat.

All the dancers were now frozen in wild positions of movements, bright-colored robes and hair flung all over the place. From a few of the loose robes, I could tell that underwear wasn't a fashion these kids believed in.

"Sorry," the kid who had hugged Ben said, still smiling. "A little loud I suppose, but figured we weren't bothering anyone."

Ben just shook his head and turned to face Stan and the rest of us. "This is my nephew, Nicky."

"From Atlantis?" I blurted out, not even wanting to know how he was Ben's nephew.

"Where else?" Nicky asked, still smiling.

Oh, wow. And I thought I had a lot to learn about history.

5

BEN INTRODUCED US ALL.

Nicky gave Patty a very broad smile and a slight kiss on the back of her hand. He was a real charmer, this guy.

After the introductions, Ben said, "Your mother and Horae have both been very worried about you."

I didn't want to even ask who his mother was.

Nicky actually looked puzzled at that and my alarm bells suddenly went off at full force. This kid had no idea where or when he was.

Not a clue.

"Nicky," I said, indicating the kid should come with me, "I want to show you something."

Ben nodded and I led the young superhero across the room toward the big windows. The others followed me through the frozen crowd until we all stood beside one of the huge floor-to-ceiling windows.

I pointed at The Strip below and then at the desert around the city. "You know where you are?"

He shrugged, looking out over the city. "Never seen the place before," he said. "North quadrant, maybe."

"North quadrant of what?" I asked as Ben shook his head and looked down at the soft white carpet.

"Of Atlantis," Nicky said. "Where else."

I turned to Ben. "What was this area called in the time of Atlantis?"

"This was mostly all ocean and swamp," Ben said softly. "This land mass was much lower at the time, so we really had no name for this area."

Nicky looked at me, then at his uncle, a look of panic starting to cross his face.

"What exactly did you do to make this building be in a time bubble?" I asked.

"Any building," Nicky said. "We all jam into a mountain cabin that I put the bubble around. I can jump the field out of time and have it go around a larger building. That gives us all a place to party and not even be gone more than an hour or so."

"How do you pick the building?" I asked.

He shrugged, looking out over the city below. "I don't. My machine does. Chronos is going to be angry at me for jumping in time, isn't he?"

I ignored that question. "How do all these people get here?"

"Portal near the device down on the ground floor," Nicky said. "Everyone was already in the cabin before I locked up the building. So a portal down on the main floor is the only way in and out. When exactly is this?"

Silence. I couldn't answer him because I honestly didn't know the answer.

Finally Ben said softly, "This time is about eleven thousand years after Atlantis was destroyed."

"Destroyed?" Nicky asked, looking like he might faint at any moment.

"You haven't been seen since about sixty years ahead of the destruction, Ben said."

Now the kid simply dropped to the floor, his eyes blank, his smile long gone.

So we had a young inventor superhero that had brought about fifty people with him through time to the present. We couldn't let him or any of them just go back, because in this history, our history, my history, he didn't go back.

This was going to take a time travel expert far, far smarter than I was to unravel the mess that Nicky had just caused.

I looked around at all the dancers frozen in a moment of pure enjoyment, then down at the young man sitting on the floor staring down at the depths of the plush carpet.

My warning voice was tingling.

Something was still very, very wrong. And I needed to figure out what.

But for the life of me, at the moment I just couldn't ask poor Nicky another question.

Not after the reality he just faced.

6

WE ALL STOOD there in silence until finally what had been worrying me

crawled its ugly way to the surface of my mind. And when it poked out, I shuddered.

I turned to my team, letting Nicky sit on the floor and stew in his own thoughts.

"If this time bubble gets shut off, the bubble is going to haul us back to the past as well with it."

"But it doesn't go back to the past," Stan said, staring at the dancers. "We know that."

"In this timeline," I said.

Stan started to open his mouth and shut it, suddenly lost in his thoughts.

"Have I ever said that time travel gives me a headache?" I asked.

Patty smiled at me as I turned and kneeled down beside Nicky.

"How is this time bubble around the building set to recall?"

"One day exactly from the moment it left," he said. "Automatically. It will return within thirty minutes of leaving."

"And it takes everyone who is inside it at that moment with it?"

"I don't know," he said, shrugging. "I would assume so. This is the first time I've ever tried it. I figured if the bubble took along anyone who didn't belong, I would just send the hitchhikers back where they belonged before they noticed."

Now my stomach was really twisting. We had an untested machine that could take us all at any moment.

I stood and looked at Patty. "Any idea how many people live in this building?"

"Oh, my," she said, her face white. "Maybe around 500 people at any given time."

It was the middle of the afternoon on a Saturday, so not all of them would be in the building, but a large number of them would be.

Stan and Ben and Screamer had been listening and all three of them were just shaking their heads slowly, Stan staring at the dancers.

All my team looked like I was feeling. Shocked.

Around us, all of Nicky's friends from Atlantis remained frozen in different positions of dance, their brightly-colored robes spread out or twisted around them, smiles covering their faces.

If we were inside this building when it shifted back, we would end up in a timeline where Nicky returned to Atlantis with his friends. And everyone from Las Vegas time in this building would go with him and suddenly find themselves thousands of years in the past. And all of them would be lost to this world and all their families.

That would be a missing person's case for the ages.

And if we stopped this, Nicky and his friends would be stuck here, lost to all their families.

And since it was a new invention, who knew if the timer was right or would even work.

Or if it went off, where or when it would send any of us.

Wonderful. Just wonderful.

We were so screwed.

I had to admit, Nicky here had really invented something to cause problems.

"I'm open to ideas," I said, glancing around at my team.

I didn't even have one of my normally stupid ideas or random thoughts.

Patty, Screamer, Ben, and Stan all just stood there looking blankly. We all seemed to understand this was a disaster where no matter what we did, no one won.

"So what's going on?" Laverne demanded as she walked into the room. Lady Luck had on her normal power suit and her hair was pulled back. She also had on tennis shoes instead of her normal dress shoes. More than likely she knew she was going to have to climb twenty flights of stairs when she came into the time bubble.

She looked at the crowd of frozen dancers with a puzzled frown, then looked at Ben. "Why are those kids dressed like they are from an Atlantis college party?"

"Because they are," Ben said.

That made the frown on Lady Luck's face just get deeper.

Behind me, Nicky was climbing to his feet. "Hi, Aunt Laverne," he said, stepping up beside me, his voice soft and his eyes not meeting hers, but instead staying focused firmly on the carpet in front of him.

"Oh, shit," Lady Luck said, seeing him. She clearly understood the situation, or at least part of it, instantly.

She stepped forward and seemed to tower over the cowering Nicky.

"So you are responsible for the greatest mystery in all of Atlantis, the Lost Fifty," she said.

She glanced at Stan, then focused back on Nicky.

Ben was nodding slowly, his gaze also aimed directly at the carpet.

Nicky wisely said nothing.

Lady Luck shook her head, clearly disgusted and saying nothing. Having Lady Luck disgusted at me was my worst nightmare. And I had some horrid nightmares at times, but having her disgusted at me was the worst one.

Finally, Lady Luck turned to look at the frozen dancers, then at Stan, touching his arm slightly for a moment, and then finally she looked at me. "We can't let these kids go back. They did not return in this timeline. They were lost to their families a very long time ago."

I nodded.

"We know that," I said. "But we have another problem as well. Nicky thinks his machine will just take everyone in the building when it automatically jumps."

Beside me Nicky nodded.

"Even the people from this time period who are in time stasis in the building?" Laverne asked, her voice as cold and as angry as I could ever imagine it getting. The windows seemed to vibrate from the tension in her words.

I know I did.

"I think so," Nicky said. "I don't know for sure. It might. I don't know."

I thought the poor kid was going to break into tears, but somehow he just kept staring at the carpet and managed to hold it together.

"Can you just shut it off?" I asked Nicky. I hoped my voice was a little less angry and powerful as Laverne's, but I was so mad at this point, I wasn't sure.

Nicky did exactly as I feared he would do. He shook his head.

"It will return the moment I shut it off," he said.

"Perfect, just perfect," I said to myself. "Where is it exactly?"

"Ground floor, very center of the building," Nicky said.

"Does it have a visible timer on it?"

Again he shook his head.

"Any other way outside this field but through the door on the ground floor?" Stan asked.

Again Nicky just shook his head.

I was stunned. Not only had this kid just destroyed the lives of fifty of his closest friends and their families, if we didn't figure something out quickly, he was going to take all of us as well and who knew how many hundreds with him in this building.

"How long do we have before the time field returns to Atlantis?" Laverne asked directly at Nicky.

"At most ten hours," he said. Then softly he said, "It might be a lot less. I'm sorry."

"Not as sorry as you're going to be when your mother hears about this," Laverne said.

Then Lady Luck turned to me and said simply.

"I'll talk with Chronos and the Fates and see if I can come up with a solution. In the meantime, get everyone out of this building. I'll have the portal downstairs hooked into real time to move with your time here in the building."

I had no idea how she was going to do that, but decided this was not the time to ask.

Then with Nicky by the arm, she turned and yanked the poor kid by the arm toward the apartment door like a mother with a misbehaving three-year-old.

7

WE ALL WATCHED them go. I looked at the fifty dancers and took a deep breath. "We're going to need help and a really amazing cover story for the residents."

"And we're going to need counselors for these kids," Patty said, indicating the dancers, "to help them understand what happened."

"They aren't even going to be speaking English," Ben said. "Nicky could because he's a superhero, but none of these kids will."

"Can we give it to them in some sort of power?" I asked, trying to imagine fifty college kids trying to learn English while dealing with being centuries out of time and their entire country being destroyed and their families killed.

Ben nodded slowly. "We might. For the Atlantis Fifty, we might be able to make exceptions. I'll go find out."

"See if you can find something that will ease their memories as well," I said.

Ben looked at the group of frozen dancers and nodded sadly, understanding exactly what I was saying. With that, he turned and headed for the door and the stairwell for the long climb down.

I turned to Screamer. "We're going to need Johnny's help on this and any other police we can trust. And a bunch more we're going to have to fool with a cover story."

Johnny was Detective Johnny State. He was also a superhero working for the police department. I had worked with Johnny on numbers of cases, including the first case when I met Patty.

"That's going to take a really good cover story," Screamer said.

"Some sort of phony virus," I said, "that everyone in the building might have been exposed to, so we take everyone to a holding area and then when the time bubble jumps, we let them return, giving them all clear."

I was making this up as I went, but that sounded like it might work. We get the Atlantis Fifty, as Ben called the dancers frozen around us, out first and isolated, then we work on the normal residents.

"I'll get some help from the gods of health," Patty said, "to come up with something logical, but not too bad, but that would require this kind of action."

"Stan," I said, turning to my boss. "If you can hold this time bubble inside Nicky's bubble, do you think it's going to be possible to release a set area of residents from his mechanical bubble?"

Stan shook his head, turning his attention from the dancers. "I don't think so. It doesn't work that way, and since this is mechanical, I doubt I can block it."

"How did I release Patty?" I asked.

"She's a superhero," Stan said.

I thought I was discouraged before, now I was really about to lose it.

"Oh, no," Patty said, shaking her head.

I took a deep breath and came up with the only solution I could think of.

"So we move maybe up to five hundred frozen people by stretcher to the entrance, down flights of stairs. Nothing to it, right?"

Silence in a room full of dancers.

I turned to the love of my life. "We're going to need even more help from the medical side of this than we thought," I said. "Because everyone has to be taken by ambulance to the hospital. Only way any cover story will work when they all snap back into real time going out that doorway Laverne is setting up."

Patty nodded.

"Our cover story could be some gas that knocked them all out," I said. "And has no lasting problems with it."

"Better than a virus," Screamer said, nodding.

I turned to Screamer. "Johnny's going to need his girlfriend from the paper to cover this as well. We're going to need help to keep this from turning into a panic that will empty the city."

Again everyone stood silently.

Then Patty said simply, "I don't think we have enough time."

"Time is the enemy no matter what we do," I said.

"Ain't that the truth," Screamer said.

I kissed Patty and told her to get going.

She nodded and went with Screamer out the door almost at a run.

I looked at my boss. "Can you hold the dancers?" I asked.

He nodded.

"I'm going to go scout out where the local residents are to save a little time while we're waiting for the cavalry to arrive."

He nodded and dropped down onto a couch, staring at the Atlantis Fifty, saying nothing.

There just wasn't any more to say at the moment. All I knew was that I didn't really want to see Atlantis. At least not on a one-way ticket to a time sixty years before it was destroyed.

8

I CHECKED OUT the other penthouse apartments. They were really nice, and luckily no one was home in any of them.

On the floor below there were six apartments, all the size of Patty's apartment.

In two I found guys watching television. In two others I found only a woman home, both of them also watching television. The other two apartments were empty.

I was starting to understand how really lucky we had gotten that this happened on a Saturday afternoon.

On the floor above Patty's, I found twelve people in the six apartments. Four were playing cards in one, two kids about twenty-something were making love and were pretty tangled up together, which was going to get interesting to say the least.

They both might need counseling after this was over, one moment going at it with their partner, the next on a stretcher going out the front door of the building.

So in three floors I had sixteen people.

I heard some commotion in the staircase outside and went out to find Patty and Screamer headed back up.

I went with them back to the top floor and back into the room full of the brightly clothed dancers.

Stan was still just sitting there, seemingly lost in his own thoughts.

"Medical equipment and ambulances are headed this way," Patty said. "We've got all the gods and superheroes who could get free working this. But not everyone outside is with us, so we'll have to be careful outside the building."

"Are they coming up with stretchers?" I asked and Patty nodded. 'They should arrive here in about ten minutes."

"No one I could find on this floor," I said. "But we'll need to check again to make sure."

"Police already have the building surrounded and roads blocked off and press held back," Screamer said. "Johnny and two people he can trust are coming up in a few minutes."

Less than thirty minutes. I was impressed.

"So now we have to get these kids moving," Stan said.

"I think we should wait for Ben and Laverne," I said. "We have a language problem."

"I speak their language," Stan said softly.

I kind of looked at my boss, who seemed very, very upset by all this. Usually he was calm and clear, but now he just sat staring at the dancers.

I glanced at Patty and she shrugged.

"You want to tell me what's going on," I said to my boss, going over and dropping onto the couch beside him.

"We don't have time," he said, shaking his head, but not moving to stand.

"I want to wait for Laverne and Ben and help from other gods to help ease these kids' transition," I said firmly. "They can all walk down anyhow. So taking the time is worth the gamble."

He nodded, clearly agreeing.

"So what happened?"

My little voice sort of told me the answer, so I went ahead and asked anyway. "Did you know some of these kids?"

He nodded.

"Which ones?" I asked, my voice gentle. It never would have occurred to me that I would have to be gentle with my boss, the God of Poker.

"The two twins," he said, pointing to two brown-haired girls dancing almost back-to-back near the center.

Patty gasped and I sort of did the same the moment I focused on them. They looked just like Stan.

"Are they superheroes?" I asked softly.

"Not yet," he said. "They will be."

"Your daughters?"

He nodded.

All I wanted to do was be sick.

9

ALL FOUR OF US remained silent after that until Ben and Laverne suddenly appeared on the edge of the room.

"Thank you," Ben said to her.

"We can teleport inside the bubble?" I asked.

Laverne nodded.

I turned to Patty.

She was ahead of me, already turning for the door. "I'll cancel the stretchers coming up, have them stage on the main floor. I'll get it set up."

Being able to teleport inside this bubble was the first good news we had gotten in this mess.

I stood and Laverne looked at Stan, a feeling of complete sadness on her face.

"Stan, you should be able to bring your daughters out before we do the rest," she said. "Get them out of here."

He nodded, took a deep breath and stood. "I'll explain what happened and they will help get their friends rescued. Give us a few minutes."

Laverne started to object, then nodded.

Then Stan moved into the dancers and touched one daughter on the shoulder, than the other, bringing them out of the time bubble he held the rest of the dancers in.

"Dad," the one closest to the window said, glancing around at her frozen friends. "What are you doing?"

"Yeah, does mom know you are breaking up our party?" the other asked.

Stan shuddered and then with another deep breath said, "Follow me."

I glanced at Ben and he waved that I should not ask, even though at that moment I would have never asked.

In my head I heard Laverne's voice. *His first wife killed herself when they lost their two daughters. Never ask him about it, ever.*

Understood, I thought back at her.

Stan took his two daughters toward a bedroom in the back of the huge penthouse. I did not envy him at all what he was about to tell those two girls.

I couldn't even comprehend it, to be honest. It just made my stomach twist into little knots.

Laverne looked at me, then nodded that I should go ahead with the plan.

"Let's give Stan the time," I said. "I will start clearing out residents, jumping them to the main floor. There should be a place down there we can store them until stretchers can take them outside."

Laverne nodded, staring at the door where Stan and his daughters had vanished.

"Ben, you stay here to help when Stan and his daughters need the help."

He nodded.

"Screamer," I said. "I know where people are on the two floors below. Go down to Patty's floor and start scouting. And work with Johnny when he gets here."

"Got it," Screamer said and turned and headed for the door.

"Stop a moment," Lady Luck said to Screamer. She waved a hand at him. "I just unblocked what was holding you from learning how to teleport."

She turned to me. "Have him jump with you on the first couple, then he can start moving people down as well. Have Johnny and his people do the scouting ahead."

Screamer started to open his mouth, his eyes wide, then he said simply, "Thank you."

Lady Luck waved her hand and sat down on the couch were Stan had been sitting. "You earned it and you would have figured it out eventually, and now you and my daughter can be together easier."

I smiled and grabbed his arm before he could say anything. He was married to Sherri, one of Lady Luck's daughters, and she lived in Reno while he lived here in Vegas.

I jumped us one floor down to where a guy was sitting in shorts and a tee-shirt watching a football game. The apartment was done in brown tones and had heavy tan drapes blocking out the sun. The television he was watching was huge and from what I could tell, the program was in commercial.

The guy looked to be around sixty and slightly overweight.

"Holy crap, what just happened?" Screamer asked, looking at me.

"Lady Luck just helped you get another power. Don't question it. You'll have time to figure it all out later. We got a lot of people and our own butts to save."

Screamer nodded.

I walked across the room. "See this spot?" I asked, pointing at the carpet beside me.

He nodded.

"Jump to it."

"How?" he asked, looking puzzled.

"I imagine myself in the new spot and then think I am there."

He nodded, focused at the spot beside me, and the next instant he was there, facing past me at the drawn drapes of the apartment.

"It worked," he said softly, shaking his head. "I thought the word *jump* and it happened."

"That sometimes works for me as well," I said. "Jump into the kitchen next." I pointed at the open kitchen on the other side of a brown counter with barstools against it.

Almost instantly he was there.

Then he jumped back beside me.

"Wow, just wow," he said. He was smiling like a kid at Christmas getting everything he asked for.

"I'm going to jump this guy and both of us to the main floor area," I said. "You can work on more there."

He nodded and I imagined the frozen guy and Screamer linked to me and I jumped to the main floor of the apartment building.

I was surprised to see so much activity going on. It was lucky I had tucked us off into a corner, otherwise someone might have seen us appear.

Patty sensed me at once and came running over.

The guy I had jumped with was on the floor, his back against the wall.

"Screamer can now teleport," I told her. "Where do we bring the residents down to so we aren't seen?"

Patty nodded to Screamer and smiled. "Great, we're going to need the help."

Then she showed us an area near the freight elevator where two people were setting up thick mats to help the residents of the building not get hurt. It was tucked around a corner and was big enough to get stretchers in close, but yet not be seen by anyone who shouldn't see people appearing and disappearing.

"We're telling people we're bringing people down the freight elevator and staircase here," she said. "We already have everyone who was on this level out and on the way to the hospital in ambulances."

I kissed her quickly. "Great job. We'll be back with more shortly."

She nodded and I turned to Screamer. "Remember the spot in that last apartment?"

He nodded.

"Jump there."

He vanished.

I followed him and he was standing there in the apartment smiling when I arrived.

"So how do I jump when I don't know where I'm going?" he asked.

"You know," I said.

He frowned.

"The apartment next door has a man in it," I said. "Can you sort of sense it, sense the apartment?"

After a moment he nodded slowly.

"Jump there, get the guy and I'll meet you downstairs."

"Do I have to touch the guy to jump him?" Screamer asked.

"Just imagine a link between you and the person. And then when you get ready to jump, imagine that link solid and that person coming with you."

"Wow, our minds are powerful, aren't they?"

"Don't question it," I said, smiling at him. "Like walking. Never think about it. Just do it."

He nodded and then vanished.

I went to get the woman from the apartment across the hall.

Screamer beat me to the main floor with his person, but not by much.

10

JOHNNY AND TWO other super-heroes working for the Las Vegas Police scouted apartments ahead of Screamer and me as we worked our way down the building floor-by-floor.

It seemed to be taking much, much longer than it needed to take, but we were making sure that no one was missed.

At one point Patty told me between jumps that Stan and Laverne and Ben had jumped all the kids to the main floor and had them all walk out into two waiting Greyhound buses. She said that they got safely away from the building and were being taken to a large lodge in the mountains where they could get the kids help and let them rest and get them started on learning what they were going to need to learn to survive in this new world.

"And counseling, I hope," I said.

"I can't imagine why not," Patty said, a very sad look on her face. "They all lost everything today. Their parents, their families, their entire world. Everything they knew and took for granted is gone."

I just shook my head. I didn't want to let myself think about the Atlantis Fifty at the moment. Screamer and I needed to keep going.

So I kissed her and thanked her for telling me and jumped to the next person.

Two other gods from hotel and apartment management areas joined in helping Screamer and me when we reached the eleventh floor since they could teleport. Four of us were about as fast as the ambulances could handle the load of people. Luckily the hospital was very close.

And since none of the residents of the building were actually sick, they all would be released fairly quickly.

As the hours went by, Patty made sure the main floor was cleared of anyone who didn't need to be in the building.

Screamer and I were bringing down the last two residents from the third floor. Both were young women who had been having coffee together at an apartment kitchen counter.

The second floor had already been emptied by the two gods from Patty's area. They were now all gone.

Patty and two others were waiting with stretchers. Both of the others looked like paramedics. Both paramedics were young women and intent in their job.

They helped the two residents we had brought down carefully on to the stretchers and covered them.

"This is it," I said. "Let's all get out of here."

We turned for the door.

We didn't make it.

So close.

11

A SHIMMERING went through the air.

It seemed the lights blinked, but I couldn't be sure on that.

The world spun for just a second, then snapped down solid again.

I glanced around.

Patty, Screamer, two superhero paramedics from the medical world, and the two building residents were standing around me in a cabin that smelled of pine and a cold fireplace. Everyone had a shocked and worried look.

I was sure I was no exception to that.

Only a couple lights were on in the big, high-ceilinged room and curtains were pulled tight over the big windows.

"Oh, no," Patty said softly.

"We didn't make it," Screamer said.

One of the residents of the building looked around and asked, "What just happened?"

Screamer nodded to the superhero paramedics and then reached over and touched the two residents lightly. They both fell instantly asleep.

The paramedics caught them both and stretched the residents safely out onto the floor.

That would take care of that problem for a while at least.

I wanted to just sit on the floor with them and bang my fists, but instead I walked over to the closed main door of the big wooden cabin and eased it open. The hinges on the big wooden door actually had the decency to squeak.

The air outside smelled fresh and warm, like the day might be getting warmer soon. The wonderful scent of pine needles hit me next.

The cabin sat on a hillside covered in tall pine-like trees and in the distance I could see the blue hint of a lake.

Tucked off to one side of the cabin were ten cars like I had never seen. They all looked like they had been designed by a 1950s movie guy trying to imagine what a car of the future would look like.

One of them even had a bubble on it that covered six different seats.

They looked very, very much out of place in the rustic mountain setting.

Those cars were the transportation for the Atlantis Fifty, more than likely.

A highway seemed to wind along the hill below. From where we were, I could hear high humming sounds that seemed to come from the vehicles buzzing past.

Not gas engines, that was for sure.

Patty stepped up beside me and looked around for a moment.

Then I pushed us both back into the cabin and shut the door.

"Are we where I think we are?" Screamer asked, standing next to the paramedics above the two residents stretched out on the floor.

"We're not in Kansas anymore, that's for sure," I said.

I took a deep breath and tried to think about jumping to my office hovering over Vegas.

Nothing. It wasn't there.

We were over eleven thousand years in the past. And who knew on what timeline.

In other words, we were screwed.

I looked around at the four others expecting me to lead them. I didn't have a clue what to do.

That silence just got too heavy.

"We stay here for a time," I said, finally, trying to sound decisive and in charge. Better than sitting on the floor pounding my fists.

But not much.

"You think Laverne might be able to get to us?" Screamer asked.

I shrugged. "Laverne or Chronos. We have no other hope otherwise, other than to get off this continent in the next sixty years and find a place to live and survive. So we sit tight for now and make it easier on them if they can rescue us."

All four of them nodded, clearly feeling as stunned as I felt. No one wanted to talk anymore about the fine mess we found ourselves in. I was okay with that.

"What happens when they come looking for the missing kids," Screamer asked.

I looked at him. "When that happens, we had better be gone. Somewhere."

That really nailed the silence so we all started looking around.

The place was bigger than it looked at first glance and that Nicky had described. It had a nice living room tucked over to one side with a large stone fireplace and a bunch of comfortable-looking couches and big chairs, all in dark brown tones that seemed to go well with the wood. The couches and chairs weren't shaped that different from anything you would see in a modern furniture store.

The ceiling was high and peaked and had wood beams.

On the opposite side was a kitchen and beyond that what looked like a bathroom. I had a hunch from the looks of those cars out front that using a bathroom in Atlantis might just be a learning experience.

Fifty people would have had no trouble being in here.

I turned to Screamer. "Help me find Nicky's machine."

He nodded and we started for a hallway that led off to what must be bedrooms of some sort.

"How long will they be out?" one of the paramedics asked, pointing at the two women on the floor.

"We haven't been introduced," I said, suddenly realizing I didn't know two of the people I was stuck with. I stopped and turned back. "I'm Poker Boy, this is Screamer, this is Patty."

The one paramedic with short blonde hair said, "My name is Katie."

"I'm Rocha," the taller one with short brown hair said.

Both were clearly in great shape and very strong from their handshakes.

We all did the pleasant stuff, as much as five people can do when trapped thousands of years from home in a world we didn't know. Then Screamer answered Katie's question.

"They will be out eight hours at least," Screamer said. "All harmless, I assure you."

The paramedic superhero nodded. "Let's get them back on a bed if there are any in this place."

"Hang on," I said, and went down the hallway and opened the first door on the right. It was a bedroom all right with a very comfortable large bed that seemed huge.

I jumped the two sleeping building residents onto the bed.

"Might want to straighten them out a little and cover them up," I said.

Katie nodded thanks at me and went into the bedroom.

"Can I do that?" Screamer asked.

I smiled at my friend. "I sure don't see why not."

"I'm going to check out the food supplies," Patty said.

"I'll help you," Rocha said, following her. "I'm hungry."

When she said that I realized I was as well, but I doubted I could eat at the moment.

Screamer and I quickly found Nicky's machine. It was in the bedroom on the left, sitting right in the middle of the floor.

Honestly, it looked more like someone had taken a motor out of a lawn mower and hooked it to the top of some plastic dome.

Only it was like no internal combustion engine I had ever seen. It had what looked like a big blue crystal sticking out of the top of it like a gearshift.

It wasn't humming or making any noise at all. In fact, it didn't even seem to have switches to turn it on or off. But it was glowing slightly.

"Any ideas?" I asked Screamer.

"Besides not touching it?" he said. "Not a one."

We headed back out and joined the other three in the kitchen area.

"Anyone here alive in Atlantis time?" I asked.

I had learned a long time ago that sometimes a superhero or a god could surprise you with how old they were. Since none of us aged much at all after we came into our powers, living a long time seemed to be an option. Ben looked moderately old, but he had been around for far longer than Atlantis. In fact, more than likely, he was here somewhere.

And we knew that Stan and Laverne were living here somewhere as well.

But I don't think we dared contact them. At least not until we gave Laverne some time to mount a rescue operation from our own time.

Of course, since it was time travel, the rescue might come in one hundred years of this time, but only in a half an hour of our Las Vegas time. No way of knowing.

If rescue came at all.

I pushed that thought away. I would deal with that possibility soon enough.

"Not even close to that old," Screamer said, answering my question about anyone being alive in Atlantis.

"I was born in 1930," Rocha said.

"I'm only slightly older," Katie said.

"Not even close," Patty said, smiling at me.

I always felt like the baby around gods and superheroes. This time was no exception.

12

I WAS ABOUT to suggest that Screamer and I explore the back rooms and around the outside of the cabin when Stan appeared.

The wrong Stan.

He was standing with his back to the front door and looked to be the same Stan from our time except for one major exception. He was wearing a brown toga and brown sandals. Even in a toga, he didn't wear anything but bland colors.

"Stan!" I said before my mind processed that more than likely this wasn't the Stan from our time period.

This was the Stan looking for his daughters. More than likely the angry dad Stan who didn't know any of us from a tree.

He frowned slightly, staring at me. "Who are you?"

I knew that tone in his voice. He was already angry.

I started to open my mouth, then stopped myself when warning bells went off in the back of my head.

I glanced at Patty and then Screamer. Both had wide eyes and both were shaking their heads.

The two paramedics were standing off toward the kitchen, just watching, clearly scared but saying nothing.

If we did something wrong here, we could really, really screw up a bunch of timelines. I knew enough about time travel to know that. I just hoped that we could keep Stan under control and thinking this through.

"I don't think I can tell you," I said. "Beyond that we are from your future."

Toga-Stan started to open his mouth, then shut it and stared at me like he was trying to get a read on me.

I had no idea if there was such a thing as poker in Atlantis, which meant I had no idea what area Stan was a god in.

The silence between us grew.

I flat had no idea what to do.

But I did know that anything I did right now that was stupid would doom us to remain in the past.

"Never thought I would ever get here," Stan said from my left.

All of us spun around.

Stan from our time was there, smiling at his toga-self. He had on the same plain clothes he had been wearing earlier.

I don't think I was ever so happy to see someone. I wanted to hug him, I really did.

He looked at me. "We needed that me to arrive here so we could track where and when you exactly were," regular Stan said.

Behind the toga-Stan, Laverne and another older man with a long white beard appeared. Laverne touched toga-Stan on the shoulder. That Stan then slumped gently to the ground.

I recognized the older man with Laverne as Chronos, the God of Time. Or Father Time as many called him. But instead of white robes, he had on a silk business suit with a vest and suspenders. He looked like any really rich old guy you would see on the street.

I couldn't believe how happy I was to see him as well. But not once did the thought of hugging him cross my mind.

A moment later toga-Stan vanished.

"I find him in an hour in my office," Laverne says. "I just put a memory block on him to forget all this until he sees Nicky today in the future. That way he doesn't tell me anything."

That made a lot of sense. It protected the timeline.

Then I thought about it. She had just planted the plan to rescue us in Stan's mind to carry for over eleven thousand years while he was in the middle of rescuing us. Have I ever said how much time travel gives me a headache?

"We need to get out of here," she said.

"Hold on, we have two residents of Patty's building with us," I said.

I nodded to the two paramedics to be ready and then instantly brought the two unconscious women to the front room. The two paramedics expertly caught the two women and held them like they did something like that every day.

"Got everyone now?" Laverne asked.

I nodded and took Patty's hand, feeling her calming influence on me.

Laverne turned to the white-bearded man who seemed to just be standing there smiling slightly as he watched like a grandfather pleased at the actions of his grandchildren.

"A ride home if you wouldn't mind, Burtram?" she asked.

Burtram Chronos? I was never getting that out of my mind.

He smiled and waved his hand.

Without even seeming to move, we were standing in front of the booth in my office that hovered over the Las Vegas Strip.

Laverne and Chronos were gone.

Stan was no longer with us either, more than likely with his daughters. I had a hunch we weren't going to be seeing him much for a time.

Around us the wonderful city of Las Vegas spread out across the desert. The sky was perfect blue, the desert perfect brown, and the planes were filling the sky on approaches to the airport. Below I could see the moving traffic and lights of The Strip.

It felt wonderful to be home.

Part of me had believed I would never see it again. Actually a very large part.

Ben and Madge were both sitting in the booth, sweating as if they had been running.

"Oh, thank heavens you are back," Ben said. "We couldn't hold this office up much longer."

I frowned and figured I would have them explain that later. It didn't feel like I was suddenly holding up the office.

Patty kissed me and then let go of my hand.

"Patty's building safe?" I asked Ben.

He nodded, using a napkin to wipe the sweat off his brow as Madge slid out of the booth and sort of staggered for the door to The Diner. "I'll get some milkshakes and fries started."

"I'll jump you two into the back area of the lobby," I said, turning to the two paramedics who were still holding up the two

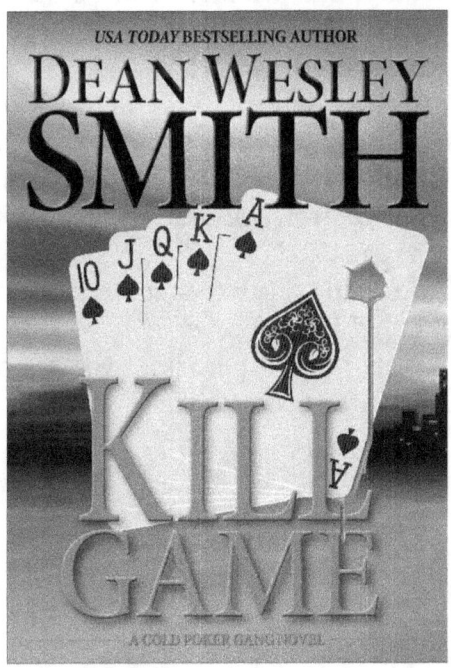

The First Two Cold Poker Gang Novels
Available at your favorite booksellers.

unconscious women residents. "From there you can get these two to the hospital."

They both nodded and I jumped them to the empty main floor of the building, thanked them for their help, and jumped back to my office.

It felt wonderful to be home.

Just wonderful.

Screamer was pulling a chair up to the booth and Patty had already slid into the side across from Ben.

"Go get Sherri," I said to Screamer as I slid into the big booth beside Patty. "Have her join us for a late lunch so we have someone to tell this story to."

He started to open his mouth, then remembered he could teleport and broke into a huge smile.

"Right back," he said, and vanished.

"Very good job today," Ben said, nodding and sipping on a glass of water in front of him. "You all saved a lot of people in a lot of timelines. How did you like Atlantis?"

"Seemed pretty advanced," I said. "But we didn't luckily see much of it."

"How are the Atlantis Fifty going to be?" Patty asked.

"The Atlantis what?" Sherri asked as she appeared with Screamer and slid into the booth as Ben slid over. "And someone want to explain to me how my husband can now teleport?"

"The Atlantis Fifty," Ben said. "They were before your time."

"Considerably," Sherri said. "If they were actually from Atlantis. I'm not that old, thank you very much."

"But we were there today," Screamer said, smiling at his wife.

"Where?" Sherrie asked, looking very puzzled.

"Atlantis," Screamer said. "Nice place, but I wouldn't want to live there. I hear it had flooding problems."

Sherri opened her mouth, staring at her husband, then shut it and looked at me.

Patty and I both laughed.

Patty finally took pity on Sherri and looked at me. "How about we start from the beginning and tell her about our day."

"Should I start with the shower part?" I asked, remembering how wonderful she looked there, naked and not moving, covered in drops of water. "With you frozen in the shower and me just staring."

"Pervert," Patty said and smacked me on the shoulder and Ben smiled like he did when amused.

"After the shower," Patty said.

"Oh, bummer," Screamer said.

And with that the laughter drained away the last of the tension I was feeling.

It was wonderful to be home, wonderful to have stopped a horrid tragedy from happening, and wonderful to be back in this time.

And even though thousands of years before in Atlantis, fifty families had been torn apart with a horrid tragedy, the Atlantis Fifty had now found a new home. They were safe and would get the help they needed.

And Stan had two daughters back he thought he'd lost forever.

All in all, I figured it was a good Saturday afternoon.

~

Now Available
from all your favorite booksellers
in trade paper and electronic editions.

Dee W. Schofield

Can romance be real
between two androids
on a poison planet
with beach sand
in all the wrong places?

Don't Rust On Me Now

A SCIENCE FICTION ROMANCE

Can romance be real between two androids on a poison planet with beach sand in all the wrong places?

Dr. Susan Taft discovers the answer to that question when her ship crashes in the middle of a lake in a very hostile place.

The only thing not hostile: Another android with her.

An Android with a great body and an even better mind.

Published under the pen name Dee W. Schofield

DON'T RUST ON ME NOW

THE ALARM BELLS were going off as I came up out of transwarp sleep, trying to remember where I was. Who I was, actually.

Oh, yeah, Susan Taft. Dr. Susan Taft, actually; originally from Canada on Earth, recently from the Mars city of Bensen.

I remembered now. Waking up from transwarp sleep was supposed to be calm and comfortable, like waking up from a long nap. Yeah, alarms blaring can really help a person be calm.

Damn I hated alarms.

The one echoing around me had a distinctive *whoop-whoop* screaming sound that I was sure could hurt a person's ears given time. What was going on?

And why didn't someone shut off the stupid alarm? And let me out of this sleep chamber. I didn't want to open my eyes because I knew there was nothing but padding about five inches above my face.

Everyone says that the human brain doesn't dream in transwarp sleep, but I'd had this uncomfortable dream about losing my body in an industrial accident, and having my mind temporarily put into an android body so I could make the journey to New Wells a couple of hundred light years away for a new and younger and healthier body.

On New Wells they grew the human replacement bodies tall, strong, and pretty in the organ beds in the light gravity. Anything would be better than the old, scarred-up and dying original body from my dream. I remember dreaming that I had ordered larger breasts as well, just to spend one life rotation seeing if the things might change my life in any way.

Then the dream firmed up and became a nasty memory, and I remembered.

No dream. I really was scarred up by an accident and I had really ordered new and larger breasts on my body replacement. Yeah, that was dumb.

And I really was in an android body right now.

Damn. I didn't want to open my eyes.

But I sure did want to shout for someone to turn off the stupid alarm. It seemed to be vibrating my sleep coffin. Even if I were dead, that sound would wake me up.

I sure hoped I wasn't dead.

I had come too close to that totally dead state in the accident back on Mars. I had plans to stay around for another ten body rotations—a good four hundred Earth years—if I stayed away from having a machine explode ten feet from me again.

The android body I was in had all the normal human shapes and bumps and curves and even the larger breasts I had ordered. It was a replica in every detail of the new body I had ordered that was waiting for me on New Wells.

The android body even functioned in all ways like a normal human body, right down to eating and drinking and other body functions. It even had soft, smooth skin over the metal alloy frame.

Only that soft-looking skin was a patchwork quilt of browns and whites, making me look more like an old movie monster that had been stitched together by an insane quilter.

Stupid Earth law. Any android with a human brain had to remain naked at all times and wear a patchwork-colored skin until the brain was transferred into a new human body.

Fear-based law. Politicians never seemed to understand anything about how androids worked. Androids were actually easier to disable than human bodies if you knew what you were doing, and they didn't last long at all because of the complexity of the systems inside.

A dumb law. I sure didn't much care to walk around naked. But with my new breasts I had gotten some nice stares while boarding from the Mars station crew.

I moved my hands and felt my android skin along the sides of my legs.

Seemed like everything was working.

Have I ever mentioned how much I hated alarms?

No one seemed to be turning off the alarm. This sure wasn't a peaceful wake-up from a long transwarp nap.

I had been told to just lay very still when coming out of transwarp sleep, but if someone didn't shut that alarm off I was going to be anything but still in a few seconds.

Back when I was a student working on my first doctorate in physics, I had used an alarm that sounded like a cross between a fire engine and a ride at Mars Disney just to make sure I got out of bed on time every day.

I kept smashing the alarms and replacing them. Cost me a very satisfactory three hundred extra credits during the term. Worth every damn credit.

If that alarm didn't get shut off, some part of this ship was going to be smashed in very short order.

Suddenly I could hear the lid of my chamber start to move. I opened my eyes.

Above me stood a very, very handsome, well-built, and very naked male android. I thought I was the only android transport on this ship. Clearly I hadn't been.

As he pushed the lid back and clicked it into place, his very personal, very male parts dangled just inches from my face. Now that also wasn't a restful way to wake up.

Nice, but clearly not restful.

"Dr. Taft?" he asked, staring down at me. His gaze first looked relieved as I nodded, but then he looked down the rest of my naked body and the part closest to my face twitched.

"That's me," I said, pushing myself up slowly as he stepped back. "What's going on? Where is the crew?"

He reached down and somehow managed to get his hands under my arms without touching my breasts and help me out of my sleep coffin.

"I don't know," he said finally, as I stood, leaning against the smooth metal of my coffin until my balance returned and the room slowly stopped spinning. "I haven't left the room yet."

There was another sleep coffin across from mine. It hadn't been there when they had put me to sleep.

"And you are?" I asked.

"Hugh Bensen," he said, smiling a smile that could knock down a dead woman, let alone an android with a human brain. I stared so long at his wonderful

Above me stood a very, very handsome, well-built, and very naked male android.

smile and his deep eyes that it took a moment for the name to register.

"Bensen of the Mars, Bensen City family?" I asked.

"Yup," he said, "Only son of the current mayor."

"So why the android?" I asked. "I seem to remember you were only into your second human cycle.

He laughed, and the laugh made me want to just hug him like a big patchwork teddy bear. "Fell off a cliff while doing some climbing up north of the city. Broke my back in three places. Lower gravity can hurt just as much as Earth gravity."

His voice also seemed perfect to my ears, even with the alarm blaring in the background.

"Great to meet you," I said.

"The honor is mine," he said. "I've been a big fan of your work since your first paper on the reality of dark space around dark matter."

Now I really stopped and actually looked at him. A rich guy with a brain *and* a nice voice *and* a fantastic body. Was that possible?

"Thank you," I said, smiling and staring into his eyes just a fraction of a second too long. God, I hoped android skin didn't blush. More than likely it did.

"Let's find out what's going on," he said, turning from me and heading for the door.

Damn, he had a nice butt as well. There had to be something wrong with this guy besides the patchwork android skin which would soon be changed for a human body when we got to New Wells.

I followed him as he opened the metal door and stepped into the hallway. He took two steps and glanced down; as did I.

We were standing in about an inch of water.

"This can't be good," he said, a hint of slight panic in his voice.

I didn't say anything, because the panic would no doubt be very real and clear in my words.

Water didn't belong on spaceships past a toilet or a shower or a glass of the stuff in the dining hall. I sure hoped this was just a sink overflowing somewhere.

His pace down the hall got faster and faster as we headed forward. The small transwarp ship was a private craft that the University had chartered to get me to New Wells. It only had a crew of four. Small ships and short, twenty-day jumps didn't need any more than that.

So where was the crew?

As we headed toward the bridge, the water got deeper, until, in front of the bridge door, it was knee-deep. And the damn alarm got louder and louder.

I hated alarms, sure, but not as much as a flooded spaceship.

The water smelled a lot like a lake I had grown up near in Canada. Not sour, just fresh and clear and wild. Not the slightly sterile, recycled smell of water on Mars.

Hugh pushed open the bridge door slowly, sending a wave of water across the control room.

"Oh, no," he said softly.

"Damn," I said, not really believing what I was seeing.

All four crew members were in their chairs and clearly dead. The front of the ship was mostly missing and the ship was nose-down and stuck in a shallow lake.

The light outside was soft, shining through high, white clouds. The air smelled slightly of almonds. I could see some sharp mountains in the distance.

The ship didn't seem to be sinking at all, so clearly the lake wasn't very deep, at least where the ship had crashed.

Hugh paused for a moment beside me, then went to the closest crew member and looked at him.

"Can you tell what killed them?" I asked, moving to stand over the captain I had met right before being put in my sleep coffin. Besides a nasty bump on the head and some saliva running out of his mouth and down his chin, he looked all right. But I had no training at all on the medical side of things.

"The air is poison," Hugh said, heading for a control panel that looked to be functioning. "We survived the impact and can breath the air because of our sleep coffins and these bodies."

I nodded. That made sense. Android bodies could actually survive in deep space for a short time without suits. Breathing was only an artificial function built in to keep the human mind inside from panic. Actually, everything about an android body was designed to react and let the brain inside feel it was actually still in a human body. I had learned that much a long time ago, long before my accident.

I moved to a blinking light and slammed my hand on the alarm controls to turn them off.

Silence, almost louder than the alarm itself, filled the bridge.

I could feel myself relax just slightly.

"Thank you," Hugh said, still bent over the communications panel. "Now I can hear myself think."

I sloshed through the water and

checked the other crew members, just to be sure, then went back over to the captain's panel and clicked on the flight record.

I had been trained a number of years back in small craft flight, and this ship wasn't much larger than the ones I had flown in short, five-light-year jumps.

I fast-forwarded to the moment of the alarms.

"Looks like the transwarp drive caught something and had a catastrophic failure," I said out loud to Hugh. "It was ejected instantly, so the failsafe worked."

"Luckily," he said, "or we would have never even realized why we never woke up."

"The ejection dropped the ship and crew into regular space, and they spent two months real-time limping their way at sub-light to this system and this planet."

"Means a bunch of people are looking for us already," Hugh said. "How fast were they traveling?"

"One-tenth light," I said, finding the reference in the record.

Hugh nodded. "Good, then it has been less than six months, real-time."

I glanced over at him again. He had his back to me, still focused very intently on the communications board. How could someone with that nice a butt have such a powerful brain? He had figured out the real-time speed time-deletion factors almost faster than I had.

I shook my head and went back to following the record. "There was engine damage from the transwarp drive ejection, so they ended up crash-landing here. When the front of the ship sheared-off, they died almost instantly."

"They are heroes," Hugh said, turning to look at me with a very serious expression. "They saved our lives."

"How's that?"

"They got sub-light distress signals out on the way here, and again before they crashed. Help is on the way."

He moved over through the water and clicked the alarms back on, killing the peaceful quiet.

"Why did you do that?" I asked. The sound just grated on me.

"Distress beacon," he said. "That's the signal that will lead the rescue ships to us."

I nodded. Made sense, but why the hell did it have to be so loud inside the ship. "Any idea how long?"

"Maybe up to two days," he said, smiling, as if enjoying a private joke on me.

I shook my head. "I don't think I can stand that noise for two days. Any way to cut the audio portion of the signal?"

Now his face was suddenly serious. "I don't want to risk our lives and even touch that thing."

Damn if he wasn't right. I didn't either, but that didn't help me with that alarm sound.

Hugh turned and took the captain by the shoulders. "Let's get the crew back into a dry room and closed off. Never know what's in this water."

That seemed like a logical plan. He seemed to be much better at emergency situations than I was.

I took the captain's feet and we headed back down the hall to the sleep coffin room.

When we had all four bodies there, we covered them with blankets from one of the crew quarters.

"When we get back," Hugh said, "Dad will make sure all their families are well cared for."

"And the university will help as well," I said. "They were very brave."

Hugh nodded. "They just didn't expect the lake to be so shallow or the nose of the ship to crack open to outside air."

In silence we went to the galley and found something to eat. Even though our android bodies didn't actually need the food, our minds believed they did, so we both felt hunger.

Sometimes the android bodies were just a little too efficient.

I just kept finding myself staring at Hugh, even though I tried not to. I hadn't had a real date for almost six months before the accident. Holo-dates, sure. Everyone did those. But no real dates, and I had been missing that.

The designers of these android shells could have easily unhooked the sex-drive part of the androids, but they hadn't. Everything was hooked-up and working from my brain.

And my brain kept my eyes staring at the naked hunk of a man I was with.

And I noticed he was staring at me as well, when he didn't think I was looking.

In the galley the alarms were muted, but even there it just pounded at my head and got in the way of my thinking. Of course, I wasn't real sure how well I was thinking considering everything that had happened.

After eating, he broke the silence and asked, "How about we take a walk outside? Get some distance from the alarm."

"I would so love that," I said. More than I wanted to admit to him, actually.

We went back to the bridge and Hugh checked the communications panel.

After a moment of my staring at his butt again, he turned to me, smiling that killer smile of his. "A ship called the *Tennison* will be here in less than twelve hours."

"Can you contact them?" I asked, feeling a huge sense of relief.

"Nope," he said. "We just have to wait and hold on."

I didn't say what I wanted to hold on to as he turned for the opening in the hull.

Carefully we worked our way outside and into the shallow water. Then holding hands like two kids at a swimming pool, we started for the nearest shoreline, a good two-hundred-paces away.

The lake looked like it could be a mountain lake back on Earth, with some sort of pine-like trees surrounding the shoreline and sharp, rocky mountains in the distance. It was stunningly beautiful.

But we were going to have to be very careful of any wildlife. Android bodies possessed almost super-human strength and the metal under the skin was tough to hurt, but a head injury would be a disaster, especially this far away from good medical help.

The water never got deeper, only more and more shallow as we slowly worked our way along the sandy lake bottom and finally up onto the beach. It was a fine, white sand, and very soft.

And on the beach the alarm from the ship was only a very distant sound, not annoying at all.

Even with the yellow sun and the high clouds, I could feel the warmth of the air and the light bouncing off of the water.

"Do androids get sunburns?" I asked, not really having a clue to the answer.

He laughed. "I honestly don't know. I don't remember reading anything about that. Guess we'll find out."

He dropped down on the beach and put his back against a tree stump so that he could stare out over the water and back at the ship.

I sat beside him, wondering how hard it was going to be to get the fine, white sand out of the intimate parts of an android body.

"So this air is poison to humans," I said, taking a deep breath of what seemed like crisp, clean mountain air.

"Very," he said. "More than likely why this planet hasn't been settled."

I laughed. "When has that ever stopped humans?"

We sat for a moment in silence just staring at the ship.

"More than likely," Hugh said, "the crew thought the lake was deep and tried a water landing. I have a hunch they

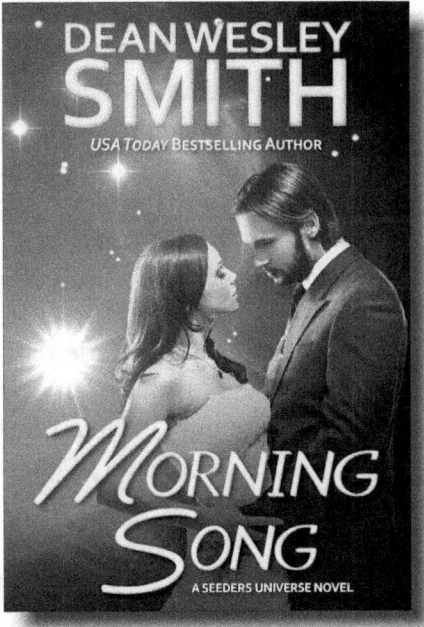

would have made it if the water had been even five feet deeper."

"Those ships float?" I asked, glancing at him.

"Like a top," he said.

"And how do you know that?"

And that question got the conversation rolling.

For the next five or six hours we talked about our pasts and discovered we had almost crossed paths a few times over the years. I was shocked to discover how really solid he was, considering his family past. And he seemed shocked to discover I was a real human with real emotions, considering my reputation and discoveries.

And he made me laugh a lot, something I would have never considered possible in this situation.

Actually, I wasn't the type to laugh much in any situation. But sitting on this lakefront with the beautiful alien sky and mountains, I seemed to laugh more than I had in years.

And I had never opened up to anyone like I opened up to him. I told him things about myself I had never told anyone.

As each hour went by I became more and more attracted to the man inside that android shell. To the brain, the personality.

Before I had wanted to jump him for sex. Now I wanted to spend time with him. A lot more time. Especially once we were both back in real human bodies.

I had no doubt I had fallen in love with Hugh. Never, in all my life, had I fallen for someone this fast and this hard.

Maybe it was the trauma of surviving a spacecraft wreck.

Or maybe it was Hugh.

I was betting it was Hugh, not the android-body-Hugh, but the mind and sense of humor and personality inside the body.

After six hours, the sun had only barely moved in the sky, clearly indicating this planet had a very slow rotation period.

"I have a hunch we need to be heading back," Hugh said, standing and brushing off sand and once again putting that magnificent body part of his directly in front of my face. "Besides, I'm getting hungry again."

Did he have any idea at all what that was doing to me?

He offered a hand and helped me to my feet.

I brushed off the sand, then laughed. "I think I need water to really get the sand out of some parts."

I headed back out into the water and when it got deep enough, I started brushing water up into my crotch, working the sand loose and enjoying the feel of the cool water.

"Need some help?" he asked, moving up beside me and splashing water in the direction of my crotch.

I sure didn't have any plans on objecting, and the two of us made sure not one grain of sand was left where it didn't belong.

Then I turned to him. "I can see you need help as well."

I splashed water at the part that was now clearly larger than it had been when he pulled me out of the sleep coffin.

"I might," he said, smiling and pulling me into his arms.

His kiss sent electrical sparks through my system like I had never felt before.

I pushed against him and he pushed back, his wonderful patched, android skin feeling like satin against me.

After what seemed like forever, yet was far, far too short, he broke the kiss and looked me in the eyes. "Wow."

"Yeah," I said. "I'm tingling all over."

"So am I," he said, smiling, the look of lust very, very clear on his face.

"Are you sure these things don't rust?" I asked after another long kiss.

"That much I'm sure of," he said, starting to kiss me again.

Then suddenly my mind clicked back in over the lust and the desire.

I pushed him away and grabbed his hand and started toward the ship as fast as I could go. My legs were actually tingling and it had nothing to do with the kiss or what body part of his that had been brushing against them.

"These don't rust *in natural conditions*," I said, the fear clouding my mind more than it had at any moment before. This was alien water and alien air and this water could be very, very corrosive to android skin and parts. We had no way of knowing.

"Oh, shit," he said, clearly understanding what I was thinking. Then, as easily as picking up a bag of snacks, he had me out of the water and into his arms and was almost running in the shallow water toward the ship.

"I can run on my own," I said, the panic filling my voice even though I tried to act strong.

"No chance," he said. "I don't want those parts of yours rusting. I have plans."

I actually laughed. How could he make me do that?

In what seemed like only a moment, he was helping me through the damaged front of the ship and we were rushing back through the ship toward the crew quarters and the fresh-water showers that were still well above the lake water.

After a short time it became clear that we had gotten out in time.

We were fine. No real damage to our android bodies.

But we decided to make sure, and that second inspection took lots of soap and very, very close personal inspection of each other.

Very close.

Careful, careful inspection, right up to the moment the rescue ship arrived.

~

USA TODAY BESTSELLING AUTHOR

DEAN WESLEY SMITH

AN EASY SHOT

A GOLF THRILLER

In the first installment, Seattle Police Detectives Bonnie and Craig, while taking a late night walk on a Scottsdale Arizona golf course happen to overhear a conversation between two men plotting to kill a United States Senator.

At the same time, a young golf professional's wife is kidnapped. Scheduled to play with the Senator, he must do what they ask or his wife will die.

A fast-paced thriller that I first published years ago under another title and under a pen name. The publishing company died just as this book came out, so I figured it would be fun to bring the book back and give it a second life here.

AN EASY SHOT

Part 2 of 8

CHAPTER FOUR

Friday, April 7th
10:07 p.m.

THE WALK BACK to the hotel and up to their room seemed to take forever for Bonnie. Her heart was racing and her mind twisting at what they had overheard out on the course. She desperately wanted to talk to Craig about it, but knew that they didn't dare until they were safely in private. Just as they had discovered, voices carried on that golf course, especially at night.

After Craig closed the door behind them in their room, she dropped down onto the bed, enjoying the softness of the mattress and the silky feel of the bedspread. "Tell me what you heard."

Craig paced between her and the dark television, a frown on his face. "Two men talking about causing a Senator to have an accident."

Bonnie nodded, her stomach now even more in a knot than it was on the walk back. "That's what I heard as well. Could we have misunderstood?"

"I've been wondering the exact same thing," Craig said, still pacing. "And the answer is yes, of course we could. They could have been talking about a game they were playing. Or the word accident could mean something completely different to them."

"Like what?" Bonnie asked, wanting to believe him, but not really following his logic.

Craig stopped and faced her. "They said they were going to do a Senator, right?"

Bonnie nodded. Those were the words she remembered very clearly.

"Who knows," Craig said, "maybe they were talking about getting a hooker for a senator and accident was how they were describing it."

Bonnie laughed, but she knew Craig was right. A single part of an overheard conversation could mean so many things, they didn't dare jump to too many conclusions. Especially the conclusions they were both jumping to.

"So what do we do now?" she asked.

"I suppose we should take things one step at a time," Craig said. He glanced at the clock on the stand beside the bed. "It's only a little after ten. Let's find out if there's a Senator registered here."

"And just how do you plan to do that?" she asked. "I doubt anyone is just going to tell you."

"You would be surprised," he said, smiling. He picked up the phone and punched a button.

Bonnie lay back on the bed. She could still feel the tingle from the fun they had had on the fairway. It had been intense,

that much was for sure. And even more startling that they could fall asleep nude like that in the middle of a fairway afterwards. The thought made her smile.

If she had her way, there were going to a few more encounters just like that one before this weekend was over.

As soon as they got all this stuff settled.

"Front desk?" Craig asked. Then after a moment he said casually, as if he said the words every day, "Would you connect me to the Senator's head-of-staff, please?"

"Good thinking," she whispered, smiling at her husband. "but it won't work." Craig was such a good detective, she knew. And he had ways of getting information that most people would never think of. But a stranger didn't just go calling a hotel front desk and ask if a United States Senator was staying there. It didn't work that way. Important people had layers between themselves and the regular public. Protective and necessary layers because of all the nut cases in the world.

Of course, Craig hadn't asked to talk to a Senator, but instead he had asked for the Senator's head-of-staff. That detail might make all the difference.

"I'm being connected," he said, his eyes suddenly full of worry. He was clearly as surprised as she was, both at his idea working, and the fact that there was a Senator staying here.

"Oh, shit," she said, suddenly remembering why Craig was making the call. "There is a Senator here. Now what are we going to do?"

He held his hand up. "Yes, hello, uh... Senator Knight," Craig said, giving her the wide-eyed shock look.

Craig was actually talking to Senator Knight! Bonnie thought her stomach was going to jump out of her body. Senator Knight from California was one of the more powerful Senator's in all of Washington. What was he doing here? And what was he doing answering his own damned phone?

Craig went on, clearly deciding to tell the truth as he went. "My name is Detective Craig Frakes from Seattle. I'm sorry to bother you, but my wife and I overheard a conversation this evening that I think we should relay to you and your security staff, if you have a few moments."

Bonnie watched as Craig listened to the Senator. Then he said, "I don't honestly know how important it is, Senator. I suspect you would be the best one to judge that."

Craig nodded, then said, "Yes, sir. From Seattle. I can give you some names to call to check on who we are."

There was another long pause then Craig finished with, "Thank you, Senator, we'll be right up."

He hung up, then turned and smiled at her. "Better comb the grass out of your hair. We're about to meet Senator Knight."

"Wonderful," she said, shaking her head as she jumped to her feet and headed for the bathroom. "He's going to think we're a couple of nutballs, you know that, don't you?"

Craig laughed. "More than likely. But at least our consciences will be clear. He can decide to do what he wants with the information we heard."

He followed her into the bathroom as she grabbed a comb from their travel kit and started to brush the dried grass from her hair. She looked ruffled, and she doubted she was going to change that much in the few moments they had.

Craig reached under her arm and cupped her right breast, giving it a light squeeze. "Just checking to make sure they got put back into the right place."

She smiled at him. "Looks who's talking." She pointed at the lump in the front of his pants. "You might want to take your underwear out of your pocket. We don't want the Senator getting wrong ideas."

Craig laughed and pulled his underwear out and tossed them at the suitcase.

"We better take our badges with us," she said, putting the comb down and grabbing her purse, even though it didn't go with her shorts and blouse. "If I were the Senator's people, I'd damned well want to see them."

"Good thinking," Craig said, moving to dig his out of his suitcase. Bonnie knew that when traveling he never liked to carry it. He figured it would get him in more trouble than it was worth. But this time was different.

"And one more thing we might want to think about before we go up there," she said.

"And that is?" Craig asked as he stuffed his badge in his back pocket.

"What happens if one of the Senator's people is one of the people we overheard?"

"Shit," Craig said softly. He had clearly not thought about that possibility. "Would you recognize either voice?"

"Easily," she said. She doubted she would ever forget those two voices.

He nodded. "I think I would too. We're just going to have to chance it. And play it by ear if one of them is there."

She didn't much like playing a situation like this "by ear," but it seemed they had no choice.

Five minutes later they were on the top floor knocking on Senator Knight's door. Bonnie could feel the knot grow in her stomach as they waited. This was just plain crazy. How did they go from making love on a fairway to talking to a powerful United States Senator in the space of an hour? This was turning out to be one really strange vacation, and they hadn't even gotten through the first evening yet.

A young-looking man that Bonnie guessed to be no more than twenty-five, opened the door and nodded. "Identification please?"

Bonnie sighed at the sound of his voice. The young man clearly was not one of the men they had heard. She could tell Craig knew that as well.

Bonnie retrieved her badge from her purse while Craig showed his.

There was a moment of uneasy tension as the man studied both badges. "Seems fine," he said, nodding and handing the badges back. Then he extended his hand, smiling. "Steve Parsons, Senator Knight's assistant. Come on in."

Craig shook his hand, then Bonnie did. Parsons' hand felt firm and warm, and his smile was winning without being too patronizing. Bonnie liked this guy at first glance. More than likely it was that skill that had gotten him the job with a powerful senator at such a young age.

"Sorry to bother you and the Senator like this," Craig said as Parsons led them into the massive suite, "but we felt we had to tell someone what we heard."

"No problem," Parson's said. "We were just finishing up some paperwork before the weekend golf tournament. You can never get away from the stuff."

"I know how that feels," Craig said.

Bonnie got into the main area of the suite and simply stopped and stared. She had thought their room to be wonderful, but now it seemed much more like a regular hotel room. This suite clearly had numerous bedrooms and a massive living room and kitchen, all decorated in the soft earth and wood tones. The square footage was clearly more than their entire home.

"You sure got me intrigued," a voice came from around the corner in the kitchen. It also wasn't one of the voices on the path.

A moment later a refrigerator door closed and Senator Knight stepped toward them. He was holding a can of soda and wearing golf slacks and a polo shirt. He was also barefoot.

Bonnie was taken aback at the man's presence. His full head of gray hair seemed to shimmer and his smile filled the room. He extended his hand to her first. "I'm Darren Knight," he said, his voice firm.

Bonnie shook his firm hand and returned his smile. "Bonnie Stanley," she said. "And this is my husband Craig Frakes."

"Pleased to meet you, Senator," Craig said.

"Likewise, Detective," the Senator said, indicating they should take a seat. "And just so you know, on your way up here Parsons there called Seattle to make sure you two are who you say you are. You got glowing recommendations all around."

"Nice to know," Bonnie said.

"So what's this all about?" the Senator asked as he dropped down into one of the big chairs. Parsons took the other, leaving the massive couch to Craig and Bonnie.

Bonnie sat back, leaving Craig to sit on the edge of the couch and do the talking.

Craig explained that he and Bonnie had gone out for a walk and decided to sit behind a rock near the cart path to watch the stars.

At that Senator Knight gave her a smile. Bonnie could feel her face redden slightly. She had no doubt the Senator knew what they had been doing, but had the good taste to say nothing.

"We heard two voices coming down the path from the hotel," Craig said. "Men's voices."

"And they were talking about me?" Senator Knight asked.

"I honestly don't know," Craig said. "Let me see if I can tell you word-for-word what we heard."

Bonnie listened as Craig went on to tell the Senator almost exactly the conversation they had heard. She doubted she could have relayed the words so accurately, but that was part of what Craig did every day.

When he had finished, Senator Knight turned to Bonnie. "Is this what you heard as well?" he asked. "Did your husband miss anything?"

She liked the man's question. He was being careful and making sure everything was clear. "I don't think he missed a word, Senator," Bonnie said. "And he added nothing."

The Senator nodded. "They didn't know you were there?"

"They didn't," Craig said. "And we made sure they were long gone before we

> ## *"What happens if one of the Senator's people is one of the people we overheard?"*

moved. We went back to our room. We didn't know of any senator near here, so I called the desk, asking to be put through to someone on the Senator's staff, to see if there was even a senator here. They connected me to you."

"They did?" Parsons said, shaking his head. "That will change."

Bonnie smiled at the guy. Clearly someone in the hotel had screwed up and Parsons was going to make sure it didn't happen again.

Craig went on. "Can you see why we thought you and your security people should be notified?"

The Senator laughed. "Sure, but I'm afraid you are looking at my security team and my entire traveling staff."

Parsons sort of half-waved at Bonnie's stunned look.

Bonnie was shocked. She didn't know why, but she expected someone as important as Senator Knight to have security around him.

"Oh," Craig said, glancing at Parsons who only looked worried in return.

You know," the Senator said, laughing, "I get threats and hate mail all the time in my line of work. Almost all of them turn out to be nut cases. Harmless fools who think that threatening a Senator will get something done."

"Has anyone threatened you here?" Bonnie asked, not really believing that the Senator wasn't worried.

"Nope," the Senator said. "Just here to play a few days golf in this charity tournament on my way back to Washington."

"Senator," Craig said, "I also deal with nut cases every day. And I don't think this is one time that should be taken lightly."

"I agree," Parsons said.

The Senator looked at Bonnie.

She nodded. "This sounded very serious. And since it is not something you knew about, or two of your staff speaking in a code, we have to assume the two men's words meant what we thought."

"Is there any kind of government protection you could get?" Craig asked.

The Senator laughed, his smile filling the room. Bonnie had never seen someone so assured and comfortable in such an odd situation.

"I'm afraid there isn't much," the Senator said.

"And really nothing that could help us this weekend," Parsons said. "The Capital security is geared to function in Washington."

"How about the Secret Service?" Bonnie asked. "Or maybe the FBI?"

The Senator shook his head. "Mostly the Secret Service is only for the President and past Presidents, vice Presidents, top White House Staff, Cabinet members, and others in direct line of succession to the Presidency. That bunch keeps them more than busy."

"We should call the local FBI," Parsons said, nodding to Bonnie.

She smiled back. She knew there had to be some branch of government who could help protect a Senator.

The Senator nodded and looked at Craig. "You don't mind telling the FBI what you heard?"

"Not at all," Craig said. "There's also an ex-Seattle cop working as a detective in the Scottsdale police force. I could give him a call as well."

Before the Senator could object, Parsons said, "I think that would be a good idea, Detective."

The Senator smiled at his assistant. "Just don't think of canceling me out of this golf tournament. I've been looking forward to this for a month."

"So have we," Bonnie said. And if she had her way, this problem wasn't going to get in the way of either the golf tournament or their vacation.

CHAPTER FIVE

Friday, April 7th
10:39 p.m.

THE HEAT HAD been almost too much for Steph Baines to bear. The men with weapons had led her out of her apartment and into the back of an older panel van. The windows in the back doors had been covered and there was a partition between the cargo area and the front seats that had no door or window in it.

When the van's doors were closed, two of the masked men had tied her up and put her on the metal floor in the back of the van. Her feet were tied with a twine that cut into the flesh around her ankles and her hands were yanked behind her back and tied with a softer rope.

Then they had left, shutting and clearly latching the van door. Then she had heard them climb into the front of the van and start the engine. She could sit up, but not comfortably. Every corner the van took had sent her sprawling on the metal floor. Finally, after twenty minutes of trying to stay sitting, she had given up and remained on her side, her feet braced against the side of the van to help stop her from sliding around.

This was all the worst nightmare she could have ever imagined. She had simply taken the morning off from school to help Danny get ready for the weekend golf tournament. During the entire drive all she could think was wonder why had they picked her?

And what did they have in mind for her?

She had tried not to think about that second question, mostly without luck. Everything her imagination had come up with was too horrible to even consider.

For an eternity the van had seemed to drive on a freeway. She had moved around enough to find a half-comfortable position. The heat also kept getting worse and worse and sweat ended up coating her skin and streaking her with the dirt and dust from the floor.

During one smooth stretch of road she had managed to move over to a sharp edge sticking out of one wall and work the rope around her wrists against it. But before she could get it cut, the van had jerked and she had cut herself. Her blood had felt warm dripping off her fingers and down her back. She had had no idea how bad she had sliced herself, but she hadn't tried cutting the rope again. After a few minutes the bleeding had stopped. She had no doubt that if she had cut herself deeply, she would have bled to death before any of the men even noticed or cared.

Finally, after a bunch of turns and starts and stops, the van had stopped and the engine had shut off.

No one had opened the door to the van.

No one had come to give her water.

The sun had just baked the van into an oven.

For an eternity she had just sat there until finally she lay down and let the heat take her.

The next thing she knew a man was saying, "Here, drink this."

She felt wonderful, cool water pour over her lips and she had managed to choke a little of it down.

"Stupid idiots," the man said. "They almost killed you."

She had let more of the water in and swallowed, then had opened her eyes enough to see the unmasked man who had kidnapped her.

The guy smiled. "Good, glad you're still with us lady." He turned to someone beside her that she couldn't see. "Take her inside and get her situated in the second bathroom."

She had felt hands roughly pick her up and carry her just before the world left her again.

Now the darkness seemed to push back one more time as she came to again. This time she was lying on a soft rug on a small bathroom floor. Her hands and feet were untied and a bright light was on over the bathroom mirror.

Slowly, fighting the dizziness, she pulled herself up to a kneeling position and turned on the water in the sink. Using her hand as a cup she managed to drink a little more before slumping back to the wonderful coolness of the floor.

She just knew that in a short time she'd wake up beside Danny and this would all be a nightmare, that he would hold her and help her get over.

All she had to do was wake up.

She lay on her back, staring up at the bathroom light, waiting.

But the nightmare just wouldn't go away.

CHAPTER SIX

Friday, April 7th
11:12 p.m.

IT HAD TAKEN Parsons two phone calls to get an FBI agent on the way.

Craig had used a second line at the same time to get in touch with Detective Hagar Daniels, formally of Seattle, now part of the Scottsdale police force.

Twenty minutes later Hagar had arrived at the Senator's suite, followed in

less than a minute by John Maxwell of the FBI.

Bonnie remembered Hagar from his time in the Seattle force. He was a big man, well over six-four, with broad shoulders, a small gut, and a sense of humor that seemed almost too dry. He arrived wearing white Bermuda shorts, a golf shirt, and sandals.

Maxwell, from the FBI, was even more casually dressed in jeans, a Grateful Dead tee-shirt, and a Phoenix Suns baseball cap. He stood about Craig's height at six foot, and was trim and clearly in shape. His most striking feature were his deep blue eyes that Bonnie felt saw everything.

Maxwell and Hagar clearly knew each other, and liked each other. Bonnie had a sneaking hunch they had worked together a number of times before and didn't have the rivalry that sometimes happened between local cops and the FBI.

After all the introductions and badge exchanges were finished, the Senator had the two new arrivals join them in the large living room area of the suite and then had Craig relay exactly, word-for-word, what he and Bonnie had heard.

Bonnie was again amazed at how exact he got everything. There were times her husband impressed her and this was one of them.

After Craig had finished with the story and how he had informed the Senator, Hagar whistled softly.

Then he said, "No wonder you called us."

Maxwell faced the Senator. "You don't have any friends or co-workers here with you besides Mr. Parsons?"

Bonnie liked the question. It was along the same lines that she and Craig had first thought might be a possibility.

"I sure don't," Senator Knight said. "It's just the two of us. I seldom travel with anyone else, do I?"

Parsons nodded his agreement, but said nothing.

"No meetings planned this weekend?" Maxwell asked.

"Just with my putter and thirty-six holes of golf," the Senator said, laughing.

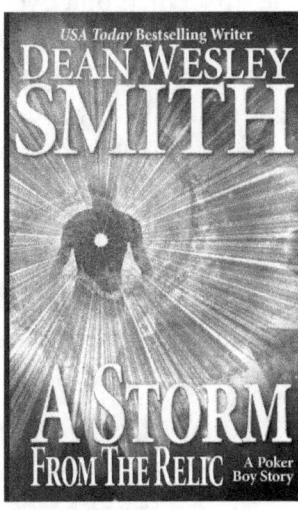

"One more question," Maxwell said. "Has any person in this area threatened you lately?"

The Senator looked at his assistant. "I never read those kind of letters," he said. "You know of anyone?"

Parsons shook his head slowly. "All the threatening letters are back in the office in Washington. I don't remember any lately from this area, but I could have that checked in the morning."

"I think getting someone to do it tonight might be a better idea," Craig said.

Bonnie completely agreed. The morning might be too late.

Maxwell nodded. "I agree. I'll have someone from the Washington bureau meet one of your staff members tonight to go through the letters."

Parsons laughed. "Jenny, the Senator's secretary, isn't going to be happy."

The Senator joined in. "Got that right. Monday in the office is going to be hell."

"Better than no Monday," Maxwell said seriously.

Bonnie agreed, but the Senator just waved a hand dismissing the somber tone. It seemed that even though this was his life they were all worried about, the Senator wasn't going to let it bother him. He was here to have fun and damned if he was going to let anything like someone threatening his life get in the way.

But if he wasn't going to be worried, Bonnie knew that the rest of them had to worry for him. Which meant they had to stay close to him, and during a golf tournament, that wasn't going to be easy to do.

"Senator?" Bonnie said, "who are you planning on playing with in the tournament tomorrow?"

"They got me scheduled with a young, hot pro from the Sedona area," the Senator said. "Beyond that, I don't have any idea."

"Well," Bonnie said, smiling at the Senator, "Craig and I are here to play as well. Mind if we join you?"

"Dear Ms. Stanley," the Senator said, "that would be my pleasure."

Bonnie could feel herself blushing slightly again. Why the Senator did that to her she had no idea. Out of the corner of her eye she could see both Craig and Hagar nodding, clearly agreeing with the idea of she and Craig playing the round with the Senator.

"Well, people," the Senator said, standing. "My tee time is at eight-forty-six in the morning, and I plan on getting a good night's sleep. Thank you all for your concern."

With that he headed into the bedroom to the right of the living area and shut the door.

His exit felt sudden to Bonnie, but correct. There was nothing more he could do now, so he left the planning in the hands of the people who knew what they were doing. He was clearly a person who knew how to delegate and was used to doing just that.

One hour later, Craig and Bonnie left, heading for their room.

Bonnie was tired, and they had to be up early for the tee time, but she knew there was no chance she could get to sleep at once after all that had happened. She wasn't sure she was going to get much sleep the entire night.

An FBI agent was standing at the end of the corridor as they headed for the elevator, clearly on post for the evening. He nodded good night to them. Maxwell was efficient and already covering the Senator. That made Bonnie feel a lot better.

Bonnie had been impressed with both Maxwell and Hagar. After the Senator went to bed, the four of them had planned what measures were needed to guard someone on a rocky, desert golf course. Much of the close-in duty was going to fall on Bonnie and Craig's shoulders, and Hagar was going to furnish them both with side-arms tomorrow to carry in their golf bags just in case. Maxwell would ride in a cart along with the group as well, with his people and Hagar's people set up along the course in an unobtrusive manner.

Everything was being done that the four of them could think to do. Even Parsons seemed satisfied with the plans after getting off the phone with the Senator's staff in Washington.

The only thing they couldn't figure out was who would want the Senator hurt, and who would pay big money, as the two men on the path had said, to have it done? Both Hagar and Maxwell said they would have full teams working that end of the problem.

Bonnie and Craig rode in silence down the elevator and to their room.

As Craig opened the door she said, "Seems we're not going to get away from work after all."

"Yeah, I'm afraid we were in the wrong place at the wrong time."

Bonnie moved inside and Craig let the door close behind them, locking the safely bolt. Then he turned and she put her arms around his neck, kissing him lightly. "I thought it was fun out there on that fairway. Didn't you?"

Craig pulled her close and kissed her hard. Then he pulled back and smiled. "Lots of fun."

"Worth all these problems?"

He pretended to be serious. "Sex with you is never a problem and always worth it."

"Ahh, the right thing for a husband to say," she said, kissing him again. "The exact right thing."

To be continued...

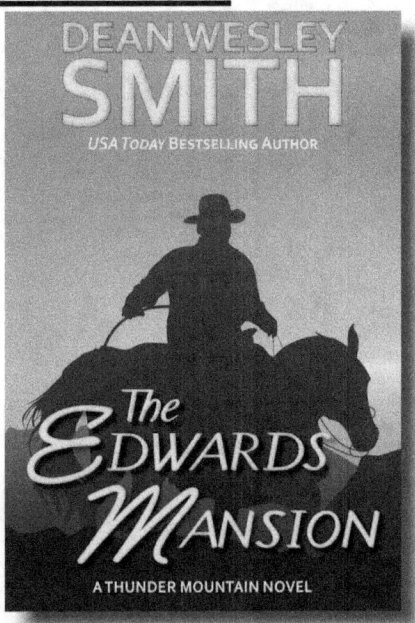

Two Thunder Mountain Novels
Available at your favorite booksellers.

USA *Today* Bestselling Writer

Dean Wesley Smith

Sometimes
You Must Go Back
to Find the Future

LONG DEAD
NEW LOVE

A Buckey The Space Pirate Story

USA Today Bestselling Author

DEAN WESLEY
SMITH

Heaven Painted
as a Free Meal

A GHOST OF A CHANCE NOVEL

Sometimes you must go back to find the future.

Buckey the Space Pirate travels back in time with his friend Fred, the talking oak tree, to learn why Fred refuses to recite his new limerick, the last limerick in Fred's first poetry book.

Over a hundred years in the past, in a forest of oak trees, Buckey finds more than just the reason for the rhyme.

LONG DEAD NEW LOVE
A Buckey the Space Pirate Story

ONE

WHEN MY BEST FRIEND is a talking oak tree named Fred who likes limericks, I suppose I shouldn't be surprised at anything that happens. I just never expected to meet the woman of my dreams, the woman I hope to marry, through Fred.

But there was only one major problem with this woman of my dreams: She has been dead for over a hundred years.

It made a relationship and a marriage just a little difficult.

Not impossible, just difficult.

It started because I needed help on a history paper due in three days and was stuck cold on what to write about. Fred could remember every detail from all his oak-tree ancestors over centuries and centuries. And oak trees could and did grow just about everywhere on the planet, so it sort of made sense to ask him for help with history.

But it still felt like a last resort as I headed for my mother's house where Fred was planted in a nice suburb of Portland, Oregon. I should have been able to come up with something myself and research it like a normal student instead of having to ask a talking oak tree. But I just couldn't think of anything to write about.

I grabbed a cookie from my mother's kitchen counter. Peanut butter, my favorite. She was upstairs watching her afternoon soaps and wouldn't see me go out back to talk to Fred.

Luckily, the afternoon May rains had stopped. It was going to be a sticky afternoon by the time the day was done, but at least in Portland, the summer heat hadn't kicked in yet.

Actually, asking Fred for help should have been my first resort, but over the last year Fred had become even more focused on limericks of all sorts and kept asking me to write them down and at some point publish them for him.

He said he wanted to be the first oak tree in history to ever write a book.

Since he was the first talking oak tree in history, being the first one to write a book wouldn't be much of a stretch. But getting his help with my history paper was going to mean some trade-offs, of that I was sure.

I slid open the patio door and stepped through, letting the damp air smother me. I had on a Star Trek tee-shirt, Levis, and my old tennis shoes that would be soaked by the grass in the back yard before I even got out to the twenty-foot-tall oak tree.

I had only planted Fred in my mother's back yard four years ago, as a seed. He should never have been this tall, but he told me because of special skills and the great soil, he could grow far faster than he normally would have. I was kind of glad he got so big so fast. It saved me looking like a fool sitting in a lawn chair trying to get shade from a sapling.

And besides, Fred hated to be called a sapling. He hated it so much he didn't even make up limericks using the word. For Fred, that was some hate.

"Well, if it isn't Buckey the Space Pirate," Fred said as I headed out toward him, as normal his deep voice sort of coming from everywhere in the air around me.

The first time we had met, I had had on my Buckey the Space Pirate costume, plumed wide hat, dark tights, black cape, and long sword. I wore the costume regularly still to science fiction conventions and Halloween parties.

Fred never called me anything else and I honestly didn't mind. He had been a huge old oak tree down in the park, about to be cut down. He made up a rude limerick about my girlfriend's private parts as I tried to get lucky, which had the result of me getting far from anything lucky or her body parts. In fact, after that night she wouldn't talk to me again since she thought I was the one who had made the crude joke about her private areas.

It hadn't been me. It had been Fred, the oak tree we were under at the time.

I didn't believe it either at first. In fact, I thought it was a joke. But he convinced me to doctor one of his acorns and plant it and I did and the next day he had been cut down to make way for a new road.

I planted the acorn in my mother's backyard and it sprouted and by the middle of the next summer, Fred was back and talking and spouting limericks once again.

It was kind of sad that a talking oak tree was my best friend. Third year of college, no girlfriends, no real close other friends. I was a typical nerd, only I talked to a tree.

Luckily the tree talked back, or I would have been in big trouble.

"Hey, Fred," I said, pulling up the lawn chair and knocking the last drops of rain off it before sitting down just under

his newly sprouted leaves. I had my chair turned so that if Mom looked out, she wouldn't see me talking. She didn't know about Fred. She just thought I used her backyard to study.

I had always been a weird kid, so this behavior didn't seem odd to her at all. Luckily Dad wasn't alive. He would have been asking a lot of questions.

"So what do I owe this unexpected surprise?" Fred asked, not starting into a limerick as I had expected him to do.

"History paper," I said. "I don't even have a topic yet."

"The learning of history is a noble enterprise for any human," Fred said, his voice booming like he was a college professor trying to wake up a sleeping student in the back row of a large classroom theater.

"You feeling all right today?" I asked, glancing up at the fresh green of the leaves over me. Everything looked healthy enough.

"I am in the top of spirits," Fred said. "Spring rain, fresh sunshine, a wonderful summer of growth ahead of me. Add in your fine company, what is not to enjoy?"

Suddenly it dawned on me why he was so happy. "You finished the last limerick, didn't you?"

"I most certainly did," he said, his voice sounding so full of pride, it was lucky his bark didn't burst from his trunk from the pressure.

"Are you going to share it with me?" I said, dreading the coming recital.

"No," he said.

I damn near fell off my lawn chair. The day Fred didn't force limericks on me was a day I really should be worried about his health.

"No?"

"No," he repeated. "Not until you see the moment in history and the person from which I took inspiration for the final limerick. Only then will you understand."

"Can I write about that period of history?"

"You most certainly may," Fred said. "It is only just over one hundred years in the past, a short hop."

I stood and moved over to touch the rough bark of the oak tree.

Fred had the ability to take me back to any point in time along what he called "his family tree." His family tree, as far as I could tell, included every oak tree on the planet.

At first I wasn't sure if he actually physically took me or not, but once he had been worried about my safety while we were in another time, so that led me to believe I actually vanished from the present and traveled somehow to the past.

He eventually told me I did.

I glanced around at Mom's house. No sign of her watching.

"Ready," I said, holding onto the trunk of the oak tree tightly. Sometimes on the other end I found myself high in the air.

A moment later I was leaning in darkness in a light rain against the trunk of a huge oak tree. Going from the bright light of a May afternoon to darkness was going to take some time for my eyes to adjust.

Plus it was cold here and the light rain felt like it might turn to snow at any moment. My Star Trek tee-shirt just wasn't suited for this kind of weather.

"Fred?"

"I am here," he said.

I glanced around. It was clear I was near a log cabin that sat nestled in a grove of oak trees. I could hear what sounded like a small river nearby and nothing else. Flickering yellow light came from the open window and a wonderful smell of bread baking.

"What time is it?" I asked. "And where are we?"

"It's only a little after five in the morning on October 21st," Fred said. "We are on the edge of the town called Boise in the new state of Idaho. The year is 1871. Take a look in the window."

"How can I do that?" I asked, staring at the open window with the light beyond. I honestly wasn't sure I wanted to go peeking in windows on someone dead more than a hundred years. There seemed to be something doubly perverted about doing that.

"You can go anywhere under the leaves of this tree or over the roots of the tree or any oak tree in this grove," Fred said. "And the roots of this tree alone extend a long distance under the house to the latrine on the other side. A wonderful source of nourishment."

"Too much information," I said, shaking my head at the idea that Fred ate from latrines. Of course he did. He was an oak tree. I just didn't have to think about it.

"Go take a look," Fred said. "See the reason, the very inspiration for the last limerick in my first book."

"First book?" I asked.

"Of course," he said.

All I could do was moan.

I glanced at the window in the side of the cabin. The drapes on the inside were pulled aside and the rough windowpane

I honestly wasn't sure I wanted to go peeking in windows on someone dead more than a hundred years.

of glass was pushed open. Every so often I could see a shadow of someone moving inside.

And the wonderful smell of baking bread just kept getting stronger and stronger. I really should have grabbed more to eat before seeing Fred than just a cookie. The smell was making me hungry.

"What happens if I happen to get beyond the branches or roots of the tree?" I asked.

"You will simply return to the backyard in your current time," Fred said, clearly starting to get annoyed.

An annoyed oak tree was not something I wanted to experience, so I stepped away from the trunk of the large tree and hesitantly moved toward the window.

It was darned cold out and I was already starting to shiver as I crouched near the window.

"You know this is illegal in all fifty states," I said. "And more than likely in most countries as well. I would hate to be arrested in 1871 for being a pervert."

"You will not startle her and there is no need to hide," Fred said. "I told her you were coming."

I stopped, stood up straight, and looked back at the large old oak tree sitting beside the log cabin. "You talked to her? I thought you couldn't talk until you were born in Portland."

"Have you noticed when and where you are at and that you are talking to me right now?" Fred asked, going into the mode where he treated me like I was as dumb as a first grader. I hated that mode.

He went on. "When I gained the ability to speak to humans, I also gained the ability to speak to humans at any point in time along my roots. I have struck up a number of friendships over the centuries."

"Oh," was all I could say. I actually felt a little disappointed because for some reason I thought I was the only one who talked with Fred.

I turned and moved toward the open window on the cabin. The wonderful fresh bread smell just kept getting stronger and stronger. And I could sense a little bit of frying bacon smell as well.

I moved up to the window sill that hit me just above my belt as Fred said, "Mary, we are here."

"Wonderful," a woman said. She turned from the stove to face me across the kitchen area of the cabin.

I suddenly just couldn't breathe and I am sure my mouth was doing the old guppy move of opening and closing.

The woman in the cabin was the most beautiful woman I had ever seen. She had bright red hair pulled back into a long ponytail, a bright smile that seemed to fill her face, and huge brown eyes. She wiped her hands off on a white towel over her shoulder as she started toward me.

She had on a thin plaid cotton dress in a white and red pattern that framed a thin, but wonderful body. The dress was protected by a long, white apron like you might see in a cooking magazine.

She seemed to be my age of around twenty-three, but that was a guess. She might be younger.

"Mary Elizabeth Smith," Fred said, his booming voice filling the area around the cabin. "I would like you to meet Buckey the Space Pirate."

She reached out her hand and I took it through the window, never letting my gaze drop from those deep brown eyes.

"Wonderful to meet any friend of Fred's," she said, her voice pulling me in even more.

"The pleasure is all mine," I somehow managed to say, even though my entire focus was on the wonderful feel of her hand and those huge brown eyes.

"Can you come in and share breakfast with me?" she asked, still not letting go of my hand.

I never wanted her to let go, to be honest.

Finally I said to the air, "Fred, is that possible?"

"Of course it is," he said. "But you will need to climb in the window or go in the back door. There are no roots under, or branches over, the cabin front door."

I smiled at her and indicated I would just climb in the window. "Do you mind?"

She laughed and let go of my hand and stepped back. "You may crawl in my window any time you would like."

At that moment I thought my heart would beat out of my chest. Somehow, with Fred giving advice, I managed to climb in the window without falling on my face. Pure luck since I could barely keep my eyes off her and didn't really pay a lot of attention to what I was doing.

TWO

OVER THE NEXT two hours we had a wonderful breakfast of fresh-baked bread, bacon and eggs, and tea. I helped her with the dishes and we laughed a lot.

The conversation with her and Fred was just wonderful, even with Fred sometimes becoming like a college professor and going into a lecture on some topic or another.

During that breakfast and conversation I completely fell in love, especially when I learned she had moved from Kansas to Boise with her brother who had gotten married a year ago and she had lived alone ever since.

"What do you do for money?" I asked and she told me about how her parents, when they died, had left her and her brother a sizable inheritance.

Finally, I realized that hours had passed in the wonderful conversation.

"Fred, is there a problem with me being gone? Is the same amount of time passing in 2011?"

I did have an assignment to get finished and classes to attend. I didn't want to, but I needed to.

"Time is always passing," he said. "But I can return you within a few seconds of when we left if that is what concerns you," he said.

"That would be helpful," I said.

"Wonderful," Mary said, clapping her hands together. "Then you can spend as much time as you would like with me here."

Then she realized what she had said and blushed. "If you want, of course."

"I can think of nothing I would want more," I said. "Fred, is that possible?"

"I see nothing at all impossible about it," he said. "I will leave you two alone. Please call me when you are ready to return."

"Thank you, Fred," I said.

There was no response. He was gone.

"He is a wonderful friend, isn't he?" I asked and reached across the wood table and gently squeezed Mary's hand.

"He is at that," she said as she put her other hand on mine and looked into my eyes.

I knew right at that moment that I had found a woman of my dreams, even though she had been dead for a long time before I was born.

After a long moment of silence, with only the sounds of the river running from the window, we went back to talking and laughing and later I helped her cook us both a wonderful dinner of venison and potatoes.

She let me wear a sweater she had knitted for her brother and promised to knit me one just like it. It had to be the softest thing I had ever put on.

And she forced me at one point to try to explain Star Trek, which got many laughs from her.

That night I slept on the couch, but for a time she sat with me in front of the crackling fire and we kissed and I never wanted to stop.

Finally she pushed me gently away and said, "We have all the time in the world."

"Thanks to our friend Fred," I said.

THREE

THE NEXT MORNING she cooked us both a wonderful breakfast and then I suggested that I needed to go home to get some clothes and run a few errands.

She made me promise to come back quickly and I did.

We also have one thing we need to do for our friend," I said as we finished up drying the morning dishes.

She smiled. "Hear his limerick?"

"You got it in one," I said, surprised Fred had recited limericks to a woman of her caliber in 1871.

"Fred, please come back."

A moment later he said, "I am here."

I didn't want to ask how he did that. I had a hunch that Fred and I would be having a lot of conversations about time travel in the near future.

"I need to return to my time for some errands and such. But before I go, we were both hoping that you'd give us a recital of the last limerick in your first book. The limerick that brought us together."

"It would be an honor," Fred said.

I could tell he was clearly touched that we had remembered and he didn't have to force his limerick on us.

"You are going to produce Fred's book for him?" Mary asked, smiling.

"I am," I said. "But I am surprised you have heard some of his limericks?"

"I have been appropriate," Fred said, "in my telling and choice of subject matter."

"I find them wonderful and funny and unique," she said.

"They are unique," I said. "Now Fred, would you please honor us?"

"I would be glad to," Fred said.

Then there was a pause and if an oak tree could clear his throat, or even had a throat, I was sure Fred would have cleared it.

"There was a woman named Mary
Who found my voice to be scary.
But I told her of Buckey
And how she'd be lucky
To find a pirate to marry."

For a moment the silence in the room seemed to grow and then Mary smiled at me and raised her right eyebrow and I smiled back and then we both started applauding and cheering while smiling at each other.

Yesterday the idea of marrying anyone would have scared me to death. Now, even though Mary died many years before I was born, the idea of marrying her just made me smile.

It would take some figuring on how to be together, but I was sure we could do it with Fred's help.

"Thank you. Thank you," Fred said.

If an oak tree could bow, Fred would be bowing.

"I would be honored to put your book together," I said.

"Wonderful," Fred said.

"I might be able to actually give you a short introduction as well," I said.

"It would have to be in limerick form," Fred said.

I smiled at Mary. "Oh, it would be."

Then I said, "How about this?"

"There was a pirate named Buckey
Who one day was very lucky
To travel in time
To listen to a rhyme
From Fred, a friend, an oak tree."

Mary smiled, stood and came over and gave me a long kiss that I did not want to break.

"That was wonderful," she said, finally, pulling away, but still holding me.

"It will do," Fred said.

"That's the nicest thing you have ever said about my writing," I said to Fred, winking at Mary.

"Don't push it," Fred said.

But I could tell the oak tree was as happy as I was.

Now Available
from all your favorite booksellers in trade paper and electronic editions.

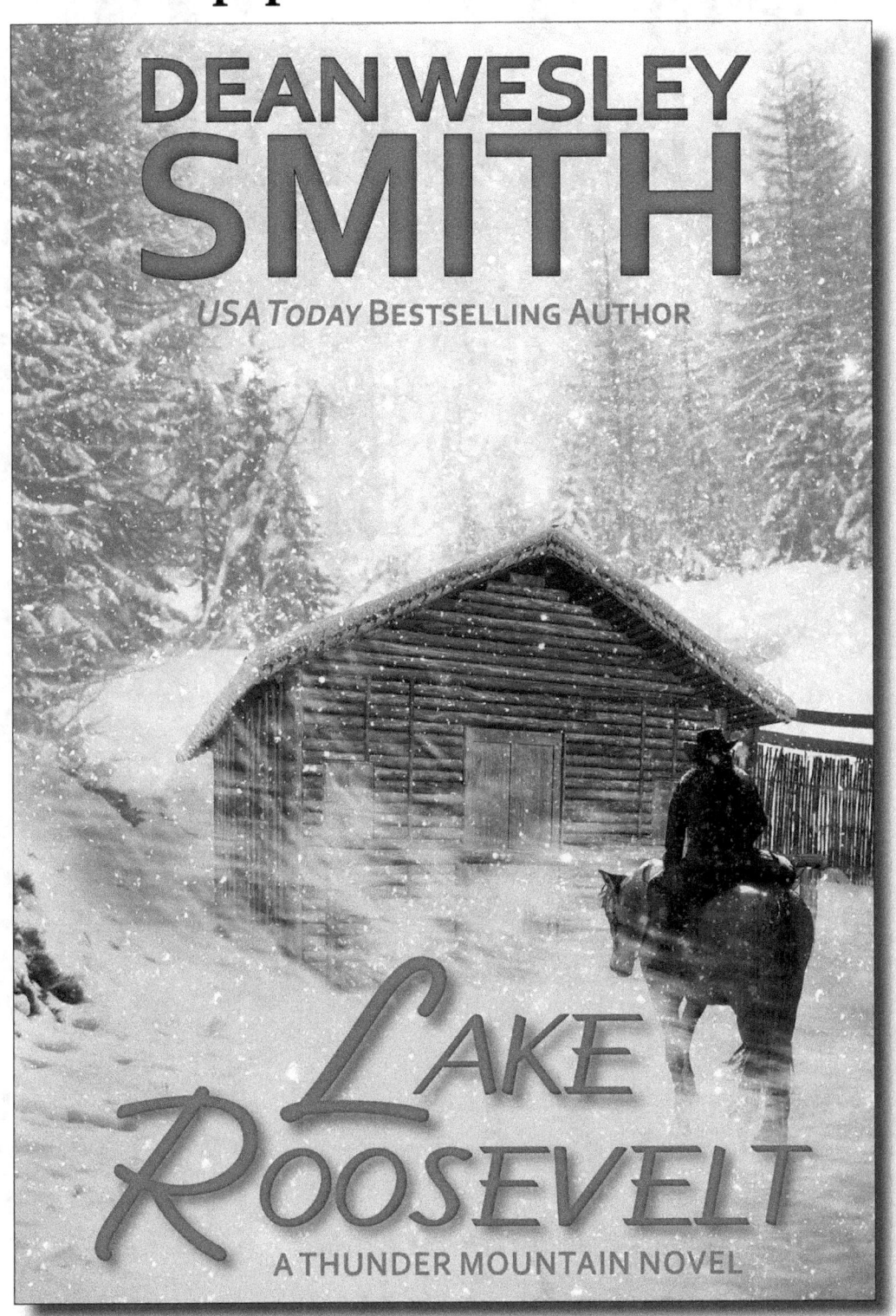

DEAN WESLEY SMITH

USA Today BESTSELLING AUTHOR

LAKE ROOSEVELT

A THUNDER MOUNTAIN NOVEL

Dean Wesley Smith
USA Today Bestselling Writer

Groceries,
Conversation
and Dreams...

SHOPPING
CART LOVER

They met on a Tuesday, a hot Tuesday in Southern California, and filled up an entire shopping cart with groceries and conversation and dreams.

Sometimes not getting a shopping cart can lead to a lot more than just carrying your food to the checkout counter under your arm.

A grocery store love story.

SHOPPING CART LOVER

I CALLED HER my "Shopping Cart Lover."

It was Tuesday.

A hot Tuesday.

Middle of June.

The parking lot to my local Safeway Grocery Store was full and I should have realized there would be a problem right there and just went back to my small apartment overlooking Interstate Five, one of the best apartments in all of Southern California. It's a nice place, one bedroom, and the rumble of trucks and cars going by reminds me of the ocean.

I love the ocean, how the waves crash on the beach, the wind always blows, the smell of brine and fish fills the thick air. I didn't often make it to the ocean due to my living circumstances and no job and not having a car, but living near the freeway reminded me of the ocean all the time and I liked that.

My ex-wife used to say I could make a silk shirt out of an old cotton rag and a vivid imagination.

I would always say, "At least I have a silk shirt."

If she hadn't left me for that manager of the hardware store last year, I wouldn't have had a chance to meet my Shopping Cart Lover.

Lucky for me my wife left.

I only go to my local Safeway grocery store once a month, when my card is refilled from the State of California. I do maintenance around the apartment complex to pay my rent and I save most of unemployment except for a few dollars to buy my Pabst Blue Ribbon beer.

Today California refilled my food allowance on my card, so I could stock up on food that would last for the month. And maybe by next month the application I had put in three months ago at the local bike shop would work out and I would get hired. The store owner liked me and said I did good work, but with the economy he just couldn't hire me yet.

I had told him I would wait.

I had always wanted to work on bikes, the peddle kind, not the motor kind, ever since I was a kid, maybe even open my own bike shop. But out of high school I had ended up working construction instead and then had gotten married and the bike shop idea sort of went the way of those old cotton rags my ex-wife used to always talk about.

So when she left me and I found my nifty apartment overlooking Interstate Five, I decided that I would work for a bike shop now and just wait until an opening came around or I had my own shop.

I saved as much as I could so that if I got the chance I would start my own bike shop. But until then I fixed a few of the neighbor's bikes for their kids and tried to watch the dumpsters for old bikes and bike parts. My apartment was pretty full of bike parts now, so I had lots to work on and fix up for the time I had enough for my own shop. It kept me busy at night, listening to the ocean of Interstate Five and fixing bikes.

Life was pretty good.

The bike I rode to my local Safeway grocery store I had put together with parts of about seven others. I had built a sidecar on it made out of parts and baskets from kid's bikes to carry my groceries and more bike parts when I found them.

It really was amazing what a guy could find in dumpsters.

I locked up my bike in the bike rack near the front door of the Safeway grocery store and went inside.

It was much cooler inside, which instantly felt good and put me in a good mood for my afternoon of shopping. It was always better to be in a good mood when shopping. I knew it never did much good to buy food angry. The food just never tasted the same.

My ex-wife thought that attitude was weird, but I tended to always get good food when I shopped happy.

Inside, by the produce section, was a big empty room where hundreds of grocery carts were normally stored in rows jammed into each other. The shopping carts were always hard to get apart like they resented being wheeled once more around the store they knew so well.

There were no grocery carts in that large area.

None.

It was cool in that grocery cart room, much cooler than the hot afternoon outside, but still there were no grocery carts.

It seemed that when California filled everyone's cards with money for food, the store got real busy.

I went back out into the parking lot and the heat to find a used cart there, but two kids with Safeway uniforms were already doing that and by the time I watched them push the rows of carts into the store, the hordes of shoppers waiting for a cart had grabbed them all.

I was left standing next to the produce section near the main door without a cart, waiting.

It was cool there, so I didn't mind. A cart would come to me soon enough.

A woman with brown hair, glasses, and a long nose stood beside me, also waiting.

She didn't look annoyed at all, which my ex-wife would have been. This woman had this calmness around her that attracted me to her and I looked at her even harder without actually looking at her and being rude and pervert-like.

She wore an old, blue-cotton tee-shirt with a light-blue cloth jacket covering it, not because it was cold, but because the tee-shirt was torn slightly from what I could tell. The jacket and shirt together still looked nice.

She had on faded jeans and well-worn leather sandals that showed toes with blue-painted toenails. She clearly was no better off than I was, except more than likely I had a nicer apartment with my ocean sounds of Interstate Five.

Her brown hair was long and pulled back and tied. Her skin looked well-washed.

A kid with greasy hair and a nose ring who worked for the store came in with one cart and pushed it toward us.

I laughed and turned to her. "Want to share?"

"That's all right," she said, her voice soft and wonderful. "You go ahead. I'm in no hurry."

"Neither am I," I said, smiling at her.

People used to say back ten years ago in high school that I had a good smile, a smile that made people feel good, so I gave her my good smile.

For the first time she actually looked at me over the shopping cart waiting to be claimed by one of us.

I wasn't a handsome man, but I had showered. I also had my long brown hair combed back and tied out of my face. And I was thin. Besides that, running around looking in dumpsters for bike parts kept me tanned.

My ex-wife said that my staying thin as I got near thirty was one of the best things I had done for myself. I don't think I gave it much thought. I just didn't eat much and now couldn't afford to drink more than two Pabst Blue Ribbons a night if I wanted the Pabst to last the month and still save money for my bike shop.

Besides, more than two and I screwed up the bike part I was working on every time. Two was my limit.

I guess that kept me thin.

"You go ahead and take it," she said, smiling. "But thanks."

I smiled back and nodded, but didn't touch the cart.

"To be honest," I said, "I thought it would be fun to share a shopping cart again. I haven't done that since my wife left last year."

"It's been two years for me," she said, smiling. "Although for the last year he didn't shop with me much."

"Come to think of it, I did all of the shopping the last year of my marriage," I said. "So I guess it's been longer than two years for me as well."

"Who knew a person could miss joint shopping," she said, smiling, a sort of wistful look in her eyes.

I really liked her smile even though she had one chipped tooth on the right side. It gave her character and made her even more unique.

"You sure you don't want to give it a try again?"

She hesitated, looking at the door to see if another cart would roll to her res-

cue, but there wasn't one in sight that wasn't firmly attached to another shopper's hand.

"You have a lot of things to buy?" she asked.

"Just basics," I said. "They don't give me a lot of money on my card every month."

At that she smiled even wider. "I don't get much either," she said. "It would feel nice to actually have a full shopping cart for a change."

"If we combine forces, we might just do that," I said, again giving her my best smile.

"You are very nice," she said, nodding. "Let's do it."

"We'll trade off pushing," I said. "You first."

I bowed like I had seen some movie star do in a movie once and she laughed and took the position behind the cart.

At that point I suppose I should have asked her name, but I just liked the idea of not knowing her name and she clearly didn't want to know mine either.

It was a great adventure.

An adventure in the aisles of the Safeway grocery store.

Who knew going to the Safeway grocery store on a hot Tuesday would be an adventure.

It is a wonderful world.

She picked up a bag of oranges.

I picked up a bag of potatoes.

Then she picked up some lettuce and bagged it and weighed it.

"How do you keep that fresh for a month?" I asked.

"I don't," she said. "I come back and buy more oranges and lettuce in two weeks. I use part of my unemployment for that."

"Where did you work?" I asked.

"Construction firm office," she said. "Bookkeeping."

"Construction as well," I said. "The driving nails department."

Suddenly, besides a shopping cart, we had something else in common. That felt good.

She kept track of what she was spending on a small calculator. I had one of those tiny spiral notebooks and an old pencil and I marked down each dollar.

"I hate to get to the register and not have enough on my card," I said, indicating the notebook in my hand.

"Yeah, I did that once," she said. "Had to leave stuff I really wanted."

Now we had three things in common. I had more in common with my shopping cart lover than I did with my ex-wife.

We kept going, me talking about how I loved to work on bikes, the peddle kind, not the motor kind, and she talking about how she was slowly trying to set up her own accounting firm.

"When I get my bike shop open, I'll hire your company to do my books," I said.

She beamed at that. "Thanks."

Finally we both had run out of money on our cards and our shopping cart was almost full.

Wonderfully full.

I had been pushing it the last few aisles, so I said, "You want to push it the last distance to the check-out line?"

"I would love to," she said. "Thanks."

She pushed it like it was the most important job on the planet and I followed along proud of the moment.

In line she sorted out her groceries first, then put that rubber thing between our stuff, which felt odd to be honest. We had shared so much in the last hour.

Now we were divided.

A simple strip of hard rubber indicated the wonderful adventure was almost over.

The clerk checked her out and she stayed under her card limit by two dollars.

A bagger with good hair and no nose ring at the end of the counter had found another cart and was putting her groceries in that.

Now we were very separated, in two carts.

And we had stopped talking.

When she was all done and had her receipt in her pocket, she turned to me. "Thank you for an enjoyable day."

I could tell she was nervous and didn't know what to say. We had shared a great deal in the last hour.

"It was my pleasure," I said. "How about next month on payment day we meet right here again at two o'clock and share a cart again."

Her smile returned, chipped tooth and all. "I would love that."

"So would I," I said, giving her my best smile again as the clerk worked at checking out my groceries.

"Until next month then," she said.

"Until then," I said.

She turned with a smile and pushed her own cart out of the door of the Safeway grocery store.

I watched her walk away like watching the end of a good movie. It felt good to have happened, but sad that it was over.

Usually I didn't feel conflicted, but for the moment I did.

I smiled at the clerk who just shook her head and finished my groceries and the bagger put them in the now only half-full cart.

My groceries looked small and sort of sad sitting in that cart all alone. It seems my food had shared the same experience I had. My food would taste great.

"Next month," I said to my groceries as the clerk handed me my receipt and I headed out of the store toward my bike.

I had a date with a wonderful woman in one month.

A date with my shopping cart lover.

I smiled and almost started to whistle.

Between my shopping cart lover, fixing bikes, and listening to the ocean sounds of Interstate Five, life just couldn't get much better.

⌒

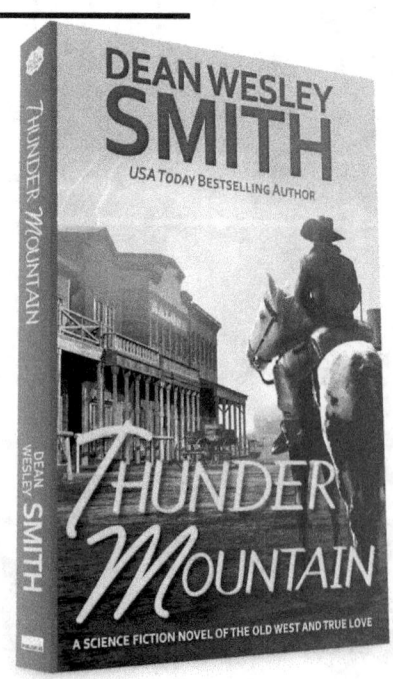

Now Available
from all your favorite booksellers
in trade paper and electronic editions.

Poker Boy and his team have saved the world countless times. The Ghost of a Chance agency follows a similar charge. Superheroes and ghosts, all working for the greater good.

But as two new members join the Ghost of a Chance team, both ghosts and superheroes face a challenge that threatens to end the world.

The Ghost Agents, including newly dead recruit Elliot and almost dead Deanna, team up with Poker Boy and his team to save the world.

HEAVEN PAINTED AS A FREE MEAL
A Ghost of a Chance Novel

For Kris
Even more popcorn for the brain.

Section One
JUMPING ON BOARD

One

THE WIND HITTING his face around his goggles felt wonderful as Elliot West fell away from the drop plane just over sixty seconds before he was going to die.

The day around him was a perfect spring afternoon. From ten thousand feet, he could see hundreds of miles in all directions over the vast Treasure Valley in Idaho. All the spring colors of the patchwork farm-lands shown in bright shades of brown and greens.

The clear air seemed to give every-thing a touch of vividness, a sharpness of detail that just couldn't be imagined by anyone standing on the ground.

Bogus Basin Ski Area above Boise looked almost small from this height, with the snow still clinging to some of the ridgelines. He could see beyond Shaffer Butte into the towering peaks of the cen-tral Idaho Mountains, still mostly cov-ered in pure white.

Below him and to the right was the wide gray ribbon of Interstate 80 that came out of the sprawling city and ran to the east toward the desert town of Mountain Home and to the west toward Oregon. Tiny dots of cars seemed to just creep along.

The Snake River twisted to his left, high from spring runoff, and he could even see from his position where the Boise River joined into the Snake River, something in all his jumps he had never noticed before.

Every time up here he noticed some-thing new, felt something different, ex-perienced a new high. Deanna, his girl-friend, called him a flat-out adrenaline junkie and at the moment he couldn't have argued with her.

The sound of the wind increased as he picked up speed, holding in stable po-sition for a moment.

Then he did a slow roll to look back up at the drop plane as two more jumpers cleared the back. One was his friend and law partner, Craig Daniels, and the other a newer member of the jump team named Ben.

Beyond the plane, white clouds drift-ed against a deep blue sky, framing the plane and the other jumpers perfectly. That would have been a beautiful picture if he had his camera with him.

This was just a free jump with all of the jumpers on their own, so since he was the first out, they needed to watch out for him. He didn't need to worry about them at all.

On the next jump they would practice for some of the stunts they were going to do for the upcoming air show in eastern Idaho next weekend.

Elliot let himself drift back into stable position, just relaxing, the wind around him a familiar feeling, the silence won-derful. He treasured the time he could get away from the pressures of defending people in courts. He loved the job, but this simple act of falling kept him grounded more than anything else.

Sometimes, in the winter, snow ski-ing gave him this same feeling, especially standing on the top of the lift, alone, just before they were to turn off the lights in night skiing. That isolation also helped him get clear and focused on the work.

And in the late spring and into the depths of summer, he loved spending time rafting the really rough rapids of the Idaho and Oregon rivers. That felt like more pure adrenaline, except for those calm, lazy times in the warm sun between rapids.

Sometimes floating down a ski hill, floating down a river, or floating down through the air at ten thousand feet all felt the same.

And all of it charged him.

On beautiful spring evenings like to-day, it just didn't get any better.

He rolled back over to see Deanna and Steve get out of the plane next. He and Deanna Teel had been dating for years now. But at thirty, he didn't feel the need to get married just yet. He and Deanna were happy with what they had. She had been a year behind him out of law school, and they had actually met while clerking for the same judge.

He had to admit, he loved her more than he could have ever imagined loving another person. They had a wonderful life together and she managed her corporate law practice with the ease and sure hand of someone far beyond her twenty-eight years. They called her one of the best corporate attorneys in the northwest.

And his reputation as a defense attorney was climbing as well, mostly because he took the fearlessness from the sports into the courtroom to save his clients.

All his and Deanna's free time away from their jobs they spent either skiing together or doing other sports or reading, sometimes far, far too late into the night when they both had to be up early the next day.

They both had a passion for reading and often shared novels they loved and often argued throughout a day about the meaning of something in a novel. Elliot found it great fun.

People said they seemed to match with their dark brown hair and dark eyes. He couldn't imagine being with anyone else, but they had made no permanent plans yet to stay together. They just both seemed to know that they would.

As Deanna had said one night a few months ago when the topic of a future came up, "Let's just not rock the boat. There will be time."

Elliot let himself just relax into the wind and drift with the wonderful view of the patchwork farmland below him. He could just feel the stress of the day's case easing away.

He let the moment last as long as he could, then checked his altimeter. Three thousand feet. He had a little time yet. He

normally pulled at just under two thousand.

So with one more look around and a final roll to make sure no one was being stupid and was right above him, he flashed past two thousand feet and pulled his ripcord.

The familiar thump of the pilot chute releasing was fine, but then nothing.

He twisted around quickly to see that his chute had not deployed in the slightest. Even with the pilot chute doing its best to yank his main wing from his pack, nothing was happening.

He did a quick by-feel check of the snaps that held the chute in his pack, trying to pry them loose.

Nothing. He could get no leverage on them at all reaching around like that.

Damn it all to hell. He hated landing with his reserve. Just annoying.

He glanced at his altimeter. He was far too low. He should cut loose of his main and go to the reserve, but he flat didn't have the time. Besides, he didn't want to lose it in a swollen creek below.

He shifted position so that he was falling almost backwards and snapped his reserve out of the pack on his stomach.

It deployed perfectly, but then caught in the pilot chute for his main and yanked his main out as well.

Shit, shit, shit!

The two chutes tangled in what was called a streamer before he even had a chance to stop them or cut one loose.

When one chute went into a streamer, it meant that the chute was tangled and the weight of the falling body was pulling the chute along toward the ground like a string flapping in a high wind.

When both chutes tangled together in a streamer, Elliot knew he was finished.

Damn it all to hell.

He studied his chutes, looking for any hope at all.

Nothing.

He had nothing to even help him start to untangle them even if he had the time.

His speed had barely decreased.

He had seconds to live.

Not staring at the ground rushing up at him, he fought to the last second to untangle the chutes, cutting away his reserve in hopes it would flash free and let his main catch air.

No chance.

It just went up and tangled with his main even worse.

Today was not a lucky day.

Both chutes were tangled far, far too much to ever hope to be free.

"Damn!" he shouted into the wind, his last word, as far above him he caught sight of the tiny figure of Deanna.

It seemed she had been wrong. They didn't have the time together he had hoped.

TWO

"SOME NEWS," K.J. said, appearing out of nowhere and sitting down at the wooden table in the Golden Nugget buffet in Las Vegas. "Our team has gotten a promotion of sorts."

"We're getting a raise?" Tommy asked, shaking his head.

Dr. Jewel Kelly glanced up from her strawberry shortcake dessert. She had just gotten a second helping and was enjoying it more than she wanted to admit. Being dead made things taste a lot better, but it also meant that if she ate more, she had to work out more. It seemed ghosts could get fat just as easily as humans. Who knew?

Tomorrow, she'd have to put in an extra few miles of running to cancel out the second helping.

And her best friend, lover, and partner, Tommy Ralston, was going to have to join her on the run, considering he had already finished two helpings and had glanced back at the buffet like he was considering a third.

The strawberry shortcake really was that good. Light white cake, fresh strawberries in a sweet natural juice, and real whipped cream. Best dessert in Las Vegas, second to none in her opinion.

"No raise," K.J. said, laughing.

"We're dead," Tommy said. "How can they promote us to being more dead?"

K.J. shrugged.

"More dead might mean better sex, better tasting food, and fewer missions to rescue people."

"Not sure if I could handle better sex," Jewel said. And she meant it. Sex was already amazing with Tommy.

Tommy looked at her. "We could try that—"

K.J. held up a hand into Tommy's face.

"Too much information," K.J. said, looking almost startled.

K.J. was a short man, with dark brown eyes and a love of partying and dressing in the wildest fashions Jewel had ever imagined.

He had been dead for over a hundred years and was their go-between with their bosses, the gods of death and dying and time and space and who knew what else.

This early spring evening, K.J. had dressed almost fashionably in a gray business suit, open pink shirt, and pink handkerchief tucked perfectly in his breast pocket.

If he had left it at that, all would have been fine, but the pink fluffy slippers and a pink Ben Hogan golf hat had just made Jewel laugh when she saw it.

K.J. was dapper all right, but just not in the normal definition of the word.

Jewel and Tommy were both dressed in their evening dinner clothes, which consisted of light shirts, jeans, and tennis shoes. Fashion statements, they were not.

Jewel had been a medical doctor before dying in the same car wreck as Tommy the year before. She had long brown hair she always kept pulled back and out of the way and green eyes that Tommy told her he loved more than anything.

Tommy had been in the Marines and joined the law enforcement after a couple of degrees in math and physics had bored him. He had been a deputy sheriff taking Jewel to a medical emergency in backwoods Montana when a deer jumped in front of them and Tommy lost control of the car and smashed them into a massive pine tree.

They had not crossed over into the next life as most dead people do. They had been left near the wreck, cold, wet, and very confused.

K.J. had appeared a few hours later and recruited them for the Ghost of a Chance organization, which consisted of a few hundred ghosts around the world who had not crossed into the next life, but who had been recruited to stay in this world and fight the bad guys and help where they could.

Since Jewel had been a doctor and Tommy a marine and a cop, they loved their new life. They got to continue to help people. It had taken some time to get used to being dead and learn all the tricks, but they had managed to do some really good things for people in the last year.

And just a few months back, near Christmas, they had helped the superhero Poker Boy and his team save the world from a real evil.

That had felt better than Jewel could have ever imagined.

Besides Jewel and Tommy, last fall Belle and Nancy had joined the team. They also now lived here in Las Vegas and were a wonderful couple. Belle and Nancy sometimes joined Jewel and Tommy for breakfast here at the Golden Nugget buffet.

This buffet had become the unofficial office for the team. They all talked about finding something official to call their office, but so far hadn't found anything.

The Golden Nugget buffet was seldom crowded, so they always had a table that wasn't bothered by living people. And the food was good at all times of the day or night.

"It seems," K.J. said, staring at what was left of Jewel's strawberry shortcake, "that the powers that be, after the job we did at Christmas, want us to focus on larger issues."

"What about fighting the Brigade?" Tommy asked a half second before Jewel could.

The Brigade was a group of truly evil ghosts recruited to do deeds that would try to twist the world into conflicts and wars because certain powers got joy and satisfaction from death. Jewel and Tommy had managed to stop the Brigade a number of times in the last year.

"We won't worry about them anymore," K.J. said, giving them a wave of his hand as if swatting a fly, "unless they get in our way. And we're going to get two more team members that we need to train before we get to the big jobs, whatever those jobs may be."

That shocked Jewel. She had thought their team was pretty balanced. She was a doctor, Tommy was a cop, Belle knew corporations better than anyone alive, and Nancy was a whiz at computers and accounting. With K.J. directing, they had functioned great.

"Another couple?" Tommy asked.

K.J. nodded. "Yes, but not at first. They are joining us a few months apart."

"Oh, that's not going to be fun for them," Tommy said, again eying the dessert area for yet another helping of strawberry shortcake.

"So who is coming in first?" Jewel asked.

"A real stud of a guy named Elliot West," K.J. said, looking slightly dreamy-eyed. "Adventurer in a bunch of sports, knows the great outdoors, that sort of thing. The fearless type. And I understand he's also a hell of a great defense attorney."

"A real he-man, huh?" Tommy said, laughing at K.J.

"A fella could do worse," K.J. said, looking suddenly embarrassed, which was hard to get K.J. to look.

K.J. sat there and pretend-fanned himself.

Over the last year, K.J. had let slip about his famous hot tub parties. It seemed that K.J. was the most famous of the dead party people around.

Jewel laughed. Clearly K.J.'s mind had gone places it should not have gone just yet with their new team member.

"So when is he getting killed?" Jewel asked.

"Skydiving accident," K.J. said, glancing at his watch. "Outside of Boise."

Belle and Nancy were both from Boise. And she and Tommy had been up in Montana. It seemed the Northwest was a prime place for recruiting Ghost of a Chance team members.

"When?" Tommy asked.

"Oh, shit," K.J. said, staring at his watch. "About forty minutes ago. I forgot about the time difference. I really wanted to be on time with this one. Honest I did."

Jewel just shook her head. The poor Elliot guy was going to be a mess. It had taken some real work to help Belle and Nancy make the transition to understanding they were dead. And it had taken her and Tommy days to finally believe they were actually dead, since this death state they found themselves in felt so real.

Better than real, actually, since food tasted better and sex was far more intense.

Jewel took one more bite of the wonderful strawberry shortcake, pushed the plate forward, and said to K.J., "Jump us to him."

THREE

ELLIOT HAD FOUND himself sitting under a large oak tree about two hundred yards from the runway the drop plane had left from. The big oak tree over him had just gotten its fresh leaves and the spring evening air smelled wonderful.

More intense than he could ever imagine.

He was still tied into his two worthless chutes and they were strung along the ground under the tree. He still had on his dive helmet and his goggles.

How in the hell had he survived that fall?

He should be very dead at this moment, or at least broken up and clinging to life. He had seen a couple other skydivers stream into the ground with tangled chutes. Neither of them had been pretty sights.

And neither had survived the impact.

He checked himself, but everything felt fine, no bones broken, no sprains, nothing. In fact, he felt better than when he had climbed on the plane for the jump.

He glanced back up through the tree, looking for broken branches. Had the chutes caught in the tree and broken his fall?

Was that even possible? If it was, he had to be the luckiest man to walk the planet.

He flexed his shoulders and back and then stood, dropping out of his two parachute packs and taking off his helmet and goggles and smoothing down his dark hair as best he could.

He felt great.

Clearly he had a lot of adrenaline still pumping through his system. He had no doubt that, when that cleared out, he would feel what had just happened.

As he moved back toward the runway, the jump plane came barreling in, far faster than normal, bounced twice and came to a grinding halt about four hundred paces down the runway.

It quickly taxied off the main concrete and stopped, its two engines cutting out.

He laughed and waved. The pilots must have seen him stream in and dove for the runway to get to him.

He glanced up.

Four wings were deployed above him and he waved up at them to try to let them know he was all right.

Deanna must be scared out of her mind. If he had watched her stream in, he didn't know what he would have done.

He went back under the big tree to gather up his chutes and get his helmet. He just couldn't believe he was alive and walking around after that. He really needed to figure out what had happened.

This might just get written up in a bunch of jump magazines.

The two pilots from the plane were both running his way as he wrapped up his chutes into a twisted mess in his arms.

Both pilots ran past him, not even seeing him.

"Over here, guys," Elliot shouted.

They didn't hear him.

After about twenty more steps to the other side of the tree line, both of them slowed, then stopped.

Then one of them turned and threw up.

Elliot dropped the chutes and headed in that direction. Clearly someone else had had a problem as well and he hadn't seen it happening. He knew Deanna was above him, so it couldn't have been her.

He ran ten steps and then slowed and stopped and looked up.

Four wings were lining up for landing near the edge of the runway.

There had only been five jumpers.

He was the fifth.

He moved slowly toward the two pilots who had backed away from what had caused one of them to lose his lunch.

Two chutes were strung out along the ground as his had been. They looked exactly like his chutes.

And tied into the end of them was a blurry image of what looked to be a human body.

He stopped about ten paces away and tried to get his eyes to focus on the body.

His stomach was twisted into a knot.

He had to look.

He had to know.

And then his vision cleared and he could see his own twisted body there on the ground, blood everywhere, bones sticking out of skin, neck twisted into a position that no neck could ever be twisted.

He was dead.

There was no doubt he was dead.

He hadn't survived the jump.

He turned and staggered away from his own body, making it back to the base of the big oak tree before dropping to the ground.

As a person who faced death in so many ways in so many sports, he thought he would be prepared.

But seeing his own body like that was something else.

Nothing could prepare a person for that.

And then, through the clear evening air he heard a scream like none he could have ever imagined.

Two of his friends were holding Deanna back from getting too close. But clearly she had seen enough.

She screamed once more and then dropped to the ground.

"I'm so sorry, Deanna," he said softly. "So very, very sorry."

FOUR

JEWEL AND TOMMY and K.J. appeared next to a small airport runway standing on soft dirt covered in a thin layer of newly sprouted grass. A fairly large two-prop plane sat to one side of the runway and a half-dozen police cars and an ambulance with lights still flashing were scattered along the edge of the runway.

Jewel noticed that all of them had left tire tracks in the soft ground.

The sun was low on the horizon and the air had a spring bite to it. Normally this would be the type of evening Jewel would love, but not when death was involved.

There looked to be four other skydivers sitting on the ground near the edge of the runway and most of the police activity was centered around a twisted body in the low-cut grass.

"Where is Elliot?" Tommy asked K.J.

K.J. just shrugged. "He's here somewhere. The newly dead seldom roam far from their bodies."

"Not miles like we did, huh?" Tommy said.

Jewel laughed as K.J. just shrugged and looked sheepish. She and Tommy had been killed far out in the mountains. It had taken them hours to leave their crash site, so mostly K.J. was right.

"Is that his girlfriend?" Jewel asked, pointing to the only woman skydiver in the group of four. She had short brown hair and seemed tall, even while sitting.

She had her head down between her knees.

K.J. nodded. "Deanna Teel. She's going to join us in two months. She and Elliot are a couple. Very close from what I understand."

"This has to be really hard on her," Jewel said.

"I see him," Tommy said and started off across the field toward the grove of oak and willow trees just starting to get their spring leaves.

A guy was sitting against the trunk of one of the big oak trees, seeming to just watch. He had on a gray jumpsuit that looked to be expensive and made of some strange material that almost shined.

"I sure hope there are no horse piles out here," K.J. said as he and Jewel followed Tommy.

"The ground does feel soft, doesn't it," Jewel said.

"Oh, yuck, I just got these shoes," K.J. said.

Tommy walked up to Elliot and stuck out his hand as if meeting the guy on a street corner. "Elliot West I presume?"

Elliot sort of looked at the hand being offered, but didn't take it.

"I'm Elliot West," he said. "Or I used to be."

He pointed to the crowd of cops around the body.

"You still are," Jewel said. "Just living outside that body now."

Elliot looked up at them and shook his head. "I didn't think people could see ghosts."

"They can't," K.J. said as he checked the bottoms of his red slipper-like shoes.

Jewel decided she needed to take over this fairly quickly. "I'm Jewel, this is Tommy, and this is K.J."

"So where's my white light?" Elliot asked. "My tunnel. If I'm dead I wouldn't mind seeing my dad again."

Jewel knelt in front of Elliot and smiled. "We can explain all that if you give us a little time."

He looked at her, clearly still very much in shock.

She remembered that feeling well.

She glanced back at Tommy and K.J. "Remember the Sizzler table we took Nancy and Belle to after their accident?"

Tommy nodded. "I'll jump there and make sure the table is open."

He vanished.

"Now that's pretty creepy," Elliot said. "I'm really seeing things now, of that there is no doubt."

Jewel offered her hand. "Come on, let's get to a place we can talk and explain what's happening."

Elliot looked at her hand and then nodded and took it.

His grip was firm, his hands slightly rough.

They both stood. And he looked over at Deanna.

"Anything I can do to help her?"

"Not at the moment," Jewel said. "You and K.J. stay here and I'll go give her some reassurance and help."

"Will she be able to see you? Or me?" Elliot asked.

Jewel shook her head. "No. But stay here and I'll be right back."

"I'll stay with him," K.J. said. "My shoes seem to have survived one transit of that cow-pie mess."

Jewel just shook her head and moved quickly over the soft field toward the group of skydivers and the woman with her head between her knees.

Jewel, without touching any of the others, moved in close to Deanna and touched her.

A moment later Jewel was completely inside Deanna.

The grief that Deanna was feeling was like a wall slamming into Jewel, but Jewel had felt this before and she sent calming thoughts through to Deanna.

Then she repeated over and over that Elliot loved her and that she would get to see him again in time and that he was all right where he was.

And as Deanna calmed some, pushed the grief back slightly, Jewel noticed something else.

Something very black and growing inside Deanna.

Cancer.

A nasty brain tumor.

And the cancer had spread from Deanna's brain through the rest of her body. Deanna had known something was wrong and had gone in for tests last week. She had just gotten the results earlier that very afternoon and hadn't yet told Elliot.

She hadn't known how to tell Elliot, actually.

She had only two months to live. There was nothing anyone could do. It had spread far, far too much.

Jewel gave the thought to Deanna that she would see Elliot shortly, that he would be waiting for her, that he would be with her through her coming trial, and then she left Deanna's body.

Jewel moved back across the field, feeling the full intensity of the tragedy around her. Two young and very smart people struck down in the prime of their lives.

"K.J.," Jewel said before Elliot could ask her anything, "get us to that restaurant."

An instant later the runway and the wide fields and ambulance and cop cars vanished, replaced by the noise of people talking and laughing and eating in the wonderful rich smell of steak.

FIVE

ELLIOT WAS CONVINCED he was now dreaming, that his accident had just been a bad dream, and now things were just twisting into silliness in his dream.

He glanced around to find himself in the Sizzler Restaurant out near the mall in Boise. He had eaten here a few times while out in this part of town shopping, but it was a long way from his and Deanna's condo against the foothills.

The place was decorated in all wood, with polished wood tables, wood beams and posts, and wood chairs and booths. It was huge, with over a hundred seats. Through the windows, he could see cars moving past and going into the mall parking lot just like any other spring evening.

The guy named Tommy, who looked nice enough and seemed to smile a lot, was sitting at a large wooden table in a closed section of the restaurant. The table could hold ten at least.

Elliot had a good feeling about all three of these people, even though they were just part of his dream. If he had met them in real life, outside the dream, he would have liked them. Even the strange guy in the expensive gray suit and pink hat and pink shoes.

He sure didn't fit in Boise, but he seemed like a good guy.

They all three seemed to be about his age at thirty. And all three seemed to be in good shape, including the K.J. guy.

Jewel, the woman who had gone to comfort Deanna and then vanished inside Deanna, indicated that Elliot should take a chair, so he did.

K.J. sat beside Tommy and Jewel sat on the other side.

Jewel seemed almost shaken by her contact with Deanna, so Elliot decided to start there.

"What's happening with Deanna?"

Jewel glanced at K.J., then shook her head. "We have time for that, but first we have to show you some things."

"And explain a few things," Tommy said.

Elliot nodded and sat back. "Explain away and then I'm going to wake up, either in bed at home or in the hospital and laugh at all this."

"Yeah," Tommy said, "thought that same thing for a short time when I died."

That death part just wasn't sinking in for Elliot. He had always lived fully. Being dead had never been part of the plan.

He was alive. He could feel it. Dreaming, sure, but alive.

"First off," Jewel said, seeming to sense what he was thinking, "you really are dead. That really was your body out there in that field."

Elliot nodded, trying to keep his stomach calm, remembering his chute tangled with his safety chute in the worst streamer imaginable.

"Most people, meaning almost everyone," Tommy said, "die and just pass into the next world."

"And before you ask," K.J. said, holding up a hand to stop the next obvious question, "no one knows what's on the other side. And I honestly don't want to know, thank you very much."

Elliot nodded again, just letting them talk. He had to admit, this all felt real, but he'd had dreams before that had felt real.

He had learned as a defense attorney that it was better to just let a client talk and get it all out before asking too many questions.

But if this was a dream, it was sure a vivid one. The steak smell was making him really hungry. If he was dead, how come he was hungry?

"You did not pass into the next world after your accident because you are being recruited for a special team," Jewel said.

"We are all Ghost of a Chance agents," Tommy said. "Our job is to fight bad stuff and help people. Sort of like you do in your job as a defense attorney."

"More like a superhero team in the comics," Elliot said, laughing. "Now I know I'm dreaming."

"Sort of like that," K.J. said, laughing with him. "Think of this as a superhero team with a bunch of dead people and a bisexual one-hundred-year-old ghost leading it. I like that. Think I could get someone to do some panels?"

Elliot just shook his head and started to stand. "If I really am a ghost, I need to get back to the airport to see how Deanna's doing."

"She's doing fine," Jewel said. "And you can see her later if you want, but we need to get you more information first."

"You need to know some of what you can do and can't do," Tommy said.

"Like this," K.J. said.

The small guy with the pink hat stood and walked with great flair, like he was on a modeling runway, right through the middle of the table, through a neighboring table, and off toward the salad bar, where he grabbed three cherry tomatoes and ate them on the way back while walking through things.

"How…? Elliot asked, but he couldn't get the question to even form.

"Everything has what we call a ghost element to it," Jewel said.

Jewel knocked on the top of the table as if it was solid, then stuck her hand through it.

There was a ketchup bottle on the table and she picked it up. Suddenly she had a bottle in her hand and an original bottle stayed in its place.

"Everything, including food, has a ghost element to it," Tommy said.

Then he smiled at Elliot. "Are you starting to feel better? Maybe better than you have felt in a long time?"

Elliot had to admit that he was. And the smells of the restaurant were more intense as well. He had been hungry before they went out for the two evening jumps. Now with the fantastic smells around him, he was famished.

"So I'm a ghost and I can eat?" Elliot asked.

"One of the many pleasures," K.J. said. "And the food is always free and tastes wonderful."

"Free?" Elliot asked. He had always believed in paying for anything he used or ate. Getting something for free wasn't the way he lived the world. He worked for his food and money.

"It's free," Jewel said, "because we don't actually take anything. Come on, I'll show you."

She stood and Elliot stood with her.

"More dessert," Tommy said, laughing and standing and clapping his hands as he went with them.

Jewel led Elliot toward the large salad bar. "Pick up a bowl."

He reached down and picked up a ceramic salad bowl. It felt real and solid in his hand.

But the stack didn't go down.

"You have in your hand the ghost element of that top bowl," Jewel said. "If you put it on the counter and leave it for an hour or so, it will just vanish."

She had him put the bowl down and then follow her over toward the kitchen door where a couple of waiters and waitresses were coming out of the kitchen with trays of food.

"How do you like your steaks?" she asked.

"Medium rare," he said.

She nodded and then motioned for them to follow a waitress with five meals on a tray toward a table near the salad bar.

She pointed to one plate on the tray as the waitress set the big tray on a stand.

"Grab that one," Jewel said. "It's got the medium rare tag in it."

Elliot didn't much like the idea of taking another person's food, even though it was clear no one could see them and this was a dream. Who knew he had ethics even while dreaming.

He did as Jewel instructed, picking up the heavy plate, feeling the heat from the bottom against his hand.

But the original meal stayed on the tray.

Jewel indicated he should bring the plate and follow her.

She grabbed some silverware and napkins on the way back to the table. Ghost silverware, ghost napkins, Elliot noted.

After he was seated back at the table with the meal in front of him, Tommy and K.J. came back, both carrying some sort of pudding dessert.

Jewel indicated that Elliot should eat.

He looked at the steak and baked potato and then back at Jewel. "I'm not eating that person's dinner?"

Jewel shook her head. "Nope, that person has their dinner, the real dinner. You are just eating the ghost element of the food."

Elliot cut into the steak and took a bite.

The sensation was like nothing he had ever imagined. The taste seemed to explode in his mouth, the steak itself seemed to almost melt. It was the best-tasting steak he had ever had, without a doubt.

Nothing else had ever come close.

He closed his eyes and just enjoyed the flavor, savoring it for a moment. Then when he opened his eyes, Tommy, K.J., and Jewel were all smiling at him.

"One of the many perks about being dead," Tommy said. "The food just flat tastes wonderful."

"You think the food is good," K.J, said, laughing. "Wait until you try sex. Worth dying for, let me say."

Elliot looked at Jewel, then at Tommy. "Ghosts can have sex as well?"

"Like rabbits," Tommy said, laughing.

But Jewel was looking serious and considering how much fun Tommy and K.J. were having teaching him the ropes of being dead, that made no sense.

Elliot took another bite of steak and tried to think, tried to come up with more questions. But the steak tasted so damned good, and he was so hungry, he couldn't think of a one.

And after he woke up from this crazy dream, he and Deanna were going to have to come out here for dinner. He had no idea the food here was so good.

SIX

JEWEL WATCHED Elliot eat the juicy sirloin steak and the baked potato. She was convinced that Elliot still thought he was in some strange dream.

She liked the guy. Her first impression of him was good and he had a confidence you didn't often see in a person. But she had no idea what was going to happen when he finally realized he really was dead.

So while Elliot was eating, she turned the conversation to K.J. in an attempt to give Elliot more information.

"So why did the powers-that-be want to add Elliot to our team?" Jewel asked. "I'm a former doctor, Tommy was a cop,

Belle is a corporation wizard, Nancy is amazing with math and money."

"The risk-taking part," K.J. said, "would be my guess. Either of you ever think of jumping out of a plane?"

Jewel shook her head, as did Tommy.

"They didn't even have planes when I died," K.J. said.

Elliot looked at him with a funny look, then went back to eating.

"My boss told me that Elliot will bring to the team that 'take chances' attitude," K.J. said. "And his legal thinking will help a lot as well. I have no idea what kind of special missions they have planned for us, but seems that Elliot's duel skills are needed."

"So you killed me to join your team?" Elliot asked, stopping with a piece of steak halfway to his mouth.

K.J. laughed, as did Tommy.

Jewel took the question seriously, because she and Tommy had thought the same thing at first.

"No, you were going to die today in that accident no matter what," Jewel said.

"When a person's time is up, their time is up," K.J. said, finishing the last of his pudding dessert and pushing the tin cup away. "No one, no god, no superhero can stop that or change that in any fashion. Kind of a real downer, but it's true."

"So how did you die?" Elliot asked K.J.

K.J. shrugged. "Beat to death because a group of men didn't like my sexual orientation."

"Oh," Elliot said, then went back to eating. He had almost finished the large sirloin.

Jewel glanced at K.J. "You want to go get Belle and Nancy so they can meet our new team member?"

"Be glad to do thy bidding, my lady," K.J. said, standing, bowing, and vanishing.

Elliot stared at where K.J. had been for a moment. "Am I going to be able to do that?"

"You are," Tommy said. "With a little time and practice."

"And this," Jewel said, floating up out of her chair until she was near the ceiling, then coming back down.

"Now I know this dream is crazy," Elliot said. "I wonder what I ate to cause this."

"It's not a dream," Jewel said.

"Whatever you say." Elliot pushed his empty plate away. "Can I have seconds and will they taste as good?"

"You can," Tommy said. "And it will."

"Great," Elliot said, standing and heading back for the door from the kitchen near the salad bar.

Jewel watched him go, weaving through the tables as if he was still alive.

"We might have a problem," Tommy said.

Jewel nodded. Elliot was completely convinced he was in a dream. That might turn into a very big problem. And Jewel had no idea at all how to stop it.

SEVEN

ELLIOT DECIDED that like a good ski run, he was just going to enjoy this dream and not fight it. And when he woke up, if he could remember it, he and Deanna would have a good laugh.

He was really going to try to remember this. Just too weird.

He went over toward the door to the kitchen to wait for someone to bring out another steak dinner. The food had tasted so wonderful and he was far from full yet. So while he was dreaming, he might as well enjoy himself. Can't gain weight eating in a dream.

A woman with a large tray of meals came out of the kitchen. She started for him and he stepped back to give her room and bumped right into a woman about his age.

Only he didn't bump into her.

He went completely inside of her. Like she had been a vacuum and he was a dust mote.

No suck, plop, or whish sound. Just one minute he was outside of her and another minute he was inside her.

Trapped.

He could feel everything she was feeling and hear everything she was thinking and see everything she was seeing.

He felt a short moment of panic, then realized this was all a dream and laughed to himself. Then he let the woman's information flow over him.

Her name was Cathy, divorced, one kid, worked for a computer firm.

Oh, god, he suddenly realized he was inside the Cathy from his math class in high school, the same Cathy who had been a cheerleader and had married the head of the cross-country team.

He remembered everything she remembered from high school, the time she knew deep down had been her best time in life.

Wow, how sad was that? He had hated high school and just wanted to get out and really start living. He figured he had a full life of living ahead of him, if he ever woke up from this stupid dream.

Or got out of being trapped inside this woman.

Cathy was headed for the bathroom. She felt kind of ill and was hoping her period wasn't going to start tonight. She had no intention of sleeping with the older guy she was on a date with, but she just didn't want the hassle of her period.

Elliot could see Cathy's entire life, the affair she had on her husband that caused their breakup and his eventual suicide. Elliot could tell she wasn't a bad person, just a very, very dumb person.

And she carried the guilt about what had happened to her husband like a tight black knot in the back of her mind. Her sex drive had killed him just as if she had taken a gun to his head.

She knew that. She still loved him, for all the good that was going to do. She was trying to forget and move on.

Elliot had no doubt that she needed professional help to get past that tragedy, but Cathy didn't feel she had the money to get it.

He had always thought she was hot in high school, but since he was a skier, not some sports jock with a letterman's award, she never gave him the time of day.

He hadn't given her one thought in over a decade. Why was he now, in this dream, inside her, listening to her thoughts on the way to a bathroom?

And from what he could see about what she liked about sex, thank god he hadn't asked her out. She had a hidden closet in her bedroom full of all sorts of whips and chains and things he now could see her using, but didn't want to know about.

As far as he was concerned, everyone had a right to his or her own sexual interests. He just didn't want to know about the interests if he could help it.

And right now, riding inside of Cathy, he couldn't help but know about it all.

Every last detail.

And how much she loved it.

No wonder her husband had left her when he discovered her naked with another man tied up and getting whipped.

Now Cathy was walking at a fast clip toward the woman's restroom. That was not a place Elliot wanted to be, even in a dream that was quickly becoming a nightmare.

How the hell did he get this dream back on track and out of this woman's brain?

Was this what Jewel had done when she disappeared into Deanna? If so, there had to be a way out.

He tried to imagine himself just standing outside the bathroom or back in the main part of the restaurant, but no luck.

He was inside Cathy, stuck.

Cathy opened the door, her thoughts on hurrying up and getting done and getting back to her date with a guy she called Bennie. Bennie was ten years older than Cathy and they had met on an online dating sight. His last wife had died, and he had money, something Cathy was very interested in.

As Cathy went into the stall, Elliot imagined himself like a little ball inside her head, his hands over his eyes and ears, cut off completely from anything going on around him.

It seemed to work and give her the privacy he wanted her to have.

And that kept him from seeing things he flat didn't have an interest in seeing up close and really personal.

He let himself come out of his ball as she combed her hair in front of the mirror, relieved her period hadn't started.

Cathy had clearly put on a few pounds since high school, and it wasn't muscle. And her hair color and style hadn't changed at all. She still wore the same style of mini-skirt, now too short for her thicker legs, and a blouse with a frilly bra that allowed her date to get a glimpse, but not the entire picture.

"Wow, really stuck in high school," Elliot said to himself.

Cathy glanced around, thinking that maybe she had heard someone, then shrugged, put her comb back in her purse and headed back out of the restroom.

Could he actually talk to the person he was inside. Wait until he woke up and told Deanna that.

As Cathy approached the table, Elliot had a bad feeling as he recognized her date.

Bennie was actually Barry Johns. Barry had been accused of killing his first wife, but no one could ever prove it, so no arrest. Elliot and the others in his firm had talked about the chance of taking Barry's case if he was arrested and all of them had wanted no part of it.

Barry, or Bennie as Cathy called him, stood and offered his hand as she returned, playing the part of a real gentleman.

Cathy actually liked that and took his hand and settled into her chair.

But as she touched Barry, Elliot could see inside his mind as well.

And the son-of-a-bitch had killed his first wife.

And another woman back in college.

Now what was Elliot going to do?

What could he do? This was a dream.

And in the dream, he was stuck in an old cheerleader's body and she was dating a man who had killed his wife.

Suddenly this was becoming something more than a dream.

This was a full-on nightmare.

EIGHT

JEWEL GLANCED UP as the other two members of their team appeared with K.J.

Belle and Nancy both were wearing jeans and light sweatshirts, their kick-around-the-house outfits, as they liked to call them. Both women were about Jewel's age and stunningly beautiful. Belle had long blonde hair that she had pulled back and tied while Nancy had short brown hair, styled wonderfully to look like a modern cut.

When these two dressed up in modern fashions, as they loved to do at times, no model could hold a candle to either one of them.

They were a couple and Jewel had never seen two people so much in love before. They just radiated joy and friendship and Jewel really enjoyed time around them, even when working on stopping some horrid thing from happening.

"The old get-used-to-being-dead restaurant," Belle said, laughing as she looked around. "Don't you just love the wood beams and columns in here?"

Jewel and Tommy and K.J. had brought them here just after they died, just as they had brought Elliot this time.

"I still like this place," Nancy said. "And I think I could use some more to eat."

"Actually," Belle said, "with that wonderful steak smell, it's going to be damn hard to resist."

"So where is the new recruit to the team?" Belle asked.

Jewel pointed toward the salad bar and kitchen door area. "He's the six-foot tall guy in the gray jumpsuit."

Then she turned and didn't see him.

"Oh, shit," Tommy said, vanishing and appearing outside in the parking lot and doing a quick scan around.

"K.J.," Jewel said, "check the men's bathroom."

K.J. vanished.

"Wow," Belle said, laughing. "A lost dead guy. Who knew that could happen."

"He still completely believes he's dreaming," Jewel said.

"Oh," Belle said, as the three of them spread out.

But after a moment they all ended up back at the table, and K.J. and Tommy both shook their heads.

"How could a tall, really, really handsome guy in a parachuting jumpsuit just vanish in a restaurant?" K.J. asked.

"He's a looker, huh?" Nancy asked, smiling at K.J.

"Dreamy," K.J. said, pretending to fan himself.

Tommy glanced at Jewel and just shook his head.

"Did you teach him how to go into someone and get out?" Belle asked.

Jewel instantly knew that was the problem.

"He bumped into someone and he thinks he's stuck," Tommy said, nodding.

"Spread out," Jewel said. "Let's see if we can find him."

The five of them spread through the restaurant, running their hands through people. Jewel knew if she found the right person Elliot had stumbled into, her hand would run into resistance, just as if she was touching a regular person when she had been alive. Ghosts feel regular to other ghosts.

Twenty people later, and more information about people's lives than she wanted to know, she was back near their big table in the back section.

"He's not in the restaurant," Tommy said.

"Again," K.J. asked, "how can you lose a hunk of a man in a gray jumpsuit in a restaurant."

"You don't think he left, do you?" Nancy asked.

Jewel shook her head. "If he did," she said, "he's going to quickly discover just how dead he really is."

At that moment, a woman wearing a mini-skirt and a blouse that didn't fit her came out of the woman's restroom and went to a table.

Jewel pointed at the woman.

Tommy nodded and shook his head. "I'll get him."

"Oh, no," Belle said, laughing. "His first time in another person and he's trapped with a woman in a restroom."

"He's going to need professional help to get over that," Nancy said.

"As if being dead wasn't bad enough," K.J. said, laughing as well. "I'd have to pay my shrink double if that happened to me."

"You have a shrink?" Belle asked.

K.J. waved his hand in dismissal. "Of course. Doesn't everyone?"

Jewel just smiled. If anything could convince Elliot he was dead, trapped inside a woman in a restroom just might do it.

Or convince him he had died and gone to hell.

NINE

ELLIOT WAS JUST barely holding down the panic. He was trapped in a woman's body who was dating a killer and he had no idea what to do.

Or how to get out.

Or why this horrid dream wasn't ending.

Suddenly, he could feel a strong hand grab his arm and jumpsuit and yank him sideways.

He was back in the restaurant and instead of experiencing the steak smell through Cathy, he could smell it himself.

Oh, thank heavens!

Rescued.

Tommy was standing beside him smiling and shaking his head.

"Thanks," Elliot said.

"Part of the training," Tommy said and turned Elliot toward the table in the back. Jewel and K.J. and two other stunning women were there.

Both women wore sweatshirts and jeans. One was a blonde with long hair and the other had short brown hair.

And all of them were clearly trying to keep from laughing.

"Elliot," Jewel said, as they got close, "this is Belle and Nancy, our other two team members."

"Welcome aboard," Belle, the blonde said, giving him a smile that really was welcoming along with a firm handshake.

"Sorry that your first time inside another person had to be in a woman's restroom," Nancy said, smiling at him. "Not a fun place."

"I imagined myself down into a small ball," Elliot said, "with no eyes and ears and managed to not see anything I shouldn't have seen."

"Wow, smart thinking," Jewel said as they all sat down around the big table again.

"For future reference," Tommy said, "think of being inside another person like

Now Available
from all your favorite booksellers
in trade paper and electronic editions.

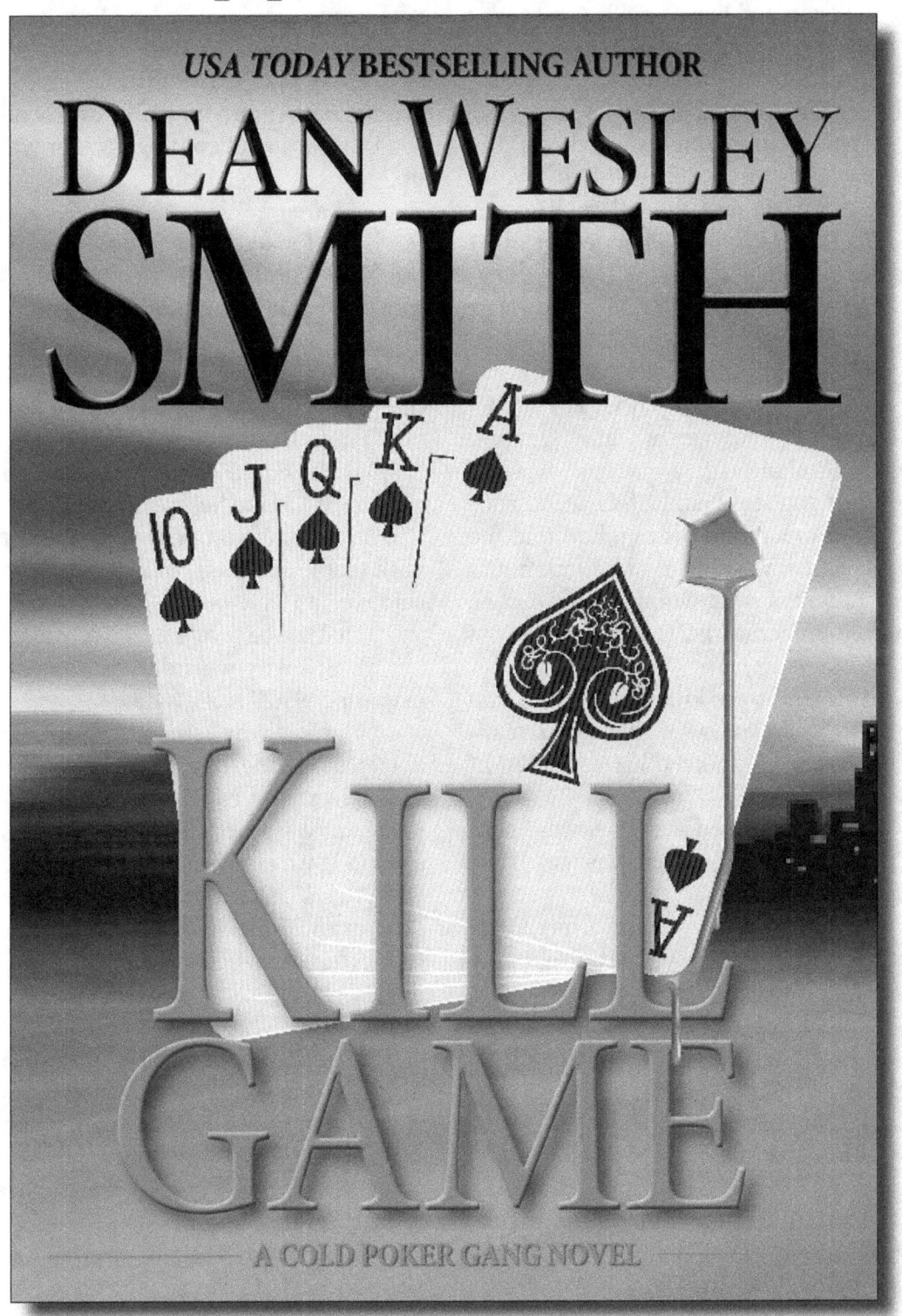

being inside a car. You just step out. It's easy once you get the hang of it."

"If they are walking," Nancy said, "I just think of myself stopping and the person walks on and leaves me."

"So I was really inside Cathy over there?" Elliot said. "She was a cheerleader in my high school."

"That's Cathy?" Belle asked, shaking her head and staring across the restaurant where Cathy sat with that killer. "Besides the weight, she hasn't changed at all. I just didn't recognize her."

"Wow, me either," Nancy said, staring at Cathy.

Elliot was surprised. "You knew her?"

Both of us went to school at Borah," Belle said, "same year as Cathy and you went to Capital."

Elliot suddenly could feel some panic start to creep into his mind around the edges. He hated panic of any kind, but at the moment it was winning because he now remembered the two sitting across from him.

"You both were killed last fall in that horrid mess downtown," Elliot said, managing, he hoped, to keep the panic out of his voice.

They both smiled as if they were happy to be recognized. "That was us," Belle said.

"We didn't stick around for the aftermath," Nancy said. "We had a world to save. Was it fun?"

"Not sure about fun," Elliot said, "but it was headlines. So that must mean I am really dead?"

All five of them nodded.

"But just remember the food's good," K.J. said.

"And we get to save the world at times," Nancy said, "and a lot of people as well along the way."

"This isn't a dream?" Elliot asked.

He was trying to let his logical brain figure out a way that he couldn't be dead, but the logic kept telling him he was dead.

Very dead.

He really had streamed into the ground earlier and he really was dead.

Dead as in not coming back or waking up.

"No dream," Jewel said.

Elliot looked at the five people around the table with him. Two he had seen pictures of in the paper last fall when they died horribly.

More than likely his picture would be in the paper tomorrow as well.

Damn, he was dead.

And he could eat and be inside other people. What the hell was going on?

He glanced around at Cathy sitting with that killer, then back at Nancy. "You said we can save people?"

"That's what we do," Jewel said.

"That's why we didn't cross over like everyone else," Belle said.

"That's why the powers-that-be above us, those I call our bosses," K.J. said, "recruited us. Since we were going to die anyway, they figured we could stick around if we wanted and help others."

"You mean I don't have to stay if I don't want?" Elliot said.

"After you learn everything we are doing," Jewel said, "you can decide to go on. It will be your choice."

Elliot wasn't sure how he felt about that. He was still fighting the idea this was a dream, but he had to find out for sure, or somehow wake up.

"How about we save someone as a test run on this craziness?"

All of them looked puzzled, so he pointed back to Cathy sitting with that killer. "That guy's she's with is named Barry Johns."

"The guy that killed his wife, but no one could prove it?" Belle asked.

"One and the same," Elliot said. "I think I was hearing Cathy's thoughts and she doesn't know who he is. And might be too stupid to care."

Both Belle and Nancy nodded at that. They must have had some connection back in school with Cathy.

"When she touched Barry's hand," Elliot said, "I could see that he had actually killed his wife and another woman back in college."

"Yeah, noticed that," K.J. said. "When I touched him while looking for you. Figured there was nothing we could do at the moment."

"Exactly," Elliot said. "If what you say is true and we are all dead, what can a bunch of ghosts do?"

At that, all five of them laughed.

"We saved the world before Christmas," Belle said, "I think we can deal with a twisted murderer just fine."

"Watch this," K.J. said, clapping his hands together. "This is just too much fun. I should get some popcorn. Who wants popcorn?"

Jewel just laughed and shook her head at K.J. "No popcorn."

"You're no fun," K.J. said, pretending to pout.

"That's not at all what Tommy says," Jewel said, making K.J. blush slightly.

Tommy stood and glanced at Nancy. "You want to back the woman out of this?"

Nancy stood. "Love to. Let me act first. I'll set the scene."

Tommy laughed and nodded.

"I'll get the manager to call the police," Jewel said, standing as well.

"I still want popcorn," K.J. said.

Tommy headed for Barry and Nancy for Cathy.

Jewel just vanished.

Elliot had no idea what they were intending, but Belle and K.J. seemed to know and were having fun watching.

"Is he going to go inside of Barry?" Elliot asked, feeling shocked. He had only touched the guy and had felt dirty.

"Memories you get from people pass very quickly unless you want to hold onto them," Belle said.

"Until you mentioned him," K.J. said, "I had already forgotten about touching him and learning about his past."

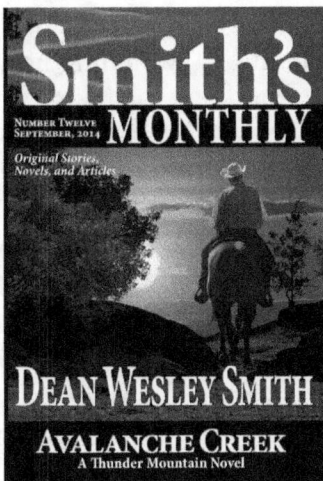

As Elliot watched, Tommy sunk into Barry and Nancy into Cathy.

Just watching Tommy go inside that slime-ball made Elliot shudder.

Suddenly Cathy slammed her chair backwards and stood, shouting at the top of her lungs, "You're that killer Barry Johns. You killed your wife!"

She picked up a glass of water and threw it in Barry's face.

Everyone in the restaurant went silent. Everyone was staring at the scene.

"So what do you have to say for yourself?" Cathy shouted.

Elliot looked at Belle who was smiling. Was this really happening? Nancy was controlling Cathy, getting her to speak.

"Really should have popcorn," K.J. said, clapping his hands.

"We can control people like that?" Elliot asked.

"You'll learn," K.J. said. "Watch what Tommy can do. He's one of the best."

At that moment, Barry started to shake and tremble. "I didn't mean to kill her. I didn't mean it. Honest. Can't a guy be forgiven for a mistake?"

Everyone in the restaurant sort of gasped at once.

Elliot was pretty sure he was one of the people gasping.

The silence in the restaurant got more and more intense as everyone, including the staff just sort of froze to listen and watch.

"No!" Cathy shouted. "You killed her in cold blood. It wasn't a mistake and the only reason you aren't rotting in jail is because they could never find her body and prove you did it."

Barry just sat there shaking, seeming to plead with her as if they were alone and an entire restaurant of people weren't watching and listening.

"I buried her in a nice spot," he said. "She can see down over the entire city."

Again about half the restaurant gasped.

Elliot was just flat stunned.

"Please just like me," Barry said, reaching out his hand. "I'm not really that bad of a man."

"What about those rumors about your old college sweetheart?" Cathy asked. "Did you bury her near your wife?"

"Side-by-side on a ridge in the foothills," Barry said.

Once more just about everyone in the restaurant gasped.

Elliot was flat impressed. Tommy and Nancy were making Barry confess to his crimes in a way that was totally believable, spontaneous, and had lots and lots of witnesses. It would even hold up in court if the police found the bodies where Barry said they were. Tommy and Nancy were good. Real good.

"Outside," Belle said to Elliot, pointing to the windows.

Police cars, three of them with lights flashing were pulling up outside.

"How did Jewel do that?"

"Got inside the manager and had him do the call," Belle said.

Of course. Same as what Elliot was watching now with Tommy and Nancy.

"I just want you to like me," Barry said again to Cathy, his voice pleading.

"You confess everything to the police and then maybe we can have a real date," Cathy said. "With nothing hidden."

Barry nodded just as the police came pouring through the door and a dozen customers pointed to Barry.

Barry raised his hands over his head and turned to face the police who had their guns drawn.

"Officers," Barry said, "I want to confess to killing my wife and my college girlfriend. They are both buried exactly two miles up the Benson Gulch Road after the pavement ends on the top of a ridge to the right."

Then he turned back from the stunned police to face Cathy. "Now will you go out with me?"

"Go to hell, you murdering bastard!" Cathy shouted.

At that, the entire restaurant burst into applause.

Cathy turned and took a bow.

"Wow," Belle said, "Nancy is good, isn't she?"

Jewel appeared beside Elliot. "Now watch this." She pointed back to Barry.

Elliot felt more stunned than he wanted to admit. But as he watched, Barry started to shudder and as the cops grabbed him and put cuffs on him, he broke down into sobs, crying over and over again, "I didn't mean to kill them. Honest, I didn't."

And then he wet his pants.

A moment later, Nancy stepped out of Cathy and Tommy stepped out of Barry.

Both laughed, gave each other a high-five, and headed back to the table as both Cathy and Barry seemed suddenly stunned.

Then Barry screamed and grabbed his crotch in pain.

"You didn't?" Jewel asked Tommy.

Tommy laughed. "I did. The guy was a real sicko."

Jewel just shook her head and kissed Tommy.

Belle hugged Nancy.

K.J. applauded and said, "Told you this would need popcorn. A real passion play."

Elliot stared at the screaming-in-pain Barry and then turned to face the group. "What did you do?"

"Just made sure that if he ever thinks of sex or killing again," Tommy said, "his crotch will feel like a thousand bees are stinging it at once."

"Oh," Elliot said.

It was all he could think of to say.

"Anyone hungry," K.J. said, "Stopping bad people always makes me hungry."

With that, all four of the others laughed and headed back toward the salad bar and kitchen, ignoring all the disruption and police talking to tables of people as Barry was hauled out of the door swearing in pain.

"Don't worry. You'll get the hang of all this," Jewel said.

Then she took Elliot by the arm. "I seem to remember that you were going for seconds a short time ago before your trip to the restroom?"

He nodded. He had been. But that was back when he thought this all a dream.

Now he was fairly certain he was dead. And damn it all to hell, he was still hungry.

SECTION TWO
The First Mission

TEN

FORTY MINUTES LATER the pandemonium in the restaurant had died down. A few police were still interviewing people and four police cars still had their lights on outside, but it seemed like the entire thing was about over.

Jewel had stuck with Elliot and managed to help him get more food. Then they rejoined the team sitting around the big table in the back.

Belle and Nancy sat together facing into the restaurant next to K.J. Tommy sat at the head of the table, and she and Elliot sat facing Belle and Nancy.

Elliot seemed quiet, but clearly aware and the conversation went on around him as he ate, every-so-often holding up a bite of steak or fork full of potato in wonder at how good it tasted.

Jewel knew that the shock of actually understanding he was dead had sunk in. That was just going to take some time to get past. Elliot had the time.

She also knew that pretty soon he would ask to see Deanna and at that point Jewel would have to tell him about Deanna's tumor. And that she would also be joining them in two months.

Jewel had no doubt that Elliot would want to be with Deanna for the next two months.

If it was Tommy in that situation, Jewel would want to be there as well.

They would figure out a way to help Elliot with some training while he was with Deanna, and then train them both completely together starting in a few months.

"Well, counselor?" Tommy asked Elliot, "Will the police be able to make that stick on dear old Barry?"

For the first time in thirty minutes, Elliot smiled and nodded. "Spontaneous confession, lots of witnesses, and his description of where the bodies are buried should lock him up for a very long time."

"They got it all on security cam as well," Belle said, indicating the small cameras up near the ceiling.

"Great job," Elliot said to Tommy. "Everyone inside the legal system knew he had killed his wife. No one could prove it and all the defense lawyers were silently glad he was never charged so that he didn't need an attorney."

"Not a fun client, huh?" Nancy asked.

"He would have been horrid," Elliot said.

Jewel was glad that Elliot was smiling and talking again. That was a good sign.

Suddenly, the entire place froze except for them. No sound, no movement, nothing.

Jewel knew instantly what had happened. They were between instants of time.

A moment later Laverne appeared right between Tommy and K.J. at the end of the table. She was a tall and powerful woman in a gray suit that shouted both expensive and power. Her hair was pulled back tight, giving her classic Greek face a stark look.

Everyone jumped to their feet and bowed just slightly except Elliot, who looked around stunned at the frozen people and then saw he was the only one sitting. He quickly stood.

Laverne nodded to him. "Nice to meet you, Elliot. I'm sorry about your death earlier this evening, but now glad to have you on this great team. You will make a perfect addition to it."

Elliot just sort of half-nodded, clearly stunned.

Jewel felt stunned as well.

Elliot had no idea he was facing one of the most powerful gods in the world, a woman hundreds of thousands of years old. The team had worked with her and other gods and superheroes to save the world just before Christmas last year. But after a Christmas visit from her, they hadn't seen her since.

It looked as if Elliot was going to learn even more on his first day dead.

Laverne turned to K.J. "I've got a situation we need your team's help with."

"Anything," K.J. managed to say.

Considering how in awe of Laverne he was, Jewel was impressed he got that much out.

She indicated that everyone should sit down and she pulled a chair over from another table to sit between Tommy and K.J. They moved slightly to give her more room.

"Frozen in another time bubble is a casino robbery going on right now in Las Vegas," Laverne said. "About a dozen armed men with machineguns took over the casino and have about three hundred innocent hostages."

Jewel felt her stomach twist into a knot.

"Why isn't this a police matter?" Tommy asked.

"Normally it would be," Laverne said, nodding. "But Kronos and the other gods who watch the future events did not see this coming in any fashion. And they have no way of knowing what the death of even a few of those hostages would mean to the future, let alone all of them."

"None of those people's time has come, huh?" Tommy asked.

"Not a one," Laverne said.

Now Jewel was even more stunned. Their direct bosses had always been the time gods who could see varied futures. And her and the team's goal was to save a certain future. Or it had been before this promotion of the team.

"Are the gunmen demanding anything?" Elliot asked, clearly dropping into legal mode and forgetting his circumstances.

"Nothing," Laverne said. "It appeared when we froze them in a time bubble that they were within seconds of just killing everyone."

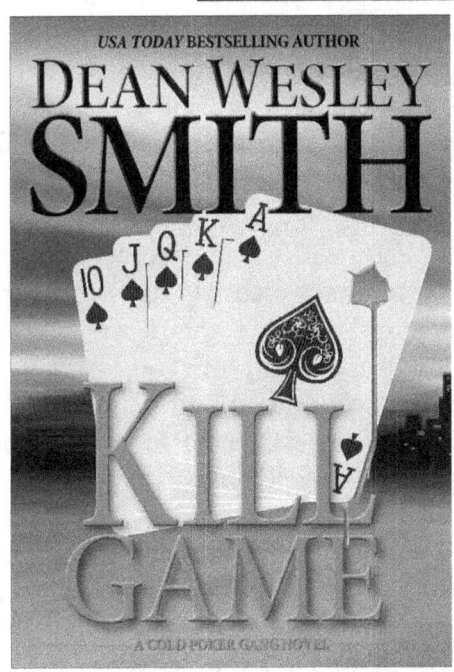

The First Two Cold Poker Gang Novels
Available at your favorite booksellers.

"Oh, no," Belle said, covering her mouth.

"No idea at all who is behind this?" Tommy asked.

"It has to be either a god or an escaped Titan or an alien," Laverne said. "We are sure that this is not real world or money motivated in any fashion. Poker Boy and his team and a dozen other teams are all on this, but it's going to take time to figure out what caused this."

K.J. looked at her. "You had a sense of another negative force starting to build, didn't you?"

"We did," Laverne said. "It's why this team will be needed. We just didn't expect you to be needed so quickly."

"What can we do?" Tommy asked.

"Poker Boy suggested that your team go into the time bubble in the casino," Laverne said, "and get in the gunmen's heads and see if you can both stop them and figure out where they are getting their orders from."

"We can do that," K.J. said.

"Hang on," Tommy said.

He vanished and appeared next to a woman sitting at a table halfway across the restaurant, a piece of steak halfway to her mouth.

He put his hand inside of her shoulder, then shook his head and jumped back. Jewel knew the look on his face. It wasn't good news.

"We can't read their thoughts and control them unless they are moving in time."

Laverne nodded.

"How many did you say there were?" Jewel asked.

"A dozen," Laverne said.

"How about having Poker Boy and his team jump inside the bubble and take all the ammunition from the guns?" Tommy asked.

Jewel knew exactly what he was thinking. "Then when you release the bubble, we can be inside some of them as they fail to kill anyone, getting a sense of who is in charge."

"Great idea," Laverne said. "Stan, you get that?"

She nodded. "Poker Boy and his team are pulling the ammunition now."

With that she jumped them all to the edge of the big Living Time Hotel and Casino.

The place was bright and had what seemed like thousands of colors. But nothing was moving, no jackpot bells going off, no people shouting and laughing.

Jewel was stunned at the gunmen. They all wore black body suits and black stocking masks over their faces. They were standing in a large circle around the edge of the casino, all holding what looked like AK-47s, if she knew her guns right.

The guns were trained on a large crowd of people in the center of the room. No doubt that if the gunmen started firing, they would kill a lot of people and more than likely kill each other as well.

That just flat seemed wrong.

"Not the way to kill people," Tommy said. "They will kill themselves as well."

"Someone clearly doesn't care," Elliot said.

Poker Boy and five others had the guns of the gunmen and were carefully taking the rounds out of them, then putting the guns back in the same exact position the gunmen had them.

Tommy turned to the six of them. "K.J., take the short guy to the right, Jewel, the guy next to him. Nancy, Belle and I will go to the ones on the left of here."

"What about me?" Elliot asked. "I was trapped in a woman in a woman's restroom. I think I can spy inside one of these guys."

Tommy glanced at Jewel.

She laughed. "I think he has a point. Just remember to just step out when you are done."

"Never forgetting that," Elliot said.

Tommy laughed and said, "Elliot, take the guy next to Jewel on the right."

Elliot nodded, looking nervous, but Jewel had a hunch he would be fine.

"We go into the men the moment they lift the time bubble," Tommy said.

They all spread out, with Elliot going to the guy with the gun beyond Jewel.

Jewel couldn't even tell what nationality her guy was with the mask over everything but his eyes and gloves on his hands.

Poker Boy in his usual black leather coat and black fedora-like hat appeared next to Tommy. "All the guns are empty. Great idea."

"Keep a sharp eye on this and if anything goes south, snap us out of time," Tommy said.

"We're watching," Poker Boy said.

"Count us down," Tommy said.

"On three," Poker Boy said loud enough for all of the ghost agents to hear.

Jewel took a deep breath, ready for anything when she stepped into the man in the mask next to her.

"One, two, three!"

The sound of the casino and all the scared humans smashed back in at her as she went into the man with the mask and black outfit next to her.

She went into the darkness, trying to find the edge of the shield.

"Fire! Fire! Fire!"

That was all she heard from the man.

That was the only thought in his head, but it didn't seem to be coming from him at all.

He had no background, no opinions, nothing.

It was as if she had stepped into a black room with a speaker shouting "Fire! Fire! Fire!"

From somewhere the order to fire was coming into the blackness. And she could feel it being relayed to the man's hand on the gun.

She could hear the screams of the people as they panicked and ran, but there were no sounds of actual gunfire.

She went into the darkness, trying to find the edge of the shield.

And trying to trace where the command to fire was coming from.

She finally found it. It was attached to a small device in one ear, embedded in the man's skull.

She stepped back out of the man and into the mass panic of hundreds of people trying to get away from men who kept firing empty weapons at them.

She shouted upward, "Freeze it!"

An instant later the sound vanished, leaving a ringing in her ears. People were almost trampling other people.

Poker Boy and his team, including Stan, Patty, Ben, Screamer, and two others she didn't recognize, instantly appeared and started pulling people off the bottom of piles and out from under other people so they would not get hurt in the mass panic.

They were careful to not move them very far so that when time restarted, the people wouldn't think much of being in a slightly different position, and it wouldn't show much on the cameras. But it would be enough to save some lives and injury.

Tommy appeared from the gunman, shaking his head. "Total blank slates," he said as Laverne appeared beside him.

"I traced the connection of the order to fire," Jewel said. "It's an implant in the bone behind their ears. I have a hunch it wipes out any idea of the man's personality."

"I traced it as well," Elliot said, coming over. "It strikes me like it also might be set to explode at a certain point."

Jewel was impressed and nodded at Elliot who just looked focused and stressed.

"Damn," Laverne said. "Think we can get the device out of there?"

"If I operated in these time-frozen conditions," Jewel said. "Yes. But we would need to have all these men in a secure location in case something triggers and goes wrong."

"We don't dare do that," Poker Boy said, appearing next to Laverne. "Everything here is getting filmed and will be on every news feed in the country. We just can't explain gunmen like this vanishing."

Laverne nodded.

A tall thin woman who had been helping get people into safe positions for when the time bubble released appeared next to Laverne. She was as tall as Laverne with the same dark hair and intense eyes.

"Mom," she said, "I was listening and if this is a device, it has to have an energy signal. I might be able to trace it."

Jewel felt shocked. She had no idea Laverne had a daughter.

Laverne nodded and then introduced her daughter. "This is Sherrie. She's a member of Poker Boy's team."

"How about we put a force field around each device," Poker Boy said. "To hold in any explosion."

Laverne nodded. "Stan?"

Stan, who Jewel knew as the God of Poker and Poker Boy's immediate boss appeared. He was the kind of guy no one would ever notice, but right now he looked as intense as the rest of them.

"I'll get the shields ready to clamp down on the devices," he said, "the instant it looks like a problem."

Then he vanished.

Jewel didn't much like what they were thinking, but they had to try it.

"I'll touch you, Sherrie," Jewel said, "and then I'll go into the gunman and show you where the device is, so you can focus on it when we release the time bubble."

Tommy glanced at Poker Boy and Laverne. "Be quick on that time bubble coming down again."

Both nodded and vanished.

The rest of Poker Boy's team vanished.

"Keep an eye out on all the gunmen," Tommy said to Belle and Nancy and Elliot and K.J. "In case one of the others gets off script."

All nodded.

Jewel reached out and touched Sherrie. She could feel the power in her and the hundreds and hundreds of years of living. And her love for Screamer, her husband and another member of Poker Boy's team.

"Can you hear me all right?" Jewel asked Sherrie.

"As if you are standing beside me," Sherrie said, laughing.

"Only I didn't say that out loud," Jewel said.

"Oh," was all Sherrie said.

Jewel put her hand into the gunman's body.

Blackness.

Nothingness.

Jewel knew that Sherrie could sense it and feel it as well.

"Drop the time bubble," Jewel said out loud to Tommy as she got Sherrie to the small implanted device in the head of the gunman.

"Fire! Fire! Fire!"

The command inside the man's head echoed even louder.

The same order was being repeated over and over as the wave of noise of screaming casino victims smashed back into Jewel.

Then suddenly Jewel could sense that everything had changed inside the gunman.

The order to fire had stopped.

A power surge was starting to build in the device.

"Shields!" both Jewel and Sherrie shouted at once.

Jewel pulled out of the gunman and let go of Sherrie at the same time.

Jewel could tell that Sherrie got no trace on the origin of the signal going to those devices. More than likely they were just on timers.

Sherrie vanished, since she was the only one of them that could be hurt from any kind of explosion.

The last of the hostages were streaming past the gunmen in all directions, just getting out of the area. The noise was deafening as most were screaming and shouting and numbers of people were helping others.

After what seemed like only a moment, the dozen gunmen were all left standing, holding their useless guns, facing the now empty casino.

Jewel shouted to Laverne. "Keep the explosions contained to as tight an area around the device as you can. It might not kill the men and we can get information from them if you keep the explosion to only the insides of the device."

"Understood," Laverne said, her voice echoing now.

"They going to blow?" K.J. asked, staring wide-eyed at the gunmen now all standing like statues. "I would hate to get ghost blood on this new suit."

"They're going to blow," Jewel said, nodding. "But no blood."

A moment later a pop-sound echoed over the empty casino and all twelve men slumped to the floor.

Jewel went back to the nearest one and put her hand in him.

His name was Ben. A carpenter and fine craftsman with two kids who should be home with his wife for dinner right now. He was very much still alive.

Jewel stood as emergency people came flooding in from a number of directions, including a Swat Team with guns drawn.

"We have a problem, Laverne," Jewel said into the air. "These men are just dupes. They had no idea what they were doing. Someone kidnapped them and blocked their thoughts."

"Understood," Laverne said, again her voice sort of echoing around the space and making a few of the emergency people glance around. "Thank you."

"The Nugget?" Tommy asked.

All Jewel could do was nod.

ELEVEN

ELLIOT GLANCED AROUND at the buffet they had transported to from the Living Time Casino floor. Stunned didn't begin to describe how he was feeling.

Stunned, disbelieving, and in need of about a thousand answers.

And who knew a ghost could feel stress.

Nancy moved over toward the hostess area of the buffet as they all took seats around a large wooden table tucked against some plants in the back.

The room smelled wonderful and since it was still in the normal dinner-time hour, the room was about half-full of people of all ages.

The room was in oak tones, with plants in a tall planter separating part of the buffet from a lobby area. Giant windows on the other side looked out over a pool area a story below, so the buffet must be on the second floor.

"This is the Golden Nugget buffet in downtown Las Vegas," Tommy said, noticing how Elliot was looking around. "We sort of consider this our team office at the moment."

"What's Nancy doing?" Elliot asked as she vanished inside the hostess, then appeared a moment later and started back for them. The hostess was a large, middle-aged woman with tall brown hair that looked like it had been done in the 1960s.

"Making sure that no one is seated at this table," Tommy said. "She just gets Diana there to mark that management called and reserved the table for an hour or so."

"Diana's grandkid survived the operation just fine and is leaving the hospital tomorrow," Nancy said, smiling and pulling up a chair next to Belle.

"Great to hear," Jewel said, smiling.

Elliot just shook his head. Clearly they came here a lot if they were worried about a grandkid of a hostess.

"So why aren't we helping with the gunmen anymore?" Elliot asked.

"They're living," K.J. said. "Laverne, Poker Boy and his team can take it from where we left it just fine."

"So they are all living?" Elliot asked.

"They are gods and superheroes," Tommy said. "It seems that every aspect of life has a god for it and some superheroes working for that god."

"Poker Boy and his team are a special group," K.J. said. "They tend to save the world a lot. We got to help them last winter on one mission. Looks like we might be helping them more often when they need our invisible talents."

"Seems they want this group to be special as well," Elliot said.

"Maybe," K.J. said, smiling. "I sure feel special. Doesn't everyone?"

Tommy laughed and Belle and Nancy just smiled.

"I don't think the problem they are facing with those gunmen is finished yet," Jewel said.

"I'm betting the same thing," Belle said.

"Bombs in the skull just gives me a headache," K.J. said. "I'm going to get something to eat."

Belle and Nancy nodded and stood.

"Strawberry shortcake to die for here," Nancy said to Elliot.

"We're already dead," K.J. said, heading toward the buffet with his pink fluffy shoes and expensive gray suit. "So I'm not afraid of some strawberry shortcake."

"So we die again for it," Belle said, laughing.

"Yeah, worth it," K.J. said.

Elliot watched them go, then turned back to Jewel and Tommy.

"I bet you have about a thousand questions," Tommy said.

"And great spot on the devices being a bomb," Jewel said.

"Just thinking the worst as any attorney is trained to do," Elliot said.

But the compliment felt good. If this didn't end up being the most bizarre dream ever, he was going to pull his weight with this team. To do that, he had a lot to learn.

"Any question you have," Jewel said, "we'll try to answer."

"The woman in gray who came and got us," Elliot said, deciding to start with the first basic question. "Who was that?"

"Everyone calls her Laverne," Jewel said. "She's a god, one of the most powerful, and has been alive for hundreds of thousands of years, far before recorded history and Atlantis. Over time she went by many names."

Elliot opened his mouth, but the question he had next got confused with the term Atlantis and he shut it.

"For the best way of thinking of her," Tommy said, "she's Lady Luck herself."

"Oh," Elliot said.

His brain just went completely blank with that.

Jewel and Tommy both sat there silently waiting for him to come up with a question. He had so many, he couldn't think of one, so he decided to just back up to the start and try to make sense of all this.

"So a number of hours ago, outside of Boise, I was going to die? Nothing to change that like we did with those people today?"

"Laverne said that today was not those people's time to die," Tommy said.

"It was your time," Jewel said, "and nothing anyone could do to stop that without violating all sorts of time stream issues far too complex and dangerous for me to understand."

"So instead of crossing over, following the white light or whatever happens," Elliot said, "I was picked to be part of this team."

Both nodded.

"Who picked me?"

"One of the major gods who can see the future in fuzzy form," Tommy said.

"A god who can see that this team needed you. More than likely Laverne was part of that decision."

"We had nothing to do with it," Jewel said. "K.J. was even forty minutes late telling us you had died because of the time difference between here and Boise."

"And clearly," Elliot said, "as I did with Cathy in the restaurant and the black-mind guy in the casino, I can be inside others and hear their thoughts."

"You will know everything about a person if you are inside them," Tommy said.

"And I can help them or get them to act in a certain way if I need?"

"With training, yes," Jewel said. "We'll train you."

Elliot remembered when Jewel went over to Deanna and went inside her to help her, Jewel had said.

Damn, with the thought of Deanna, he wanted to just curl up in a ball. Even though in a couple of hours he had helped put a killer in jail and saved hundreds of people's lives, what he had done to Deanna by dying was almost too much for him to bear.

"I need to tell Deanna I'm sorry," Elliot said, his voice soft. "I never wanted to leave her. Can I do that? Can I tell her I'm sorry for leaving?"

Jewel glanced at Tommy, then back at Elliot. "You can."

The relief and the gratitude were almost more than he could take.

TWELVE

"CAN DO WHAT?" K.J. asked as he sat down with a large bowl of strawberry shortcake.

Jewel glanced up at him. "Tell Deanna that he's sorry for leaving her."

K.J. started to open his mouth, but Jewel shook her head and thankfully K.J. caught the signal and stopped. It just wasn't time quite yet to tell Elliot about Deanna.

Belle and Nancy both came back with shortcake as well and Jewel had to admit it looked great.

"Will I also be able to teleport to different places as you guys do?" Elliot asked, continuing on with his questions.

"Again, yes, with training," Jewel said.

Elliot nodded. "So how many ghosts like us are there?"

"A couple hundred around the world," K.J. said. "We're the only six in the western part of the United States."

"You ever see the others?" Elliot asked.

"No reason to, actually," K.J. said, shrugging and working at the shortcake.

Jewel just let the questions go on like that for a few more minutes.

At one point Tommy touched her leg and signaled she should go with him to get some food, leaving the question-answering to Belle, Nancy, and K.J.

She did, walking hand-in-hand with Tommy over to the area where there was a big bowl of fresh strawberries, some wonderful light cake, and fresh real whipped cream.

She went and got a soup bowl since the dessert bowls were too small.

"You know," Tommy said, "that Elliot's going to want to go back to his apartment tonight to see Deanna."

Jewel nodded. She knew he was. She had been hoping that they might get him distracted enough with finding a room to stay here in Las Vegas for a day or so before going back, but she knew that wasn't going to work by the look on his face.

Then she had an idea. She glanced at Tommy. "Since Deanna is going to be going downhill quickly from what I saw of that tumor in her head, and on pain meds a lot, think there is any chance we can start Deanna's training before she comes over?"

Tommy looked at Jewel and smiled. "Never hurts to ask."

They headed back to the table. Jewel set her bowl down, then asked K.J. to come with her. She had a question.

He shrugged and followed her back toward the buffet line. "Since Deanna is joining us in a few months, and most of that time she's going to be knocked out with pain meds or in a coma, any chance we can start her training early?"

K.J. started to say something, then smiled. "You know, in over a hundred years, that's never come up."

"Ask, would you? And find out if that stuff with the gunmen is done with us for a while."

"Will do," he said, and vanished.

She went back over to the table and sat down, getting ready to dig into her bowl of strawberry shortcake.

"Where did K.J. go?" Belle asked.

"Off to find out if we're done for the night with the gunmen problem or if we have to stand ready," Jewel said.

"Great idea," Tommy said. "I bet we're done."

"I'm hoping," Jewel said.

She was done with her shortcake and had answered a few more of Elliot's questions when K.J. showed up smiling.

"We're done for the time being," he said. "Laverne will come and get us if they need help again."

"And?" Jewel asked.

"The answer is that the bosses couldn't see why not. That we should try."

Belle and Nancy both looked puzzled, but Jewel smiled, as did Tommy.

Elliot asked simply, "Try what?"

"It's time we jump you to Deanna," Jewel said.

Belle and Nancy both nodded, then Nancy said, "We're headed home."

And they vanished.

"I have a hot tub with my name on it," K.J. said. "And I got to check my shoes to make sure I have no cow dung on them from that field."

And he vanished.

Elliot just shook his head. "Why do I get the feeling they are rats leaving a sinking ship and I'm the sinking ship?"

"Because it's been a long day for you already," Jewel said.

"And you have a little more of a rollercoaster ride ahead," Tommy said, "before it can calm down and you can rest."

"Deanna?" Elliot asked.

Jewel nodded.

"Let's go," Elliot said, taking a deep breath. "I need to say I'm sorry and goodbye."

"Well, maybe," Jewel said.

And with that they jumped to Deanna and Elliot's condo.

Deanna was sitting on the couch, her head back, her eyes open, just staring at the ceiling. She had clearly been crying.

She had taken off her jumpsuit and had on jeans and a plain white blouse and slippers.

The living room was tastefully arranged with a number of chairs, a large couch, and a coffee table stacked with sports magazines. Everything was in brown tones and to one side there was a large dining room table with a laptop on it. There was an open kitchen beyond with stainless steel appliances.

Books on oak shelves filled one long wall and Jewel could see a couple reading devices on the end tables.

The place looked comfortable and lived in.

A woman about Deanna's age sat in a reading chair near her. The woman had long brown hair and had also been crying.

There was a deep silence in the room.

"That's her sister Carla," Elliot whispered. "She's nice, but not too bright."

"They can't hear us," Tommy said.

Elliot nodded and went to sit beside Deanna on the couch.

Jewel watched as he carefully reached over and touched her.

He jerked back, but kept his touch with her.

Jewel knew that Elliot had run into the wall of grief. That's why he had jerked back.

Then suddenly Elliot seemed to sit up straight, as if listening for something in the distance.

Jewel knew he was seeing the news that Deanna had gotten from the doctor that very morning.

Suddenly Elliot stood and moved away from Deanna like he had been shocked.

Then, after a moment, he looked at Jewel. "You knew and didn't tell me?"

"It wasn't my place to tell you," Jewel said. "It was her place and she just did. In the only way she could now."

Elliot nodded slowly, tears filling his eyes. "Is there any way we can make her death easier? Can I be there when she passes to the next world?"

"That's the other part we didn't tell you," Tommy said. "That she doesn't even know. The powers want both of you

as agents. She's going to join you, not leave you."

Elliot opened his mouth, then shut it, then opened it again, shut it again, and turned to look at Deanna. "We'll be together again?"

"For as long as you both want," Jewel said, her voice soft.

With that, Elliot sat on the couch and just stared at Deanna.

And Jewel could see he was smiling.

THIRTEEN

ELLIOT JUST LET himself sit and stare at Deanna, the woman he loved more than anything in the world. He had come here to say goodbye. Now Jewel and Tommy were telling him that Deanna was going to be recruited with him as an agent.

And that they would be together.

She was dying. But by dying, just as he did today, she would become a ghost agent. And together they could save people.

Behind him he heard Jewel say to Tommy, "Head home. I'll be fine here."

"Sure?" Tommy asked.

Elliot turned and smiled at them both. "You can both go get some sleep if you want. I assume we ghosts sleep because I feel worn out beyond belief."

Jewel laughed. "We sleep. And everything else as well. But I want to stay here because we have some other things to discuss about what's going to happen to Deanna during her last two months of living. I'm a doctor, remember."

Elliot nodded. "Thank you."

Tommy kissed Jewel and then said, "See you at home."

Then he vanished.

Elliot wanted to ask how ghosts could have homes, but figured there was more than enough time to figure that out later.

Jewel sat down in an open chair facing Deanna. "When you touched Deanna, you felt the grief, right?"

"I did," Elliot said. "Like hitting a wall."

"And then how did you figure out she had an inoperable brain tumor?" Jewel asked.

Elliot pointed at Deanna's sister in the other chair. "She just told her. She had planned on telling me tonight."

"She did, actually," Jewel said, smiling.

"Yeah, she did, didn't she?"

"So we have been given permission from our bosses, whoever they might be," Jewel said, "to try to do some training with Deanna before she crosses into our state."

Elliot looked at Jewel, clearly stunned. "How can we do that?"

"Deanna is going to be drugged for most of the next month," Jewel said, "and the last month she will almost certainly be in a coma considering where that tumor is and how large it is."

"Wow," Elliot said, staring back at the woman he loved who was still sitting on the couch, her head back, staring at the ceiling.

"The doctors will mostly just keep her out of pain," Jewel said. "So we can, in theory, train her mind. But I need to warn you, this hasn't been tried before and it might not work."

Elliot nodded. "Worse comes to worst, I can just comfort her until her time comes. How long?"

"Two months from today," Julia said.

Elliot nodded. "I'll keep training while I stay with her. Think I can do that?"

He hoped like anything that he could do just that. He didn't want to leave Deanna's side.

"Except for being called for duty as we were tonight," Jewel said. "I think we can make that work."

"Wonderful," he said.

"So I would suggest that you touch Deanna again," Jewel said, "tell her you are here and not to worry, that you will be with her through it all."

Elliot looked at Jewel and then just blurted out what he was worried about. "What happens if I see she doesn't really love me, or has secrets in her past that I shouldn't know about."

Jewel smiled. "Just love her and that will be all that matters."

Elliot nodded. "You are a wise woman, Doctor."

Jewel actually laughed. "Give me another century or two and I really might learn something."

Elliot had no idea what to say to that, so instead he just turned and moved over beside Deanna.

He put his arm up and around her and pretended to pull her close.

She sort of turned toward him and settled her head down, as if she was settling against his shoulder.

Elliot could see that her mind was spinning in a thousand ways at once. Horror at seeing Elliot's body, anger at him leaving, total grief that he was gone and not willing to believe he really was gone.

And then the reality of her own cancer. Part of her was glad for it now, glad she would be following Elliot quickly.

Another part of her was so angry, she could punch walls.

The day had just been too much.

"Calm," Elliot said. "I'm here. I'm not completely gone. I'll be with you through all this."

He could feel her heart slowing a little.

"Calm," he said out loud. "Just rest. I'm here."

Her thoughts slowed, and he could feel her exhaustion taking over her body.

"Just sleep," he said.

She closed her eyes.

And a moment later she was asleep.

Then inside her mind she sort of stood up.

She didn't wake up, but she stood up and looked at him.

She could see him. Her mind could see him.

"Elliot, is that you?" she asked.

"It is," he said. "I'm right here and I'm going to be right here helping you through this."

She hugged him and he hugged her back and they stayed that way for the longest time.

"I'm dreaming," she said. "But it's a wonderful dream."

"It sort of is a dream and isn't a dream," he said. "But we have lots of time to talk about that later. Just know that I am still here, with you, to help you. I haven't left, even though my body has left."

"I'm dying," she said.

"I know," he said. "I'm already dead."

She half laughed. "So what happens when I die?"

"Then the fun begins," he said.

"You know," she said, "this is a very strange dream."

"It is," he said. "But as long as we're together, I sure don't mind."

"Neither do I," she said.

"So I need you to now wake up, get ready for bed just like you normally do, and crawl into bed. I'll join you there."

"You promise?" she asked.

"I promise," he said. "Now, just as I often had to say when you fell asleep reading, wake up and go to bed."

She laughed, but stirred and he moved away from her.

She stood, hugged her sister, then said she was going to bed. That she would call her in the morning.

The sister wanted to stay, but Deanna insisted and locked the door behind her and headed for the bathroom to get ready to go to bed.

Elliot turned to Jewel. "I got her to go to bed. I'm going to curl up with her and just sleep."

Jewel nodded. "I'll be out here if you need me."

"Why not just go get some sleep yourself and come back early in the morning," Elliot said. "I'm a ghost. I'm not going anywhere but with Deanna and to sleep."

"You're sure?" Jewel asked.

"I am sure," Elliot said. "And thank you for letting me remain with the woman I love."

Jewel nodded. "Get some sleep."

And then she vanished.

Elliot went into the bedroom, stripped off his jumpsuit for the first time, then his clothes under that. He went to his closet and grabbed another pair of pants. The ghost pair came away while the regular ones just remained. He nodded. At least tomorrow he wouldn't have to put on the same clothes.

Deanna came out of the bathroom in her pale-blue robe as she always did, took it off, and crawled into bed.

She looked more wonderful than he had remembered, and he had only seen her this morning.

What a long day.

Elliot went into the bathroom and turned on the faucet. Only he didn't actually turn it, but it seemed water came out, so he splashed water on his face.

Then he realized he needed to use the toilet. Luckily Deanna had left the lid up, but he couldn't raise any more than a ghost seat, so he did what he needed to do, sort of stunned that as a ghost everything still worked.

Then he went into the bedroom just as he always did.

Deanna was on her side of the bed, lying on her back, staring at the ceiling.

He crawled in his side, raising ghost blankets around him, but not disturbing the real blankets. The ghost blankets felt as real as any blanket.

Then he put his arm over Deanna.

Again he could feel her mind starting to spin out of control and the grief building.

"I'm right here," he said.

She moved toward him and sighed.

"We need to sleep," he said. "Just sleep."

Her mind calmed and she closed her eyes and after a moment she was asleep, but he was with her.

"You really are here?" the real her inside asked.

"I am," he said.

"If I told anyone they would send me to a grief therapist, you know that?"

"You're dying, remember. I'm going to be here with you all the way through that and beyond. You won't have time for anyone to judge you."

"Oh, thank heavens," she said.

"Now our minds need to sleep," he said. "I'll explain more tomorrow and as time goes on."

"Promise?" she asked.

"As soon as I learn a bunch of it," he said, "you'll be the first to know."

"What does that mean?" she asked, feeling more and more tired to him.

"Being dead is complicated," he said. "Now sleep."

And with that he shut his eyes and let himself relax with the woman he loved.

SECTION THREE
Another Attack

FOURTEEN

ELLIOT WASN'T REALLY surprised that after a full night's sleep, when Deanna awoke she wasn't as welcoming to him trying to talk with her. She kept shaking her head, so he backed up and just worked to keep her calm.

When she went into the bathroom to take a shower and get dressed for the day, he got dressed and went out into the living room and kitchen. He so wanted to go take a shower with her, as they had done many times, but he felt this morning she needed her privacy and to just get through the day.

Jewel was in the kitchen, drinking a glass of orange juice, sitting at the kitchen bar. She pointed to another glass of juice on the counter and he took it. With one sip he knew it was the best orange juice he had ever tasted.

"Does everything taste this good after death?"

Jewel laughed. "It does. And I see you figured out that clothes have a ghost element about them."

"I did," he said. "So not only do we get free meals, we get free clothes?"

"We do," Jewel said. "And I'll explain how we end up living in places later on."

"I was wondering about that," Elliot said, again sipping the incredible orange juice. He was hungry. He was going to need to eat pretty soon.

"So how did it go?" Jewel asked.

"We slept together and a couple times when she started to have nightmares, I was able to keep her calm and get her back to sleep."

"Good," Jewel said, nodding. "She's going to need that."

"This morning," Elliot said, "after she was rested, her mind didn't want to accept that I was there with her, so I didn't push it."

"Again, smart," Jewel said, nodding. "I'm assuming you would mostly like to stick with her today. Keep her calm where you can, keep reassuring her."

Elliot nodded. He had hoped he would be allowed to do that. He hadn't figured out just exactly who was in charge of this ghost job he found himself in. A question he would ask later.

"What's Deanna's plan for the rest of the day?"

"Her sister will be here in just over an hour," Elliot said. "From there, I couldn't get any plans. I don't think she knows other than a second opinion doctor appointment at three this afternoon. She had figured I would go with her on that."

"You will," Jewel said.

"Thank you," Elliot said. He couldn't believe how relieved he felt with that. He wanted to help Deanna as much as he could.

"So how about now we meet Tommy for breakfast at the Golden Nugget," Jewel said. "We can answer more of your ques-

tions and give you some first basic training. Then you can come back here and be with Deanna for the rest of the day."

"I like that idea," Elliot said.

A moment later they were standing beside a table tucked into the back of the Golden Nugget buffet. The place looked pretty crowded and there was a table of two elderly couples sitting pretty close to their table. Both men had walkers.

The golden tones of oak and wood really felt comforting, and the bright light coming through the tall windows was warming and welcoming.

And the smell was wonderful. Bacon, waffles, it all smelled so wonderful.

Tommy was threading his way through people back from the buffet with a plate full of food. He was smiling as he sidestepped people who couldn't even see him like he was playing a game of tag.

A couple times he brushed through a person, but he didn't seem to notice or care.

Tommy reached them and put his plate down on the table and shook Elliot's hand. "Heck of a first day yesterday. You okay?"

Elliot liked Tommy a great deal. He was a man who made decisions and acted. He must have been a great Marine and cop when alive.

"It went as well as could be expected," Elliot said. "I actually talked with the true Deanna when she was exhausted, but this morning she wanted nothing to do with the idea that I was with her."

"Logical," Tommy said, nodding.

Elliot looked at all the people around the horseshoe-shaped main part of the buffet. None of those people could see him.

"How do I manage to not get trapped in anyone accidently again?"

"Just move through them," Jewel said. "You will hear and know their thoughts and memories and details of their lives with a single touch, but if you don't focus on the details, those memories vanish quickly."

"Thankfully," Tommy said, sitting down and pulling his plate toward him.

"So try to avoid them," Jewel said. "But if you can't, just go through."

Elliot nodded, took a deep breath, and headed toward the buffet.

He managed to grab a plate that felt warm to his hands, and actually get some scrambled eggs scooped up before a man turned and bumped right into him.

Actually, he didn't bump, he just went inside Elliot, or better put, Elliot went inside him.

The guy was about sixty, gray hair, overweight, and in a hurry to get to the blackjack table. He was an accountant, happily married, and enjoying his vacation with his wife.

Elliot stepped sideways away from him and focused on getting some bacon. Jewel was right, if he thought about something else, the man's thoughts and memories just sort of vanished.

Elliot managed, with two quick retreats from others, to get some bacon with his eggs, then while grabbing a waffle, a thirty-one-year-old woman walked right into him from behind.

Her name was Candice and she had her husband tied up and naked back in their room in some strange game he had wanted to play last night. She had wanted nothing to do with it, even though it was Vegas, but he had insisted, ignoring as he always did what she wanted and only focused on what he wanted.

So she had gone along, tied him up so well he would never get loose on his own, and then left with him yelling against the gag in his mouth. The housekeeping staff were going to be in for a shock this morning.

The First Two Ghost of a Chance Novels
Available at your favorite booksellers.

But more than likely, since this was Vegas, they had seen it before.

Candice had gone across the street, used some mad money to get a hotel room, and ended up enjoying a very drunk evening with another woman. It turned out to be an evening she had never realized she would enjoy as much.

An evening Elliot could see and remember every detail of, even though he didn't want to.

This morning, knowing that her marriage of four years was over, Candice had drained her and her husband's joint bank accounts, checked out of their room with him still tied up in there, just leaving her luggage, then she drained all his credit cards as well and cancelled his plane ticket home.

He was stuck here with no money and no way home.

After a bite to eat, she was headed to the airport to head home. She had already called an attorney friend back in Chicago and the divorce process would be in the works before she landed.

She was still mad at her husband, disgusted at him was more like it, and finally happy to be moving on. She flat didn't love him anymore and had enjoyed the experience with another woman last night so much, she wanted to test those waters more.

Elliot got all that in the moment that he had passed through her trying to back away.

"Tough, isn't it?" Jewel said from beside him. "Especially when it's this crowded. We like to come here on off hours to avoid most of this."

Elliot shook his head. "People are interesting, that's for sure."

"Infinitely," Jewel said. "But sadly, so many fall into the same patterns."

"Haven't got that far yet," Elliot said, laughing. Then with one more look at the smiling Candice, he took his waffle, bacon and eggs and headed back for the table.

This being dead sure had its interesting moments.

FIFTEEN

JEWEL AND TOMMY both answered questions from Elliot about various things, then told him their story of dying in the car wreck, waiting in the rain, and then ending up saving a girl's life within their first five hours.

Then they took turns telling him how Nancy and Belle had figured out for all of them last fall how to teleport and float.

"So what do I learn first?" Elliot asked.

Jewel liked his attitude. He was going to be a great addition to their team. And from what little she had seen of Deanna, she would be as well.

"I think we better get you teleporting before anything else," Tommy said. "That way in some bad situation, you can just get out of the way."

Jewel nodded. She agreed with that. When they had started, they had learned to hide inside people. But Elliot had been inside his fair share of people already. The extra tricks on that he could pick up easily.

She turned and pointed to an area with no people near an elevator in the buffet diner. "See that over there? The area in front of the elevator? Right there near that big plant with the big leaves?"

Elliot nodded.

"Just imagine you are standing there," Tommy said.

Elliot looked puzzled.

"We're ghosts," Jewel said, "living in this real world, experiencing it, but not bound by it like we used to be."

"So our minds and souls are what we live with," Tommy said, "since we have no bodies."

"And if your mind thinks you are standing in front of the elevators, you will be," Jewel said. "That simple."

"Just focus on it," Tommy said. "It's amazingly easy."

Jewel could see Elliot frown.

"Just be standing there by the elevator," Jewel said.

An instant later Elliot vanished and was standing beside the elevator.

Jewel watched as he looked around, clearly shocked, then smiling he quickly sidestepped an obese woman and appeared back in his chair.

"Damn, that was fun," Elliot said.

"Jump to that open spot in front of the desserts and bring me back a piece of cherry pie, would you?" Tommy asked, smiling.

"Gladly," Elliot said.

He turned, looked at the dessert bar, and appeared there. He picked up a piece of pie and jumped back.

"Your pie, sir," Elliot said, laughing.

Jewel and Tommy both applauded.

"So anywhere you can imagine," Jewel said, "you can be there."

"Can I go see what Deanna's doing at the moment?" Elliot said.

Jewel nodded. "But come back so we know everything is all right."

"Will do," Elliot said and vanished.

"He picked that up quickly," Tommy said, shaking his head and digging into the cherry pie.

A moment later Elliot appeared back in his chair. "Deanna is just sitting on the couch, resting, waiting for her sister. I calmed her for a quick moment. She seemed to appreciate that."

"Good," Jewel said. "So we have a little more time?"

Elliot nodded.

"So how about we get you used to walking through walls," Tommy said, "and controlling people's actions."

Elliot sort of opened his mouth, then shut it, then glanced at Jewel.

"Yeah, like Tommy controlled that guy last night," Jewel said, "and Nancy controlled the woman, you can learn to do that as well."

"I figured that," Elliot said. "The walking through walls has me a little spooked, though."

All Jewel could do was laugh.

SIXTEEN

FOR THE NEXT two weeks, they met Elliot for training in the morning, then he had spent each day with Deanna. Jewel checked in with him often, and at one point checked on Deanna's condition. She was going downhill fast.

She had made it through Elliot's memorial service just fine, and every night Elliot had stayed with Deanna. Slowly she was beginning to believe he was really with her.

Then two weeks after the first attack, Laverne froze time around Jewel and Tommy as they were eating dinner in a small Japanese restaurant near the strip and then appeared beside their table.

"Same attack," she said simply and transported the two of them to the Living Time Casino.

Jewel could not believe what she was seeing in the large area that was the casino. Again, there were twelve men, all with machine guns circled around a large mass of tourists trapped in the casino area. Some of the tourists were hiding behind tables, others just hugged each other in sheer terror.

Poker Boy, in his black hat and leather coat, appeared next to them as K.J. brought Belle and Nancy and Elliot.

"We've got them disarmed again," Poker Boy said, "at least none of the guns they carry have ammunition."

"Do you have any leads as to who is behind this?" Jewel asked.

"None," Laverne said. "There didn't seem to be any connection at all between the gunmen, and the first group had all vanished from their jobs at different times over the day ahead of the event."

"Frustrating doesn't begin to describe it," Poker Boy said.

Tommy looked around, then turned with a frown on his face to Jewel. She knew that expression. It meant he had an idea of some sorts.

"All these men are standing in exactly the same spots as the previous group."

Poker Boy glanced around and nodded.

"And the same casino," Jewel said.

Laverne and Poker Boy both nodded.

"I'm betting," Tommy said, "this has something to do with this exact location and that circle they are forming."

"Someone wants this land?" Poker Boy said.

"No doubt this isn't doing this casino's stock price any good," K.J. said. "Or their reservation bookings."

"Let's see if these guys are wired the same," Jewel said.

The six ghost agents spread out as they had done the first time.

Jewel put her hand inside the man she was going to check out.

"Drop the bubble," Tommy said.

The sound of the casino and scared customers came smashing back in like a hammer.

Instantly Jewel knew they were in trouble.

The device had already built up explosive power and was about to explode.

Both she and Tommy shouted for the time bubble at the same exact moment.

Everything froze again instantly.

"Clamp tight shields over those devices in their heads," Tommy shouted.

"Done," Laverne's voice came clear.

"Release the bubble," Jewel said.

A moment later there was a uniform pop and again all twelve men slumped to the ground at the same time, which set off a stampede of people trying to escape.

Poker Boy and his crew had to freeze things three times to make sure people didn't hurt themselves in the stampede to leave.

"K.J. is right," Elliot said. "This can't be helping the casino's business. Unless this is solved quickly, this is going to drive the price of this casino and this land through the floor."

"I think it has something to do with the circle," Jewel said. "Circles through time have vast power in many different cultures."

Poker Boy appeared with Patty Ledgerwood, another superhero that Jewel really liked. Patty was Poker Boy's girlfriend. She had her long brown hair pulled back and actually was dressed in an MGM Grand front desk uniform. She must have left work over there to join this.

Laverne and Stan, the God of Poker also appeared.

"That might be the point of all this," Poker Boy said, freezing time once again as the last of the people got past them. "I think you are on to something."

Poker Boy and Laverne and Patty and Stan all walked to the very spot in the center of the circle of gunmen and stood there for a moment.

"I'll be go to hell," Lavene said. "Why didn't I see this before?"

Then she and Stan sort of drifted down into the floor like there was an elevator there.

Jewel and Tommy could have easily followed them, but neither of them did. There was still far too much unknown power in this new world and both of them had come to be respectful of it, even though they were already dead.

Patty and Poker Boy sort of stood there, holding hands.

"Sure is fun to watch the gods work, isn't it?" K.J. said, moving over beside Jewel.

"Know anything about the ancient history of this area?" Jewel asked K.J.

K.J. shrugged. "Las Vegas area has always been a major area of extreme power. A lot of the gods and power people tend to end up living here. And not just for the great night-life, which I must say is really fun at times."

A moment later, Laverne and Stan appeared and the four of them walked over to the ghost team.

"Ancient power ring," she said, indicating the circle the twelve passed-out gunmen outlined. "I think I might know who is doing this now."

"Good," K.J. said.

"You all helped us save a lot of lives today," Laverne said. "Thank you again."

With that, the time bubble vanished and all the police and swat team came swarming in.

"Going to be interesting to see the cover story they work up for this one," K.J. said.

"Anyone up for dessert after saving so many people once again?" Belle asked.

"Always," Jewel said, laughing.

And a moment later the six of them were at their favorite table in the Golden Nugget buffet, laughing and talking and heading for strawberry shortcake.

SECTION FOUR
Needed Training

SEVENTEEN

DEANNA STILL WASN'T believing that Elliot was with her. She had seen his body after the accident, had been at a memorial service for him, had not been able to tell him that she was dying.

He had died first. Part of her was very glad he had been spared watching her waste away.

Yet from the first night he seemed to be with her, calming her, believing in her as the cancer started to get worse. And especially when she was tired or under a pain medication, he seemed to be with her even more.

And it was as if they were alive together, only living in her mind. She was convinced she was making it all up, that it was part of some coping mechanism she was using.

Or part of the brain tumor. More than likely that was it.

But at the moment, five weeks after the accident and her diagnosis, she just didn't care. She wanted him with her and he was there. That was all that mattered.

Today had been a pretty good day. She had managed to drink a little and keep it down and then to get from her bed out to her couch. She now had a day nurse, and in a few days or so hospice would start the round-the-clock care to keep her comfortable and drugged up. When they came in they would put in a hospital bed for her. She knew from that point onward she would never leave that bed alive.

At least the cancer was taking her quickly. She wouldn't be in that hospital bed for long.

The day nurses alternated. Today was a wonderful woman about Deanna's age of thirty, but much heavier. She had a friendly smile and short brown hair. And she always seemed to smell of fresh bread.

She had praised Deanna for getting to the couch, which was just annoying. Deanna wasn't like some child just learning to walk on her own. Today might be the last day she would be able to walk. Period.

And maybe remember it as well. So far the brain tumor was leaving her memory and speech functions alone. It was the cancer in the rest of her body that was taking her down.

She let the nurse put a pillow under her head. Deanna hadn't even bothered to learn the names of the different day nurses that came and went, since it wouldn't matter much longer anyway.

Deanna had on a new nightgown and a new robe she had bought after Elliot's funeral. She had stocked up on a number of them, figuring that most of the next two months she would be living in them. And after the second week she had been right.

She closed her eyes. The walk to the couch had tired her out. How far she had fallen. Wow.

After a moment she saw the smiling face of Elliot standing over her.

"Want to take a longer walk, beautiful?" he asked, offering her his hand.

She loved when he was there with her. She could feel her mood lifting.

"And how am I supposed to do that?" she asked. "I barely made it out here."

She asked that without saying anything out loud. She didn't know how she did it, but it seemed that her delusion of Elliot was like talking in her head. She didn't have to actually speak to have him hear her.

"Just give me your ghost hand and I'll help you up."

"Ghost hand?" she asked.

He laughed. "Yeah, that takes time to get used to. Here, let me take your hand."

He reached down and took her left hand. She could feel it, just as she could feel him cuddling with her at night and brushing her forehead to ease pain at times.

"Open your eyes and look at your real hand," Elliot said.

She did, focusing on her hand. It took a moment. Her skin was dry and tight over the bones. She could feel his hand holding hers, but she couldn't see anything.

"That's really weird," she said in her ghost voice, closing her eyes again.

"Now when you feel me pulling gently," Elliot said, "just stand up as if you are healthy again."

"Yeah, and that's going to happen," she said, laughing.

"Try it and you might be surprised," he said.

She could hear the humor in his voice.

He gently pulled on her hand as if working to help her stand up, so she did.

She stood up as if cancer wasn't eating at her body like termites at an old house.

They took a few steps toward the front door and stopped. It felt wonderful, not tiring at all.

"Now look at me," he said.

She did. Not with her real eyes, but her ghost eyes. And Elliot was standing there, holding her hand, beaming like she had just crossed the finish line of a marathon.

"Wow, some dream," she said. "I love it."

"No dream," Elliot said. He pointed back toward the couch and she turned around.

There she was, looking like she had felt a moment ago, near death. Her once beautiful hair was pulled back and looking fragile. Her face was far, far too thin. She had her eyes closed. She actually looked peaceful.

"Did I just die?" she asked.

"Not yet," he said. "Got some weeks yet before that happens. This is what could be called an out-of-body experience."

He walked her over to a large mirror near the door. "No one else can see us, but we can see ourselves."

She looked in the mirror. The healthy person she knew was there, looking stunned, standing in her new bathrobe next to a smiling Elliot. Her hair was healthy, her face filled back out.

"You are so beautiful," he said. "I love you."

"And I love you," she said. "And miss you so much. I'm making all this up, aren't I?"

He laughed. "Well, not really."

He kissed her and that felt real to her. Very real.

"So what do you mean by not really?" she asked.

She was making this dream complex, of that there was no doubt.

"Let's go for that walk," he said. "It's a beautiful evening in Boise."

She nodded. "But what about that part of me?"

"You're still attached to your body," Elliot said. "So no worry, you'll return to it when you want and when needed."

"Well I sure don't want," she said, laughing.

He held out his hand. "Then come with me."

A moment later they were outside their condo in the warm evening air. It was if they had just transported there.

She could smell the freshly mowed grass and the drying sagebrush from the foothills behind their place. She had loved walks with Elliot before his death. Now she was getting to experience it again.

At least in her imagination.

They started off down the wide sidewalk beside the parking lot. On one side was her red Blazer in its normal spot. She was never driving that again. Her sister would like it, since it was only a year old.

Then they turned to the left to go around one of the buildings and into the park-like grass area behind the condos. The sidewalk skirted the grass on the left and the sagebrush covering the foothills on the right. The sidewalk went all the way around the entire complex and on nice nights they used to walk it and talk about their days.

The temperature this evening was perfect, a slight breeze to cool her a little. She was outside and still wearing her nightgown and robe and slippers. But it didn't feel that wrong for some reason.

After a few minutes of walking in silence, hand in hand, she finally said, "You really want me to believe this is real, don't you?"

"It is real," Elliot said. "But after I died, I thought I was dreaming for a while as well."

"I'm not dead yet," she said. "So this has to be a dream, right?"

He squeezed her hand. "No, this is real. And when you die, you'll join me like this."

"What is this?" she asked.

"Ghosts," he said. "I'm a ghost and you will be as well, but not like some scary ghost thing haunting an old mansion. Normally everyone just moves on to the next life, whatever that is. But you and I have been recruited to stick around in this world and help people."

She laughed. "Dream just got real silly."

"Let me tell you silly," Elliot said. "I don't know if you paid any attention or not, but on the evening of the day I died, Barry Johns just up and confessed out at the Sizzler Restaurant near the mall. Did you hear about that?"

"I remember I thought it sort of odd," she said, surprised at such a strange topic coming up in her dream. "And they found the women's bodies where he said they would be. I remember reading about that as well."

Elliot nodded. "Here is where it gets really silly."

"That's not silly enough?" Deanna asked.

"No, listen to this," he said. "I was thinking that I was dreaming as well, and Jewel and Tommy and K.J. were trying to convince me I was not."

"Who are they?" Deanna asked.

"Three of the five members of our team we have been recruited to join," he said. "You'll meet them."

"Other ghosts?" she asked.

"Other ghosts," he said. "Remember the two women killed downtown last fall by that car the police were chasing?"

She nodded.

"They are the other two members of the team. Nancy and Belle."

Deanna just shook her head. They were about three quarters of the way around the complex and she could suddenly feel pain in her side and her right leg and she started to limp.

"So you're telling me you had something to do with Barry confessing?"

At that moment on the sidewalk, a short man wearing a bright purple suit and red shoes and bowtie appeared. His shoes looked more like ruby slippers and they both had bows on them that matched his red bowtie. He had a fedora-like hat, also red, with a bow on it as well.

"Elliot, we have a situation," the man said. "Meeting at the Nugget buffet."

"Give me one minute, K.J.," Elliot said.

"Nice seeing you, Deanna," the man in purple said, nodding. And then he vanished.

Deanna just opened her mouth, but had nothing to say she was so shocked.

A moment later she and Elliot were back standing over her body in their condo.

"You need some pain meds and need to get back to bed," Elliot said.

"But you're not finished with your story," she said, feeling more exhausted by the moment. Her dying body was dragging her back. "And was that the K.J. you mentioned?"

"We'll have more than enough time for that," he said. "And yes, that was K.J."

Elliot helped her ease down onto the couch and stretch out with her own body.

And then Elliot was gone and she was awake in her cancer-riddled body. It had been such a strange dream. It had felt real, but yet not.

"Could I get my pills, please?" she asked just barely loud enough for the nurse to hear, once again missing the young body that had just taken a walk around the complex.

The nurse jumped from a chair at the dining room table and scrambled to the bathroom for the pills. And then a few minutes later Deanna had her dying body off the couch and shuffling, with the help of a walker and the nurse, back to bed.

In her mind she said, "Elliot, what you are telling me had better not be a joke."

He wasn't with her.

And she felt the pain, both real and not having him with her, more than she wanted to admit.

EIGHTEEN

JEWEL WAS SITTING next to Tommy at a six-person table in the far corner of the Golden Nugget buffet when Elliot appeared.

When Jewel had arrived the buffet smelled of prime rib and baking bread. Even though she and Tommy had just had dinner, the smells had made her hungry again. It was amazing she didn't gain a lot of weight as a ghost.

"How is Deanna doing?" Belle asked as Elliot took a chair next to Belle and across from K.J.

"We went for our first walk today out of her body," he said, smiling. "She thinks all this is part of her brain tumor and cancer causing dreams, which is as expected."

"Go slow," Jewel said.

"Very slow," Elliot said. "And we'll have more than enough time in three weeks after she gets out of all the pain."

Jewel only nodded to that. As a doctor, not being able to save someone was always the worst part of trying to help people. There was just nothing good to say about any of it. She liked how Elliot was thinking about it. Deanna wasn't dying, she was just getting out of pain.

"So what's happening?" Elliot asked.

"The gunmen," K.J. said. "Seems that Poker Boy and his team have not yet found who was behind those gunmen."

"So the gunmen haven't returned yct, have they?" Nancy asked, looking worried and sitting forward.

"No," K.J. said. "But they are expected in two hours. Something about the times of the ring, the power cycles, and so on. I don't understand exactly, but it seems the gunmen appeared to try to give blood sacrifices to the ring at power high points. The next high point is in two hours."

"I know a little about the ancient tribes that were in this area," Jewel said, feeling very puzzled at all this. "None of them did blood sacrifices of any type."

K.J. nodded. "This dates back into the time when this valley was lush and mostly marshland. This is actually coming back to haunt us from the Atlantis period. It seems a splinter group of humans lived here that thrived on the black magic from blood."

At that moment Laverne appeared, causing K.J. to scramble to his feet and lose his red hat.

Laverne had on a gray power suit, had her long brown hair pulled back, and looked intense and focused.

Everyone started to stand and Laverne indicated they should all stay seated. She pulled a chair over to the table and then put a time bubble around them. All sounds in the room stopped.

Jewel just found Laverne amazing. She radiated power and control and yet seemed very likable under the surface.

"The splinter group were called the Blackrow," Laverne said after K.J. got his hat back on his head and got seated again.

Laverne went on, smiling at K.J. "The Blackrow, about forty of them, were rounded up by Atlantis authorities, charged with mass murder, and put in jail, where they all died when Atlantis submerged. Blackrow was forgotten until those men arrived around that old Blackrow power circle."

"So who even remembers Blackrow?" Tommy asked.

"Anyone alive back in the last days of Atlantis," Laverne said, frowning. "So upward of a few thousand or more."

Jewel felt shocked. There were that many gods and superheroes who had been around that long? Wow, just wow? She and Tommy really needed to find someone to tutor them in the history of the gods, superheroes, and Ghost of a Chance agents.

Elliot and Nancy and Belle looked as stunned as she felt. Maybe the entire team needed a tutor in the history of things.

"How about ghost agents?" K.J. asked.

Laverne nodded. "A few have stayed through that long. But they work in Europe and China, if memory serves."

"So this is black magic?" Jewel asked.

"All magic goes black eventually," Laverne said. "Which is why all real magic is forbidden for anyone to use."

Jewel and the other ghost agents all just sat there stunned. All of them but Elliot remembered how close they had come just before Christmas fighting black magic. The world had almost ended. So black magic scared Jewel more than she wanted to think about.

"Seems we have two problems," Elliot said. "How to stop those men before they get started. They are not going to wait to detonate this time, since we stopped them twice."

Laverne nodded.

"And secondly trying to figure out who would gain from this?" he said.

Jewel agreed completely.

"Poker Boy and his team," Laverne said, "have gone after the idea that one of the longer-lived gods who have lost power over the centuries want to bring back Blackrow. They have learned, putting it bluntly, that if enough blood is spilled inside that ring at a high power moment, it just might resurrect all original Blackrow members and give them a lot of black magic power."

"Creating an instant magical army," Jewel said, not liking the sounds of that at all.

"Exactly," Laverne said.

"No luck on that path yet?" Tommy asked.

"Poker Boy and his team are right now following some very promising leads," Laverne said. "But they believe that those twelve men with bombs in them are already set and moving."

"And that's where we come in," Jewel said, finally understanding. "We need to find those men and get shields on those bombs without them even knowing they were discovered."

"Exactly," Laverne said. "If whoever is doing this manages to bring back the original group of Blackrow followers, I have no idea what would happen. But I can guess we would be in for a very long and bloody war."

"So let's go," Nancy said.

Laverne held up her hand. "One other problem. After today, the most powerful of the power points is in three evenings. Then the power points will be finished for over two hundred years."

Silence.

Then Elliot said, "I wish Deanna could help us on this."

Laverne looked at him. "She can, as of about midnight tonight. At that point she will slip into a coma and never wake up again. Her essence will be free to leave her body and help you."

Elliot nodded. "Thank you."

"We'll deal with that after we get this first one stopped," Jewel said, seeing that Elliot was not focused on this problem, but on Deanna. And she didn't blame him in the slightest.

Again Elliot just nodded. Then he took a deep breath and Jewel could see he was back in his eyes again.

"When we find the bombs," Tommy said, "we'll shout. Right?"

Laverne nodded. "Stan and I will be monitoring and will clamp shields tight around the bombs and teleport the bombs to a safe spot. So the men with the bombs this time won't even pass out."

"And the guns?" Nancy asked.

"The security at the casino, working with our people, have set up scanning equipment to find any gun being brought onto the property," Laverne said. "All guns have been tagged and will be teleported to another safe location about thirty minutes ahead of the power high, even if they are not part of the attacking team."

"So we got a lot of people to scan," Jewel said. "And we can't assume it will be only men this time."

Laverne nodded. "It could be anyone, including children. Those who follow the Blackrow do not value human life in any form."

Jewel did not like the sound of that. Not one bit.

NINETEEN

DEANNA SAT ON the edge of her bed, waiting for the nurse to bring her some pain meds. She loved this condo more than she wanted to admit, and was glad she had insisted on staying here.

She had a large closet to the right of the bed, Elliot had a smaller walk-in closet to the left, so they had just decided that their sides of the big king bed were closest to each person's own closet.

The bathroom door was at the foot of the bed and the bathroom was huge and modern, with a large shower and two sinks and enough room for both of them to get ready for work at the same time.

They had had a lot of fun in that huge shower. Now Elliot was gone and she doubted she could even stand long enough to take a short shower at this point.

No reason to even try.

Her time was almost up. She could feel it.

The doctors said her last few weeks would more than likely be spent unconscious. She honestly wasn't going to mind that as long as they kept the pain under control.

Hospice had promised it would and every morning they had someone check in on her very early. She called it the "pulse check" to see if she still had a pulse.

Sitting on the edge of the bed, she looked around the bedroom, studying every detail. The large framed pictures of skydiving covered one wall on Elliot's side. All of them had been taken by Elliot. She loved the colors of those. Bright greens of new spring fields and reds of a sunset. She hoped those pictures found a good home.

She had some of her family pictures on a dresser near her closet door. And a picture of some of her office co-workers. She honestly hadn't thought much about missing her job. After Elliot's death, she just never went back. Corporation law just went on and on. Her office managed without her, she was sure. She had good people there.

Her grandmother's hairbrush lay on top of her dresser. She didn't use it often, but she loved it. More than anything.

This condo was hers and Elliot's place. Everything in their lives were mixed together in here.

Neither of them had ever expected it to end.

At that moment, the nurse came in and gave her three pills.

Still seated on the side of the bed, Deanna took them with a small glass of water. Then she asked for her grandmother's brush.

The nurse got it and Deanna tried to brush her own hair, but the nurse ended up finishing for her and then put the brush back on the dresser.

"Thank you," Deanna said as the friendly nurse with a smile on her face helped Deanna get out of her bathrobe, lift her legs around and get into bed.

The nurse pulled up the sheet and blanket and made sure the glass of water was where Deanna could reach it on the nightstand.

Deanna just lay there. She felt exhausted. More than she had felt in weeks.

She stared at the ceiling until the nurse said goodnight, then shut off the light and half-closed the bedroom door.

Deanna closed her eyes, hoping the dream of Elliot would be there to greet her.

But he wasn't there.

He was dead.

She knew that.

And part of her was glad he couldn't see her like this.

And a larger part really wanted him here to hold her.

She took a deep, shuddering breath and let herself relax.

Then she said softly to the room, "It was fun."

A moment later the sleep took her.

TWENTY

JEWEL HAD NEVER walked through so many people in her short year of being a ghost. She tried to just let the people's memories and feelings wash over here as she kept focused on looking for those carrying bombs.

They couldn't actually scan for the bombs. Tommy had suggested that. Seems the bombs were shielded as to not be picked up by regular equipment.

Laverne and her people needed to know there was one of the devices present.

But luckily, what could be seen by the ghost agents was the carriers' blank minds and focus on moving to one spot.

Normal people had hundreds of thoughts. Bomb carriers were like jumping into someone with a blank screen with just one sentence playing across the screen.

Ten minutes after they started, Jewel was the first to find one. It was a woman carrying a large purse with a gun in it.

"Got one," Jewel shouted into the air. She went quickly inside the woman and found the small almond-sized explosive in the same place the others had been planted before.

"Bomb is in same location in their brain," she said.

A moment later Stan's voice said, "Bomb removed, gun removed."

As the bomb was removed, the woman staggered a moment, then looked around surprised at where she was. Jewel was still inside her and the poor woman had a thousand thoughts flood through her mind, all confused.

The woman turned and headed for the front door of the casino at a fast march.

So much for not alerting anyone that the bombs were being found. Clearly something in the mechanism of the bomb was part of the control of the carrier.

K.J. found the next one, again a woman.

Same thing happened. When the bomb was removed and the gun taken, the woman carrier seemed surprised at where she found herself and left in a hurry.

Jewel went back inside the woman K.J. had found to see her thoughts. The woman was only confused and worried about a headache that might have caused her to be here.

Nothing more.

It took thirty minutes for the six of them to find all twelve women and get the bombs and guns removed.

But Jewel didn't think that was enough.

"They might be sending in teams in waves," she had said to Tommy and K.J.

Both had agreed.

So they kept searching people, anyone walking anywhere near that casino main floor and that power ring.

There were six pretty major entrances to the casino floor, so they started from the center of the main casino floor and went through everyone on the floor and then each agent took an entrance and scanned everyone coming in.

This time it was Tommy who found the next one, clearly part of a new twelve. This was a man and the guy was confused after the bomb was removed and he left.

They found eleven more, all coming in from different exits. All were cleared, guns taken, bombs removed from their bodies.

"Fifteen minutes left until time," Belle said.

"I'm betting there are more bombers coming," Nancy said.

Jewel could only agree.

So they all moved just outside the ring in the entrances and kept scanning through each person who approached. Jewel again found the first one of the next wave, and then the bombers just kept coming.

To Jewel it seemed like every fifth person had a bomb in their head. All were moving toward that edge of that old power ring.

It turned out that there were six groups of twelve bombers this time.

Thirty seconds before the time of the power ring surge, Laverne appeared and froze time.

"One more sweep," she said.

So they each would check someone, she would stop time, they would all check another person, she would stop time again.

They had found them all.

Jewel had never felt so relieved in her entire life.

But if this person was willing to send seventy-two people to this ring this time, what would he or she do for the large and last power time in three days?

If they didn't get this figured out and quickly, a lot of people were going to die.

And a very nasty war was going to start.

TWENTY-ONE

DEANNA FELT ELLIOT cuddle in beside her.

"I missed you," she said.

"Off saving the world," he said. "How do you feel?"

"Inside, with you here, fine," she said. She tried to check in with her body, but found nothing really to check in with. "Numb outside."

"Makes sense," he said. "Your body has gone into a coma. You won't wake up."

She could feel the panic rising in her mind and Elliot just sort of calmed her. She loved that he could do that.

"It was expected," he said. "Remember?"

"I do," she said. "But not really fond of the idea of dying."

"Yeah," he said, clearly amused. "Can't say as I blame you there. But I didn't have weeks to think about it like you have had. Kind of glad, actually."

"So if I am in a coma," Deanna said, "how am I talking to you?"

"Come on," he said, standing beside her bed and holding her hand. "Let's get you dressed and go talk for a while."

"I am so delusional," she said, laughing. "I talk with my dead boyfriend, tell myself I am in a coma, then want to go get dressed and talk."

"Well," Elliot said, holding her hand while he stood beside the bed, "I am personally glad you are delusional. So let's go."

He pulled on her hand a little and she just stood like she would have normally gotten out of bed. No problem at all.

"That's just weird," she said, standing there looking back at her body on the bed.

Her closet door was closed, so Elliot showed her how to get into her closet by sticking her hand through the wooden closet door. She couldn't feel anything but the clothes inside. She pulled a white blouse through the door and held it up.

Then she went over and with Elliot's help stuck her hand through into one of her clothes drawers and got some jeans.

She was wearing underwear, so she just slipped out of her nightgown and put on the blouse, then the jeans.

The entire time Elliot just stared at her. And she had to admit, she liked that and had missed that from him.

"You are so good-looking," he said after she went for her tennis shoes and sat in a kitchen chair to put them on.

"I really love this delusion," she said, shaking her head. "I'm complimenting myself."

He laughed. "Nope, that was me and I meant it."

"Wow, my own delusion trying to convince myself. Getting kind of twisted."

She stood, enjoying the feel of being healthy, even though she knew she was just dreaming it.

"So what time is it?" she asked.

"Just after one in the morning," he said.

"So where are we going?" she asked. "Now that I'm all dressed."

"You hungry?"

She checked in with her stomach and nodded. "Actually, I am. Haven't been able to keep food down lately for some reason or another."

"I know exactly the place," he said.

He took her hand and squeezed it and then a moment later they were standing in the hallway outside a really nice café. People were walking by in the wide hallway and on one side of the hall glass windows looked out over a darkened large pool area.

The place felt alive and active, even at this time of the night. And she could smell hamburger and steak smells coming from the open front of the café.

"Where are we?" she asked.

"We're in the Golden Nugget Casino and Hotel complex in downtown Las Vegas," he said. He pointed to the café with a lot of tables beyond a reception desk and some low planters. "I sometimes come down here to eat at night."

"Come down here?" she asked.

He nodded. "I have a suite up in the Rush Tower in this hotel that I have been living in since I died."

She opened her mouth, but no question came out. This delusion was going far beyond anything she could have ever imagined. And she had never been in this hotel before. In fact, she couldn't remember even seeing pictures of it.

"I figured I would need some help telling you what has happened," Elliot said. "So Jewel is meeting us."

He indicated a woman about their age sitting at an open table in the back. The woman had short hair and a nice smile and waved when Elliot pointed at her.

"One of your ghost team members," Deanna asked as Elliot took her hand and started toward the back.

"Yes, a former doctor," Elliot said. "She died in a car accident with her boyfriend, Tommy, last year."

Elliot led her toward the back, but he didn't attempt to go around tables or the planter. He just walked through them and since she was walking with him, she did the same. Tables, chairs, everything just seemed to not exist for them.

When she got to the table with Jewel, Deanna glanced back and just shook her head. "That was very strange."

"You get used to it," Jewel said, smiling and extending her hand. "Nice finally meeting you, Deanna."

Deanna shook Jewel's hand, which felt solid and strong.

"Thanks for joining us," Elliot said as he sat down.

Deanna did the same, feeling like any moment she should go through the chair. But she didn't. It felt solid under her. And the table in front of her was solid, even though she had just walked through a couple of others on the way here.

Deanna looked at Jewel and the worried expression on Elliot's face. She needed some answers, even if she was making them up herself.

"So want to try to explain all this?" Deanna said. "I'm kind of curious what my delusion is going to come up with next. I didn't know cancer could cause this sort of thing."

"It doesn't," Jewel said. "If this was a normal situation and you were going to just pass on to the next life when you died, you would have no thoughts at all right now, since your body slipped into a cancer-caused coma about an hour ago. In most cases, brain function pretty well stops at that point."

"So this is part of the brain tumor, huh?" Deanna said.

"No," Jewel said. "This is all very real."

"You and I have been picked," Elliot said, "to stay in this real world, as ghosts like I said, to help save people."

"There are only a few hundred of us around the world," Jewel said. "Now that you have joined us, our team has seven."

Deanna just sort of shook her head. "Wow, this delusion has taken entire new paths. I'm not even dead yet and I'm a ghost."

Suddenly a tall woman in an expensive business suit appeared. She had intense dark eyes and her long hair pulled back tight from her face.

And suddenly all around them everyone froze in position. And all background sounds of other talking and eating and laughing as they walked down the wide hallway in front of the café vanished.

Both Elliot and Jewel started to stand, but the woman motioned them to stay seated. She pulled over a chair and sat next to Elliot. Then she extended her hand. "Welcome, Deanna. My name is Laverne."

Deanna shook the woman's hand, feeling extreme power and confidence coming from her.

"You are the first ever to join a team before dying," Laverne said. "So it's going to be almost impossible, until your body finally dies, for these two to convince you that what you are experiencing is any more than a delusion."

Deanna nodded. "Got that right. But I am sure enjoying this. Better than being in that bed in pain."

"You are no longer attached to that body in that bed," Laverne said. "So that pain won't bother you. You have crossed over even though your body will continue to breathe for two more weeks."

That matter-of-fact statement from the clearly powerful woman sitting across from her rocked Deanna back.

"So I really am now dead?" Deanna asked.

"To put it bluntly," Laverne said, "yes."

Jewel and Elliot were both nodding.

"And you are dead as well?" Deanna asked.

"No," Laverne said. "I am very much alive. But I am here to speed up your training so you can help us in three days. I suspect we will need your help."

Deanna started to ask what was the problem, but Laverne put up her hand. "They will explain to you what is happening. Just let me be clear here. Earlier tonight these two and the rest of their team saved hundreds of lives and helped avert a very nasty war."

Deanna glanced at Elliot, but he only seemed embarrassed by the compliment, as the Elliot she loved would be.

"Take my hand," Laverne said. "I will give you the larger picture and clear out the idea of this being a delusion so you can work on training the next few days."

Deanna hesitated, then took Laverne's extended hand.

Suddenly she knew she was dead. That her essence that made her who she was had crossed over into this new state.

That she and Elliot both were being recruited to be Ghost of a Chance agents.

And she understood that there were gods and superheroes working in every walk of life, that the ghost team she was to be a part of would be special and report mostly directly to Laverne.

It was as if a huge curtain to parts of the world had suddenly been drawn to one side and she could see a larger, formally hidden aspect of life.

Then Laverne let go of her hand and smiled.

All Deanna could do was smile back. Her body was dying, sure, but she and Elliot got the chance to keep on living and being together again.

It was real.

She knew it now.

"I'm very glad you two have joined the team," Laverne said, standing and nodding to Elliot and then Deanna. "We're going to need you."

With that, she was gone, and the sounds from the restaurant came smashing back in. And people went back to moving.

"Wow," Deanna said, smiling at Elliot. "Who was that?"

"One of the most powerful of all the gods," Elliot said.

"You know her as Lady Luck," Jewel said, smiling.

"And that's exactly how I feel right now," Deanna said. "Lucky. And damned hungry. Ghosts had better be able to eat or we're all going to be in trouble."

Elliot and Jewel both laughed. And Deanna had her training start with learning how to get food.

SECTION FIVE
A Mission

TWENTY-TWO

JEWEL SPENT THE next two days with Elliot and Deanna, helping them both get trained, including how to be inside live people and how to go shopping for clothes.

Laverne had been correct. Deanna was completely disconnected from her dying body up in Boise. As a doctor, Jewel found that fascinating, how going into a coma like that would cause such extreme disconnection.

And Deanna sure seemed to mostly forget she actually had a body still alive in Boise. She spent the night with Elliot in his suite at the Golden Nugget and on the second afternoon. Belle and Nancy showed her how they reserved the suite through the hotel computers so no live humans slept in it.

On the morning of the third day, while all seven of the team were having breakfast at the Golden Nugget buffet, time stopped around them and Laverne appeared.

Laverne pulled a chair over to their table and sat down next to K.J.

K.J. was dressed almost conservatively in a powder-blue suit and red tie and blue shoes. His hat matched his suit, so only his red tie brought the outfit a streak of color.

The rest of them were in their normal jeans, light shirts, and tennis shoes.

Laverne had on a black pinstriped suit and had her dark hair pulled back tight.

As always, she looked powerful and impressive.

"Any luck finding out who is behind the attacks?" K.J. asked.

Laverne shook her head. "We are no closer than we were two days ago I'm afraid. And the peak power point is at 6 p.m. this evening. We will have a lot of people there to stop this."

They talked for a time about when the team should be at the Living Time Casino and decided on an hour ahead. Jewel had never seen Laverne look so worried and down. This really, really had one of the most powerful gods of all time worried.

Finally it was Belle that asked the question that Jewel had been thinking.

"Can't we just close off the hotel, make sure no one is in there for some reason?"

Laverne nodded. "If we haven't figured this out by thirty minutes before the power point, we're going to do a fake fire alarm and evacuate the entire hotel. If that doesn't do the trick, we're going to shut off all cameras and just teleport people out of there and wipe their memory as they go."

"So what can we do?" Jewel asked.

"Be there ahead and see if you can figure out anything that might be going on that we don't see."

"How about we go in there right after breakfast?" Tommy said. "We'll spend the entire day in the hotel, scouring everything and everyone."

K.J. nodded and so did Laverne.

"Thank you," Laverne said.

Then she vanished and the sounds of the buffet came smashing back in as all the live people eating breakfast and talking resumed.

"Let's hope she is thanking us when this is all finished." K.J. said.

Jewel glanced at the worried look on Tommy's face. "Looks like we had better get a good breakfast. We're going to be very busy for the rest of the day."

TWENTY-THREE

DEANNA WAITED UNTIL they were mostly finished with their main breakfast plates before asking a couple of questions that had been bothering her.

"This power ring from the ancient past hits its peak at 6 p.m. tonight. Right?"

K.J. nodded.

"So why is that ring right on the casino floor?" Deanna asked. "Land around here has risen, if my ancient geography lessons are remembered right."

"You remembered that stuff?" Tommy asked. "Wow, I'm impressed."

"Can't access actual details," Deanna said, feeling slightly embarrassed. "Just a general memory."

"I think you might be right, though, now that you mention that." Nancy said. "I'll check that."

Deanna watched as Nancy stood and went over to a woman working on a laptop near the big window overlooking the pool. Nancy then disappeared into the woman. Deanna knew that Nancy was having the woman look up the information.

It was amazing what ghosts could do without ever actually being able to touch anything in the real world.

Everyone went back to eating until Nancy came back.

"Deanna is right," Nancy said. "The ground area here has risen a long ways since it was marsh lands back in the time of Atlantis."

"That's why Laverne and Stan went down into the ground that first time," Belle said.

"So the casino floor means nothing," Deanna said. "It's not a ring but a tube coming up from the ground that needs to have the killing done inside of it. Right?"

"Sub-basements, any upper floors," Elliot said, nodding. "We need to really, really expand our search."

"There could already be hostages and bombers in suites and rooms on upper floors," Deanna said, "just waiting to cause a blood bath."

That was what had been bothering her, but she hadn't wanted to say anything until now.

And there was one other thing that was really, really bothering her.

K.J. started to stand to go tell Laverne when Deanna said, "I have one more problem I can't seem to figure out."

K.J. sat down. His funny comments held in check at the moment as he focused on the task at hand.

"I understand I'm only a few days into this and all," Deanna said.

"We're all new at this," Jewel said. "So go on."

Everyone nodded to that.

"This feels like a distraction to me," Deanna said, worried about what they would think.

"What kind?" Elliot asked, looking very serious.

She loved how he always listened to what she had to say. Sometimes he laughed, but he always listened.

"In the corporate world," Deanna said, taking a deep breath and trying to make sense of her worry, "disruption in one area is often used to soften and take the attention away from an action in another area. And the distraction often has a build-up as this has had."

K.J. looked up and shouted, "Laverne?"

An instant later Laverne appeared and time froze in the buffet. She waved that everyone stay seated and she pulled a chair over.

"Go on," Laverne said to Deanna. "I was listening. Your first point is spot on and we're scanning the hotel now for developing problems on all floors and into the sub-basements. So far nothing."

Deanna felt stunned. She hadn't really seen Laverne since that first night. But she had been told so much about her.

Deanna took a deep breath and kept going. "Even if there are some deaths today and the original Blackrow members are resurrected, you are completely prepared to trap them instantly and neutralize them. Correct?"

Laverne nodded. "We are ready for that now. We were not the first times."

"And the person behind all this would know that. Correct?" Deanna asked. "If they knew where the ring was at in the first place."

Laverne nodded slowly.

"So where is the real attack happening?" Deanna asked. "In corporate mergers and takeovers, that was always the question."

"And what is the goal?" Elliot asked. "In my line of work, when looking at the motive of any criminal, you always ask what is the overall goal? Usually it was money. Or revenge. Both extremely powerful driving forces."

"So what other major events from history are happening this evening?" Deanna asked. "Something that needs you and everyone else to be distracted."

"Damn, damn, damn," Laverne said softly to herself.

And then she vanished, dropping the time bubble around them as she did.

"Never a good thing when Lady Luck starts swearing," K.J. said, looking very worried.

Deanna had no idea what to think. She just hoped she had helped some.

They sat there in silence for a moment, then Tommy said. "We have a job to do, a hotel to protect, some lives to save. Let's get going."

"I love it when he makes speeches," K.J. said.

Jewel kissed Tommy on the cheek. "He is cute, isn't he?"

"Very," K.J. said, batting his eyes at Tommy.

And with that, they all jumped to the Living Time Hotel and Casino.

TWENTY-FOUR

JEWEL DIDN'T MUCH care that Laverne and the gods and superheroes could stop the dead from creating an army. That all sounded well and good, but she was much more interested in making sure no innocent people died in the failed attempt.

And she mentioned that to all of the team after they arrived in the lobby area of the big Living Time Hotel and Casino. All of them agreed. No one died today on their watch.

The hotel lobby was huge, with gold and white stone floors and towering stone pillars. An expansive light oak front desk ran along one wall on the right and a waiting area with couches and chairs were on the left, along with some shops and such. Tourists came in through the front door

elevated above the lobby, which gave the massive room with the towering ceilings an even grander feeling, if that was possible.

And straight ahead, across from the front entrance was the entrance to the lower-ceilinged casino area.

The massive lobby echoed with talking, laughing, and people having fun, combined with the sounds of the machines drawing customers forward into the depths of the hotel and casino.

Piles of baggage were still stacked around, mostly against pillars or on carts as people checked out.

The seven Ghost of a Chance team members stood off to one side out of any traffic area.

"I have a question," Deanna asked. "Can all the gods and superheroes see us?"

"Nope," K.J. said, shaking his head. "Very few of the gods can. Laverne gave Poker Boy and his team the ability to see us last fall, but to everyone else, we are completely invisible."

Deanna nodded.

"Why?" Jewel asked.

"Just wanted to make sure that if the gods who are planning these attacks come here," Deanna said, "we can't be seen. We have more value that way."

"Agreed," Tommy said. "How about we go into the casino, check those there, and then float up through the hotel checking everyone as we go."

Jewel looked at all the people streaming in and out of the casino area and suddenly realized that would be a waste of time. Deanna had been right. This was a diversion. She understood that now.

She touched Tommy's arm and shook her head. "I think Deanna is right and we need a different plan. Let's go back to the buffet for a few minutes to talk in comfort."

He frowned at her, but then nodded. "Sounds fine. We have a lot of time between now and six."

At that, they were all back at the Golden Nugget buffet in downtown Las Vegas. At some point they really, really were going to need to find a place of their own.

The breakfast crowd still filled about half the place, mostly over by the tall windows looking out over the pool area. And the wonderful smell of bacon and waffles made her feel hungry again, even though she had just eaten.

They quickly bussed off their ghost dishes from earlier and each got themselves something to drink and a snack before going back to the table.

"So what are you thinking?" K.J. asked, facing Jewel as he worked on a Danish, managing mostly to not get any frosting on his face or his bright red tie.

Jewel took a deep breath and tried to gather her thoughts. "I think Deanna is right. This is a diversion, but one we can't ignore or let people get killed in."

All of them nodded, staring at her.

"So I think we might be better served to help out by splitting our attentions."

"How do we do that?" K.J. asked. "This isn't a simple three-way in my hot tub, you know."

Jewel said nothing to that and Tommy just shook his head.

Jewel then turned to Belle and Nancy. "I'm thinking that you two find some very powerful computers and dig into who wants the Living Time corporations stock depressed. If memory serves, it's part of a very large group of casinos."

"It is," Nancy said. "We can dig into stalled projects and other money reasons that are large enough to want this to happen."

Belle nodded.

"Try to figure out," Tommy said, "who would gain vast sums if this entire town was shut down."

Jewel frowned at Tommy. "Think it could be something like that?"

He shrugged. "If we're going to look, let's look. A war with black magic here, if we hadn't stopped those first attacks, would have shut down this city forever."

"So someone might have a backup plan to shut the city down," K.J. said, nodding.

Jewel agreed that made sense. "Even if it is a god, they have to live here as well. Laverne and Poker Boy and his team are researching that side of things, let's look for the business connections."

Jewel then turned to K.J. "I think we need you next to Laverne and Poker Boy, reporting back anything they are doing that might help us."

K.J. nodded. "I can do that."

"And we can look from the legal side," Deanna said.

Elliot nodded. "There might be some pretty angry people out of the past that felt wronged in some land grab or legal way that are just waiting to get even. I would imagine gods hold grudges just as anyone else."

K.J. laughed so hard at that, Jewel was afraid he would have a stroke, if ghosts could have strokes. When he finally calmed down, he said, "They are masters at holding grudges. I think it has to do with living so long."

Jewel nodded and turned to Tommy, the man she loved more than anything on the planet. "That leaves the hotel for us."

"But we don't start looking in people yet," Tommy said. "We go down to that ring and see what we can find, if any-thing. And search the hotel from top to bottom for anything odd in the slightest."

Jewel nodded. "I love that idea."

Tommy turned to look at everyone. "We check back in here at 2 p.m. unless someone hits pay dirt."

K.J. nodded. He took one bite of the Danish, then dropped the remains on his plate. "Off to tag along like a well-house-trained-puppy with the gods and superheroes."

He vanished.

"Courthouse," Deanna said to Elliot.

And they vanished.

"Living Time corporate main com-puters," Belle said to Nancy.

And they vanished.

"Let's go find an ancient ring of power," Tommy said.

"You take me to all the nicest places," Jewel said, laughing.

And a moment later they were in the subbasement of the Living Time Hotel and Casino.

TWENTY-FIVE

DEANNA WASN'T SURPRISED that only two people were sitting deep in the Clark County Courthouse, working at computers.

The windowless concrete room was stacked with files and seemed to go off into the distance with shelving holding file boxes. The place felt cool and Deanna wished she had worn a sweater.

One of the two people sitting there was a woman about thirty, with short brown hair and jeans and a thick blouse that looked more suited for a winter

climate. She seemed to be studying some file on her screen, almost straining and leaning forward to look at it.

Around her she had made her area feel a little like home, with a couple plants that must have not minded the artificial light, a small coffee maker, and some pic-tures of a family that did not include her.

The woman had a nice blue sweater draped over a chair behind where she was working. Deanna figured she could bor-row that if she needed to later on.

The other person was a man, wearing a t-shirt and jeans and clearly checking Facebook at the moment. His desk only had a box of snack bars on it and piles of paper and not much else.

These two computers were the re-cord-keeping entry points for all the legal records of the area. Luckily, both Deanna and Elliot were experts in fast research through legal documents.

But finding anything today was going to need both of their skills since there was really no way to divide up what they were doing. They were just going to follow trails in legal documents like a hunter would fol-low an animal trail through a forest.

And from the looks of the physical storage in this huge room, they were in a very, very large forest.

"Check the woman for anything she has noticed unusual first," Elliot said. "And I'll check the guy for the same be-fore I get started."

That made sense to Deanna. Sometimes these data computer workers saw things that were never reported, or put pieces together that never got put to-gether in any other fashion.

Elliot kissed Deanna. "Have fun."

"Actually I will," she said, smiling at him. "I love doing research, you know that."

Now Available
from all your favorite booksellers in trade paper and electronic editions.

Elliot laughed, kissed her again, then turned and vanished into the guy doing Facebook.

An instant later the guy sat up straight and closed Facebook and his fingers started dancing over the keys.

Deanna smiled. Elliot loved the rush of danger and discovery and this assault on Vegas was giving him both.

She turned to the woman. "Sorry to take your body for a while," she said. "But mine seems to be in a coma up in Idaho at the moment."

Deanna sunk into the woman and was instantly surprised. The woman's name was Stephanie Williams, at least in this lifetime. She had lived for hundreds and hundreds of years under many names and she was a superhero working in the area of governments.

She loved computers and loved digging into the history of governments. Except for this cold, sometimes damp office, she loved this job as well. It suited her.

She was married to another superhero who worked for the gods of landscaping. They had no kids and loved to travel and see and learn about history together.

Deanna had no idea that there were so many gods and superheroes.

Deanna looked back at Stephanie's memories and only found one or two references to even knowing there was a part of her world where ghosts existed in a team. She had heard only a few mentions of that, mostly from last fall when K.J. and the others had worked with Poker Boy to save the world.

Stephanie knew about the coming problem, had met with her boss, a woman named Claire, who was also a superhero, just more powerful and older. So she had already started the search back through records, looking for anything that seemed odd, to see if she could help.

Deanna moved off to one side in Stephanie's mind and spoke to her.

"Hi, Stephanie. You are not hearing things or making things up. My name is Deanna and I'm a Ghost of a Chance agent."

To Deanna, that sounded very weird, but she liked the sound of it a lot at the same time.

Stephanie swung around quickly, looking in both directions, then frowning and being surprised that Adam, the guy she worked with, was actually working.

"My partner, Elliot, is inside Adam running searches," Deanna said. "I didn't know you were a superhero."

"You are inside my head hearing my thoughts?" Stephanie asked, without saying anything.

"I am," Deanna said. "Elliot and I believe that the attacks at the Living Time Casino might be distractions for another attack or takeover or something happening at some other place today."

Deanna could see that Stephanie was pleased. "I was working on that same theory. And really nice meeting a ghost agent, if you call this meeting."

"About as close a meeting as it gets," Deanna said.

"It is," Stephanie thought back. "So where do you want to start?"

"I can see what you were thinking about the early land grabs," Deanna said. "And the fact that so much of the land to the north of Las Vegas is off limits."

Deanna could tell that Stephanie didn't know why that land was off limits, but it worried her. It seemed that one man named Warren Numa had made many legal attempts to acquire the land to the north, but the county always stopped him cold.

"Let's get a picture of this Numa guy," Deanna said.

Deanna was pleased she didn't have to take over Stephanie and run the search. Stephanie was fast, very fast, maybe faster than Deanna would have been.

They pulled up a picture of Numa. The guy looked handsome, with the standard square chin and an expensive suit. He had dark eyes, perfectly styled brown hair, and a smile that didn't reach his eyes.

"He's not the dating kind," Stephanie said, shuddering.

Deanna could tell that Stephanie was repulsed by the guy.

"Not a normal reaction to a picture," Deanna said. "But I feel the same way. So how about a picture of a business person who tried to get land to the north back in the 1950s?"

Again Stephanie's fingers flew over the keys as Deanna watched her exact thought process in the search, only suggesting one change.

Within ten minutes they pulled up a picture of William Numa. He had been trying to buy the land under another company, but there was no doubt it was the same guy. He had just changed his first name, more than likely pretending he was just family.

"We're dealing with a god or superhero there," Stephanie said.

They spent the next thirty minutes going back into the 1930s and discovering the same man trying to buy the same land, and then they discovered that at one point he had owned a bunch of it, considered it family property, but it was taken from him and he was forced to move off his family ranch.

That was when all the attempts to regain it started and escalated for the last eighty years.

"So why is that property so protected?" Stephanie asked in her mind at the same time Deanna was thinking it. "It is vast amounts of land, actually, with only roads going through it."

Neither of them had an answer to that question.

The two of them spent the next hour digging into everything they could learn about Warren Numa. They discovered he was very, very rich and diversified under many companies. But he owned little land in Las Vegas. Very little, actually.

Only the land to the north of Vegas interested him in the slightest.

It wasn't until they found the corporate structure of one of his well-hidden corporations that Deanna suddenly got very worried. It seemed he owned an explosives corporation.

And a cutting edge medical research corporation.

And a corporation specializing in drone advancement.

"Oh, no," Stephanie said.

Deanna could feel the panic starting in the superhero. And Deanna wasn't sure if some of that panic was hers as well.

"I'm leaving you now," Deanna said. "Then I'm going to call Laverne for help."

"Lady Luck?" Stephanie asked, now even more afraid.

"Yes," Deanna said and gave Stephanie a calming feeling and stepped out.

Then as Stephanie stood, Deanna said to Elliot. "Found a huge problem. Put that guy to sleep and come on out."

The guy slumped over his keyboard as Elliot stepped into sight.

"Laverne!" Deanna shouted into the air. "I think we found something."

An instant later Laverne appeared and smiled at Stephanie, who looked like she was about to faint.

Laverne stepped toward Stephanie and stuck out her hand. "Nice meeting you, Stephanie. You've done great work over the years."

Stephanie nodded, shook Laverne's hand, then managed to say, "The pleasure is all mine."

Laverne turned to Deanna and suddenly it was clear that Stephanie could now see Deanna and Elliot.

Deanna smiled at her. "Wonderful job you did there."

"Nice having you along for the ride," Stephanie said, smiling.

"So what did you two find?" Laverne asked.

"Warren Numa is his current name," Deanna said. "He has been angry and frustrated he hasn't been able to acquire land to the north of Las Vegas since Las Vegas was only a train stop. His family settled out there and then were forced to leave their ranch."

Laverne nodded. "I remember that. He is a god in the farming area, a powerful one, and hates what happened to him and his settlement he had out there in the desert."

"It seems almost an obsession," Deanna said.

"He has hidden corporations," Stephanie said, "that control state of the art explosives, medical technology, and drone research."

"Everything needed to build those bombs in people's heads," Deanna said. "And the drone company really concerns me."

"But why would he want to depress the economy of Las Vegas?" Elliot asked.

"He doesn't," Laverne said, her voice cold. "As Deanna came up with earlier, the attacks at the casino are a distraction."

"So what is his target?" Deanna asked.

"The desert he can't buy," Laverne said.

"Why can't he buy it?" Stephanie asked.

"Because the Silicon Suckers live there," Laverne said. "He's going to start a war much worse than fighting a small army of black magic beings from the past. He's going to start a war with the Silicon Suckers. That's a war humans cannot win."

Deanna had no idea what to say to that.

Nothing.

Because she had no idea who the Silicon Suckers were.

Laverne turned to Stephanie. "You want to help more in this fight?"

"I would be honored," Stephanie said.

Laverne pointed back at Stephanie's computer. "See if in the next thirty minutes you can find dates and times that the land to the north was blocked, or that Numa was removed from his ranch. See if any of them have an anniversary today."

Stephanie nodded.

"I'll be back to get you in thirty minutes."

Then Laverne turned to Deanna and Elliot. "Meeting in Poker Boy's office in thirty minutes. Round up your team."

Then Laverne vanished.

"Poker Boy's office?" Stephanie said, almost in awe.

"Wait until you see it," Deanna said. "I'm told it is something. I'm going to stay and help you. Elliot, you want to get the team, bring them up to speed, and warn them. And get Belle and Nancy digging into Warren Numa's corporations for thirty minutes. See what they can find from that direction."

Elliot nodded and vanished.

Stephanie sat down and faced the screen. "Come on in."

Deanna smiled and joined Stephanie in her body.

And then the two of them went to work, combining both their skills to dig as deep as it took.

SECTION SIX
Attack

TWENTY-SIX

JEWEL AND TOMMY had found nothing at all that was out of place anywhere in the hotel or casino. So they had started to scan people when Elliot and K.J. appeared.

They were on the top floor and just happened to be in the wide, carpeted hallway.

K.J. was not looking happy in the slightest.

"Deanna and a superhero named Stephanie might have gotten us a lead," Elliot said.

"The lead they found has the gods scared beyond words," K.J. said. "And me too, to be honest."

"What is it?" Jewel asked, wondering what could be so bad as to scare the gods like K.J. said.

"I never met a Sucker and I don't want to now." K.J. said, then took a deep breath. "It seems that there is a chance that a god named Warren Numa wants to attack in some fashion the Silicon Suckers home to the north of town for revenge."

Jewel and Tommy both glanced at Elliot, who just shrugged.

So Jewel turned back to the distraught ghost in the blue suit and red tie and asked, "What is a Silicon Sucker?"

"Humans who see them think of them as aliens," K.J. said. "They are called 'The Grays' by flying saucer believers. But they are actually an ancient race of beings that has been on Earth far longer than humans and giants and the Titans."

"Oh," was all Jewel could say.

"They live in huge sand caverns and one of their main cities is under the desert to the north. All that land is Silicon Sucker land. And they protect their land."

"So does this god named Numa know this?"

"He would have to," K.J. said, "since it seems after Atlantis went under, he built a compound to the north of here and was removed from it by treaty with the Silicon Suckers at some point a number of years ago. He's been trying to force governments ever since to give him his land back."

"So what makes him a suspect in the gunmen here?" Jewel asked, trying to connect the dots.

"He owns a company that does high-tech explosives," K.J. said, "and another company that does state-of-the-art health inventions. And, on top of that, he's a god who was alive in the days of Atlantis and settled near here after Atlantis went down, so he would know about this power ring."

"Okay," Jewel said, now seeing why K.J. was rattled. "What do we do next?"

"Meeting in a couple minutes from now in Poker Boy's office," K.J. said.

"Deanna is still with the superhero searching history for more legal issues with this guy," Elliot said. "And Belle and Nancy are now doing a fast dig through the man's multiple corporations to see what they can find."

Jewel nodded. "So let's go a few minutes early."

K.J. took a deep breath, nodded and a moment later they were standing in Poker Boy's office.

Jewel still found the office stunning, not in a normal office way, but in the fact that it was a giant invisible cube floating about a thousand feet above the Las Vegas Strip. And besides a few chairs, the only furniture was a large 1960s style diner booth in the middle of the room.

K.J. had told her after their last visit here in the fall that Poker Boy and his team had started out meeting in a diner off of Fremont Street, and when Poker Boy learned how to build an office, he had just replicated the diner booth.

For a glass cube with a railing against the glass all the way around, the diner booth made the place feel comfortable.

And the view was amazing. She could see the mountains all the way around and planes approaching and taking off from the airport. Far below the cars looked like small toys on the busy streets.

Since today was a bright sunny day with deep blue skies, this office just felt perfect.

"Wow," Elliot said softly, turning slowly to get all the view.

They had arrived near one corner of the office and Poker Boy in his black leather jacket and black Fedora-like hat was sitting in the booth talking with his girlfriend, Patty. Only one other person was there, an older god named Ben who seemed to be the memory for Poker Boy's team.

Patty and Ben both waved hello at them, but kept talking.

Jewel turned to the north and looked out over the vast open desert area in that direction. So all of this might be caused by some god wanting that land. How really, really stupid.

At that moment, everyone else seemed to arrive at once.

Laverne arrived, pulled up a chair and sat at the end of the booth,

Deanna stood next to a woman who looked scared and nervous that Jewel didn't know. Both of them just gawked at the fantastic view, both turning slowly as Elliot had done.

Belle, and Nancy arrived holding hands and looking upset.

Jewel moved over and stood next to Tommy. She just felt stronger that way.

It seemed the meeting was about to start. And most of Poker Boy's team were clearly off doing something else.

Jewel had no idea what that something else might be.

TWENTY-SEVEN

DEANNA NODDED to Ben as she and Elliot were officially introduced as new Ghost of a Chance agents by Laverne.

The ghosts, plus Stephanie, were all standing around the right of the booth. Laverne had turned her chair to face them and Ben had moved around to also face them beside Poker Boy and Patty.

Then Laverne introduced the superhero named Stephanie who managed to nod and say, "Nice meeting you." But she was clearly shocked to be there.

Deanna didn't blame her in the slightest. This office was enough to knock a person's socks off. For a moment Deanna

felt like she might fall off the edge, even with the wooden rail all the way around.

The bright blue sky and views of the mountains in all directions around Las Vegas were just breathtaking.

And Deanna knew that Stephanie was in awe of Laverne and Poker Boy and his team. Stephanie had heard so much about them over the years, but had never dreamed of meeting them, let alone helping them.

The only reason Deanna wasn't feeling the same way was Elliot's reaction. He had worked with them and had described them and liked the team members he had met. So that had helped her a lot.

And learning about them through Stephanie's thoughts had helped some as well. Poker Boy and his team were impressive. Not scary.

"We somehow need to find out what Warren Numa has planned for this evening," Laverne said. "And do it quickly."

"Are we convinced he is behind all this?" Poker Boy asked.

Laverne nodded.

"We traced the money and programs," Belle said, "that Numa used to build those bombs he put in people's heads."

Nancy nodded. "We even traced the guns back to him through a number of shell corporations."

"And Stephanie and I found what today is the anniversary of for him," Deanna said.

"He and his family," Stephanie said, "were evicted by the police on this date in 1916 from his homestead in the desert. One hundred years ago."

Deanna smiled at Stephanie and nodded. The woman had courage, even in the face of meeting some of her idols.

Laverne turned to Ben. "Is this kind of behavior possible from Numa?"

"He has always been very vengeful," Ben said. "Some pretty major famines in history were caused by him because of his anger. And since he is the god of agriculture, his powers have been fading with so much food now being manufactured and so much land being put under concrete. I can vouch for the fact that when a god's powers start fading, it is upsetting, to say the least."

Deanna didn't like the sound of that. They were dealing with a real god, and an angry one to boot.

"So how do we stop him?" Poker Boy asked. "If he attacks the Silicon Suckers, we will never be able to repair the damage. And they will kill in retribution a hundred humans for every life they lose."

Laverne nodded and the silence filled the room.

"Do we know where he lives, where he is located at the moment?" Tommy asked.

"He has a fort-like compound in the rocks just to the east of town," Laverne said. "He allows no visitors, including me, without an appointment. I would imagine his shields are major."

"We can get in," Jewel said. "Give us an hour to figure out his plans."

Deanna had a hunch that shields didn't hold ghosts. And that someone like this Numa god wouldn't even give ghosts a second thought.

Laverne looked at Jewel and then the rest of the Ghost Agents, then nodded.

She turned to Poker Boy. "Ask for a meeting with the Supreme Ruler of the Silicon Suckers. Tell him what is happening, that we plan to stop it, but that he needs to mount his defenses as much as he can."

"Should I tell him who is at fault?"

"Yes," Laverne said.

She then turned to Patty. "Work with our people at the casino. At five get that fire alarm going, get everyone out of that hotel and keep them out until after the power point has passed."

Then Laverne turned to the Ghost Agents. "Get into Numa's compound, find out his plans exactly and what we can do to stop them."

All of them nodded.

Laverne look at K.J. "You be the relay back to me here in this office, since none of us who are alive dare go near that compound until this is all cleared."

"After that why don't we let the Great Leader and his people deal with Numa when we have this solved?" Poker Boy asked. "I am sure such a trade would be the honorable thing to do in sight of the threat involved."

Laverne nodded. "Let me check with the powers that be and the Fates, but I like that idea. But first things first, we have to stop what he is planning. And we have to know what that is first."

Suddenly an image of a large walled compound built into the rocks appeared in Deanna's mind. She knew exactly where it was at and what each building held.

"I have given you all the location and plans," Laverne said. "Good luck. Now I'm going to go talk with Ceres, his boss, see if she can get this guy under control."

Laverne vanished.

Deanna felt stunned. Lady Luck herself had just wished her luck. That had to be interesting. And Deanna hoped it was powerful as well.

"Teams of two," Tommy said. "K.J., you keep track of all three teams, listen for our calls. We are after information first, remember, to get back here."

Deanna glanced at Elliot and smiled.

She had no idea what she was walking into, but it couldn't be worse than dying alone, wasting away to nothingness. And no matter what, she was with Elliot.

"We'll take Numa's computer area," Belle and Nancy said.

"We'll take his walls and guards," Elliot said.

Tommy nodded. "Jewel, you and I are going right to the head of the snake."

Jewel nodded.

And with that they all jumped to the compound of an ancient and angry god.

TWENTY-EIGHT

JEWEL AND TOMMY jumped into a massive library. The ceilings towered overhead and books filled all four walls, with walkways about halfway up the walls. A spiral staircase in one corner led up to the walkways. A giant chandelier hung in the middle of the room, casting only faint light over the books.

The room smelled like really old paper, with a slightly musty smell added in. From what Jewel could tell, some of these books had to be hundreds of years old.

The floor was stone and covered with expensive-looking thick Persian rugs. A giant dark wood desk larger than some bedrooms filled one corner of the room with a huge wooden chair behind the desk that looked more like a throne than a desk chair.

A man who looked to be in his sixties, with short gray hair sat behind the big desk, studying some papers. Jewel assumed that was Numa.

There was no door into the room. None. Every inch of the room's walls was covered in books.

Jewel really liked the feel of the place except for the hate and anger radiating from the man behind the desk.

When they arrived, Numa looked up and frowned, glancing to one side, then the other.

Jewel panicked a little as she and Tommy froze, not moving. She was ready to jump out of there instantly if needed. She had no idea what Numa could do if he sensed them or could see them, but she had no desire to find out.

At that moment, a knock echoed through the large room and the man behind the desk said, "Come!"

A bookcase slid back and two men wearing modern three-piece suits entered and bowed slightly.

"Everything ready?" Numa asked.

"Completely," one man said.

Tommy indicated that Jewel should go into the one on the right, Tommy would take the one on the left.

A moment later Jewel was inside the man.

Evil did not begin to describe this man. Not an ounce of conscious remained. He had no family and had been a mercenary for a dozen years.

And then Jewel saw the entire plan. They were to send a couple dozen people to the casino to continue that ruse, but the man knew that would fail.

The drones were to attack the desert with massive bombs right at six p.m., along with a dozen trucks full of high explosives.

Jewel could see the image of the entire desert to the north of Las Vegas exploding in giant fireballs.

The man Jewel was in was not a god, or even a superhero. And he had no idea why his boss wanted to blow up the desert. But he didn't care. He was getting paid enough to not question.

"Then get it started," Numa said, turning back to study the papers in front of him.

The two men nodded and turned.

Jewel stayed inside the man until he was outside of the main office and the two men were out a back door.

Then she dropped out and shouted for K.J.

K.J. appeared instantly.

Tommy appeared after the men had taken a few steps and came back to join her.

"K.J.," Jewel said, "get inside that one man on the right, get the plan, and report it to Laverne. We're going to try to stop it from here."

K.J. instantly faded into the man.

After the man had taken three more steps, K.J had returned.

"Got it," he said. "I'll tell her you are trying to stop this as well and then come back."

He was gone.

Jewel glanced at the two men headed for a building that Jewel knew from the information that Laverne had given her as a communications center near one wall of the compound. There were a dozen other buildings around the compound and the large house they had just come out of.

"We have them give the order to stand down?" Tommy asked.

"Yes," Jewel said. "But did you see those papers our host was reading?"

"An ancient map of some sort," Tommy said.

That's what Jewel had seen as well, and it made no sense. Why would Numa be studying an ancient map at this point, when his plan is being set in motion?

"Let's take care of stopping this all," Tommy said. "Then we'll go back and see what we can see."

Jewel nodded and a moment later she was inside the man again just as he entered the communications room with banks of computer screens and a dozen men and women behind the screens.

"The boss has pulled the plug on this entire operation," Tommy's man said.

"Shut it down," Jewel had her man say. And she planted the thoughts that the boss had really said that and if he disobeyed, he would be killed.

Then she left the guy and moved to one of the women sitting behind one screen. The woman, also a former mercenary, was puzzled, but followed the order.

Jewel checked three others as Tommy checked some on his side of the big room.

All orders were going out to stand down and shut down. With each person she was in, she made them believe that the boss had ordered the shutdown and it was the right and only thing to do.

After five minutes the entire attack on the Casino and the Silicon Suckers home had been called off.

Tommy looked at Jewel. "Did that seem too easy?"

"Way too easy," Jewel said.

And that thought scared her more than she wanted to admit.

TWENTY-NINE

DEANNA AND ELLIOT had found the main guard center within seconds after jumping into the compound. And in ten minutes, they had every guard in the place without weapons headed out of the compound and down the road.

It had been amazingly easy to get the trained mercenaries to just lay down their weapons and walk away. The right com-

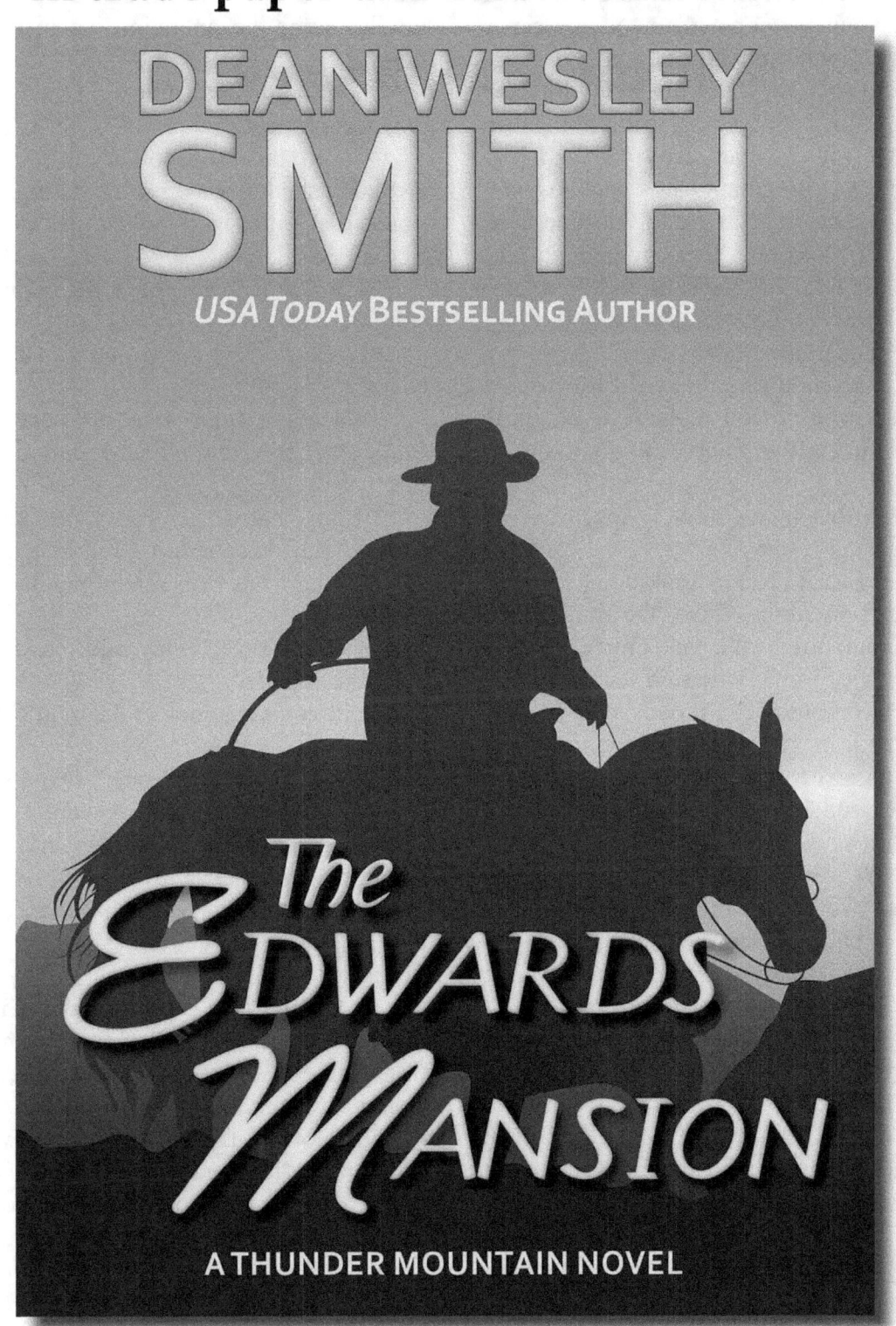

mands, the right beliefs, and even hardened killers walked from a job.

And Deanna and Elliot both made the guards believe that their boss was broke and would never pay them. No mercenary was going to fight without pay.

So once they had finished with every guard, they jumped up to the top of one of the walls near a defense gun and stood there, watching the guards walk away.

Deanna felt very odd. No one could see her except a few gods and other ghosts, but she had the ability to control people just by planting beliefs and thoughts in their heads.

It seemed like an awful lot of power for one person to have over another. Especially a nearly dead person like her.

At that moment, K.J. appeared with Belle and Nancy.

Belle and Nancy took one look at the guards streaming down the road outside the compound walls and smiled.

"Nice job," Belle said.

"Computers?" Elliot asked.

"All of his computers and communications with the outside world will shut down suddenly in exactly ten minutes," Nancy said.

"We didn't want to destroy it," Belle said. "But we're the only ones that can get it back up and working again if we need to."

Deanna loved the sounds of that.

A moment later Jewel and Tommy appeared.

"Success?" K.J. asked.

"Yes," Tommy said. "We got all the attacks stopped and all attackers standing down. The entire mission is called off."

"But it seemed far too easy," Jewel said. "As if Numa didn't really care about any of this."

Deanna didn't like the sounds of that at all.

"Numa was studying some ancient map," Tommy said, "when he gave the go-ahead for the operation we just shut down."

"It was almost as if he didn't care one way or another."

"Could this be another diversion?" Deanna asked, her stomach twisting. She glanced at Elliot who looked just as worried as she did.

"I'm afraid it all might be," Tommy said.

"What is this guy after?" Deanna asked.

"We could jump into his head and find out," Elliot said. "I'll be glad to give it a try."

Deanna hated, flat hated, the sound of that. But of course it would be Elliot to jump out front with something dangerous.

"Last resort," Tommy said.

Elliot nodded.

"Did you get a look at the map?" K.J. asked.

"I got a pretty good one," Jewel said. "But I have no idea what it meant."

"You all stay here and keep an eye on our host," K.J. said. "Jewel and I are going to go figure out what that map is all about."

Jewel and K.J. vanished.

At that point a dozen unarmed men and women came from the communications center, went out the front gate, and started down the road, walking as if they had just gotten off work.

Tommy laughed. "Jewel and I told them that once they got this all shut down, that the boss was broke and wouldn't pay them. That they needed to just get out of here."

Deanna laughed, pointing down the road outside the walls. "Elliot and I did the same thing with all the guards."

Tommy laughed.

Then all five of them just turned and stared at the big house from the top of the compound wall.

Deanna didn't want to get any closer and clearly none of the rest of them did either until that angry god was out of there.

THIRTY

JEWEL ENDED UP with K.J. back in Poker Boy's office.

Poker Boy, Patty, Ben, and Laverne were still there.

"We got the attacks we know about shut down," K.J. said to Laverne who stood when they appeared.

"But we're worried that all this might have been a diversion as well," Jewel said. "Numa was studying an ancient map when we were in his office and I sort of got a look at it, but don't understand it."

K.J. turned to Ben. "Would you mind Jewel showing you that map?"

"Not in the slightest," Ben said.

Jewel moved over and put her hand inside Ben's shoulder.

She was overwhelmed for a moment by the vast amount of information Ben had in his mind and the thousands and thousands of years he had lived. He had once been a major god of lamplighters. But Poker Boy had rescued him from fading away into obscurity.

Jewel gathered herself and tried to remember the image of the map on Numa's desk.

"Just let me look at it," Ben's voice said gently in her head.

So she focused on the map in front of Numa and after a moment Ben said, "That's enough."

Jewel stepped back next to K.J. as Ben shook his head.

Numa was looking at the Map of the Crystals," Ben said softly.

Laverne stared at him for a moment, then just shook her head and sat down.

"Can you fill us in, Ben?" Poker Boy asked after a moment.

"The Map of Crystals is basically a map of all the major crystal points in the Earth's crust. Crystal points are pressure points on what scientists today call the boundaries of tectonic plates."

"I gave the Map of Crystals back to the Fates after Atlantis," Laverne said. "There was only supposed to be one."

"He seems to have found a second," Ben said.

"He wants his power back," Laverne said softly. "He wants to send this planet back to the Stone Age, back to when we depended on agriculture."

Jewel felt more shocked than she wanted to admit. "He can do that with that map?"

"He can," Ben said. "He could cause earthquakes and volcanic eruptions so large, it would destroy this civilization. And the next crystal point is tonight."

"He wanted all of us so busy with a war with the Silicon Suckers," Laverne said, "that we wouldn't notice the buildup in energy at the points."

"So how do we stop him?" Poker Boy asked.

"We don't," Laverne said.

She stood and squared her shoulders. "I'll go plead my case to the Fates and the Powers that Be, but I doubt they will much care."

Then she was gone.

Jewel turned to Ben. "Why wouldn't they care?"

"Civilizations come and go," Ben said. "It is the nature of humanity. They will consider this nothing more than a squabble among the gods."

"Wiping out civilization is a squabble among the gods?" K.J. asked, clearly as stunned as Jewel was feeling.

Poker Boy and Patty just sat silent in the booth.

"Civilization always returns," Ben said. "It has many times in the past, it will do so in the future."

Suddenly Jewel had an idea.

"Ben, I was just inside your head," Jewel said. "If you sensed me, could you block me?"

"Possible," Ben said. "Why?"

"What happens if all seven of the Ghost Agents climbed into Numa's head. Think we could slow him down, confuse him, get him to miss some deadlines or do things wrong?"

Ben just shrugged. "At this point I see very little else to try."

Jewel turned to Poker Boy. "If he is holding some shield up around that compound that is not electrical, but power based, watch for holes. And come storming in when you see one."

Poker Boy glanced at Ben, who nodded.

"Let's go, K.J." Jewel said.

"Be careful," Patty said.

"We're already dead, remember?" Jewel said, smiling.

"But there are worse things than being dead," Ben said.

"Oh, that's what I needed," K.J. said. "A pep talk."

"Just watch for the hole in his shield," Jewel said.

And with that she and K.J. jumped back to their team standing in the sun on the wall of the compound.

SECTION SEVEN
The Battle

THIRTY-ONE

TOMMY DECIDED THAT K.J. would find someone in the house, a cook or housekeeper, then have that person knock on Numa's library door. The distraction would be enough for the other six of them to jump into the library and merge with Numa.

Or at least that was the plan.

Deanna couldn't think of a better one, so they all agreed and K.J vanished.

"We try to stay hidden in Numa's mind," Tommy said. "Just confuse him, give him faint suggestions, and so on."

"And remember when you get in there," Jewel said, "get small so the rest of us can crowd in."

"If he spots one of us," Tommy said, "the others use that distraction to take his mind apart if you can. This man wants to kill billions, so don't worry about damage. He deserves what he gets."

Deanna didn't like the sound of that either, but she sure understood.

"Watch for the mechanism in his mind controlling the screen around this place," Jewel said. "We need to knock that down to get help in here."

"I go in first," Tommy said, "then Jewel, Belle, Nancy, Elliot, and Deanna. One right after another. Be fast. We want to catch him by surprise. K.J will join us if he can."

Deanna nodded and squeezed Elliot's hand. She was dying in a bed in Idaho, days away from her final breath, and right now she felt like she was risking her life and everything.

Very strange.

"I'm in," K.J.'s voice came back strong in her mind. "Knocking on the door now!"

They all jumped at the same time into the huge library room. Deanna didn't allow herself to look around at all, but watched as Tommy, Jewel, Belle, Nancy, and Elliot vanished quickly, one right after another.

Deanna hesitated just a second to see if Numa had a reaction. "Then he said, "Come on in and join the party."

The man that K.J. had found walked in and K.J. bailed out of the man as the guy fell to the floor and burst into flames.

Deanna put her finger to her lips to tell K.J. to freeze. She had a hunch that the other five were trapped in some part of Numa's mind.

Numa didn't need to know there were more ghost agents around.

"You ghost agents didn't think I wouldn't notice how you got my people to shut down my wonderful diversions," Numa said, leaning back in his chair and laughing. "So I was expecting you because no human or superhero or god can get in here."

Numa leaned forward and looked at the old map in front of him.

"Can you all see the wonderful map I found in one of my old books?"

Deanna eased slowly toward Numa, doing her best to not make a sound and indicating that K.J. not move.

Numa pointed to a place on the map and said, "This is the first point of attack.

It will sink the west coast of the United States."

As he pointed, Deanna eased over and touched his finger and let herself be drawn inside Numa.

His mind was holding the rest in what looked like a prison in his head. Bars and all.

He did not seem to notice she was there.

He pointed to the next place and his mind imagined all the death and seemed to take joy from it.

That just made her angry, but she managed to contain her feelings. There was nothing joyful about death.

She should know.

She had watched Elliot die and now she was dying.

In one of her lessons with Jewel over the last few days, Jewel had shown Deanna the one place in a human brain that could be broken to shut the brain down completely. It was like a fine rope leading from the back of the brain to the spine. Jewel had had a medical term for that rope that Deanna couldn't remember.

But she sure remembered where that was.

She eased her way there now, ignoring as much as she could what Numa was saying, bragging to the others trapped in his brain about how many would die.

The guy really wanted the world to return to the Dark Ages where everyone farmed and he had power again. It seems the gods took power from how many were basically worshipping them.

No wonder Lady Luck was so powerful.

Numa had been very powerful in his day. Only Ceres was more powerful, and she was nothing more an old lady now tending to her own gardens and mostly ignoring the world.

Deanna could tell that Numa had great contempt for Ceres and all the other gods, actually.

Jewel had told her to only use what she was about to do in extreme emergencies, if she needed to stop someone from killing someone else.

And this seemed like a very large emergency.

It wouldn't kill Numa, but it would shut him down.

Deanna imagined a large knife in her hand and without giving it another thought, cut through the cord that Jewel had told her to cut.

Numa's brain went blank and his head banged on the table and the map.

Deanna left Numa and stood next to the wide-eyed K.J. as the rest of the team climbed out of the old god.

"Great work," Elliot said, moving over and kissing Deanna.

An instant later Laverne and Poker Boy and Patty appeared.

Tommy pointed at the map under Numa's head. "Might want to make sure all those points are defused."

Jewel nodded. "He was going on and on about all the death and destruction he was about to cause."

Laverne pushed Numa back and he slumped in his chair.

She picked up the map and stared at it, then nodded.

"What did you do to him?" Patty asked, moving around and touching his neck. "He still has a heartbeat."

Deanna couldn't imagine how glad she was to hear that.

Deanna turned to Jewel and said, "I cut the string that you told me to cut only in emergencies. I figure him killing

billions and you five trapped was an emergency."

Jewel laughed and turned to Laverne. "He will live, but never awaken."

"Thank you," Laverne said. Then she looked at K.J. and all the agents. "Your team's work is finished. You have once again helped us save the world."

At that moment Numa's body vanished.

Laverne turned to Poker Boy and Patty. "We are far, far from finished."

With that, all three of them vanished leaving the seven ghosts standing in the massive library.

Jewel walked over to one shelf and pulled off the ghost copy of one of the books there and looked at it, thumbing through the pages before putting it back. "Think Laverne would let us use this library and compound?"

"Yes," Laverne said, her voice echoing in all their heads. "Keep the entire place for your team."

Everyone smiled and laughed.

Deanna could hardly imagine having access to all these ancient books. This room was heaven to her.

She glanced over at Elliot and he was just looking upward at all the books and smiling like a kid at Christmas.

"Looks like we finally have a team headquarters," Jewel said. "We just got to figure out a way to have real people staff the compound and cook and all that."

"We can make that work," Tommy said as he walked around and looked at all the books.

Elliot looked at Deanna. "Wonderful, huh?

"Couldn't be better," Deanna said, hugging Elliot.

"Lunch first," K.J. said. "Then we can come back and haunt this mansion all we want. But if this is going to be headquarters, I vote for a hot tub up on the compound wall so we can look out at the stars at night."

Books and hot tubs and wonderful food.

Deanna just smiled.

Elliot took her hand, smiling back at her.

She had a hunch that she and Elliot had just found heaven.

THIRTY-TWO

EXACTLY TWO MONTHS from the day of Elliot's accident, Deanna and Elliot jumped back to their old condo and into their old bedroom.

It was seven and outside was one of those perfect evenings that Boise was famous for. And that Deanna loved. Clear blue sky, cooling breeze, the promise of a cool night ahead.

She and Elliot had spent so many wonderful walks on evenings like this one.

A machine beeped softly in the background like a ticking clock, noting the last few minutes of a life.

The room smelled of antiseptic and something sour. Deanna couldn't believe the thin, frail body in the bed was all that was left of her.

The consistent beeping continued and Deanna could see the sheet rise slightly as her body took a shallow breath.

"You all right?" Elliot asked.

"I feel fine," Deanna said, taking his hand. "Just glad I'm not in that body anymore."

"I'll have you know I love that body," Elliot said.

"And you did that very well last night," Deanna said, turning and kissing Elliot solidly on the lips.

She held that for a moment, then pulled away.

She looked around at their bedroom.

When alive, this had been a haven for them, a sanctuary they retreated to after long days in the real world of law and criminals and corporations.

She wanted to remember this place for all the good times they had had in here. She didn't want to think of it as a death place.

"What do you say we go get something to eat," Deanna said. "Find a nice quiet restaurant off the Strip in Vegas and have some wine to celebrate our new life together and then go back to the compound and enjoy our new apartment a little."

"I love that idea," Elliot said. "You sure?"

"Very sure," Deanna said. "And maybe get K.J. to vacate his hot tub for an hour so we can watch the stars."

"That might be asking too much," Elliot said, laughing.

Deanna had to agree. Since they had taken over Numa's old compound, Deanna and Elliot had taken one entire upstairs wing of the main house as their own and turned it into an apartment.

They loved the huge bed up there and were slowly having the living staff make the place into something more to their taste. It seemed that superheroes needed jobs to live since they were not paid to be superheroes. And Laverne had given the Ghost of a Chance team all of Numa's assets as a reward, so the entire Ghost of a Chance team were all very rich in real world money, even though they didn't need it.

Laverne had let the superheroes working at the compound be able to see the team, so it didn't seem like they were actually working for ghosts, even though they were.

Belle and Nancy were having a blast learning and running the corporations and Jewel was already digging into the medical corporation to figure out what advances they could do there.

K.J. had taken a guesthouse near one wall as a second residence and put a hot tub on the compound wall above his guesthouse in one of the old guard posts. The view of the desert sky and the valley below was amazing from that hot tub.

Belle and Nancy had decided to stay in their home in Las Vegas, as had Jewel and Tommy.

But all seven of them were already getting into a habit of meeting in the large dining room, also full of books, for breakfast every day and talking about the activities ahead, including the corporation holdings and what they were doing with them to help lives.

Besides helping with the legal aspects of the corporations and taking over control, Deanna and Elliot had spent every day in the main two-story library, just trying to get a sense of what books were there. It continually stunned them both at the scope and scale of the collection.

There were books in that large library that had not been seen in hundreds of years. Knowledge existed there that many thought lost.

But now, this evening, they were back in Boise because tonight was the night Deanna's body was supposed to die.

The mechanical sound of beeping counting the moments down continued unstopped.

Deanna took a long look at her old, frail body under the thin hospital bed sheet. Her hair had mostly fallen away and her face was nothing but bones and sunken skin.

She looked awful. She didn't need to stay here and watch this. As Laverne had said weeks ago, Deanna was already dead.

And now very much alive as a Ghost of a Chance agent living with the man she loved more than anything in the world.

She turned to Elliot. "Dinner, wine, hot tub, and sex. I can't think of a better way to celebrate dying, can you?"

"Nothing comes to mind better than that," Elliot said, smiling at her. "I don't expect you want me to think about any other options, do you?"

"Not a chance," Deanna said, laughing. "Let's go. You pick the restaurant, I'll pick the wine."

And as they jumped back to Vegas, Deanna thought she heard just as they left the beeping stop, to be replaced by a level, steady sound.

She was dead.
She was alive.
She was free.

Coming Next Issue in Smith's Monthly
The Full Novel All in One Place
That was First Serialized in These Pages!
THE LIFE AND TIMES OF BUFFALO JIMMY

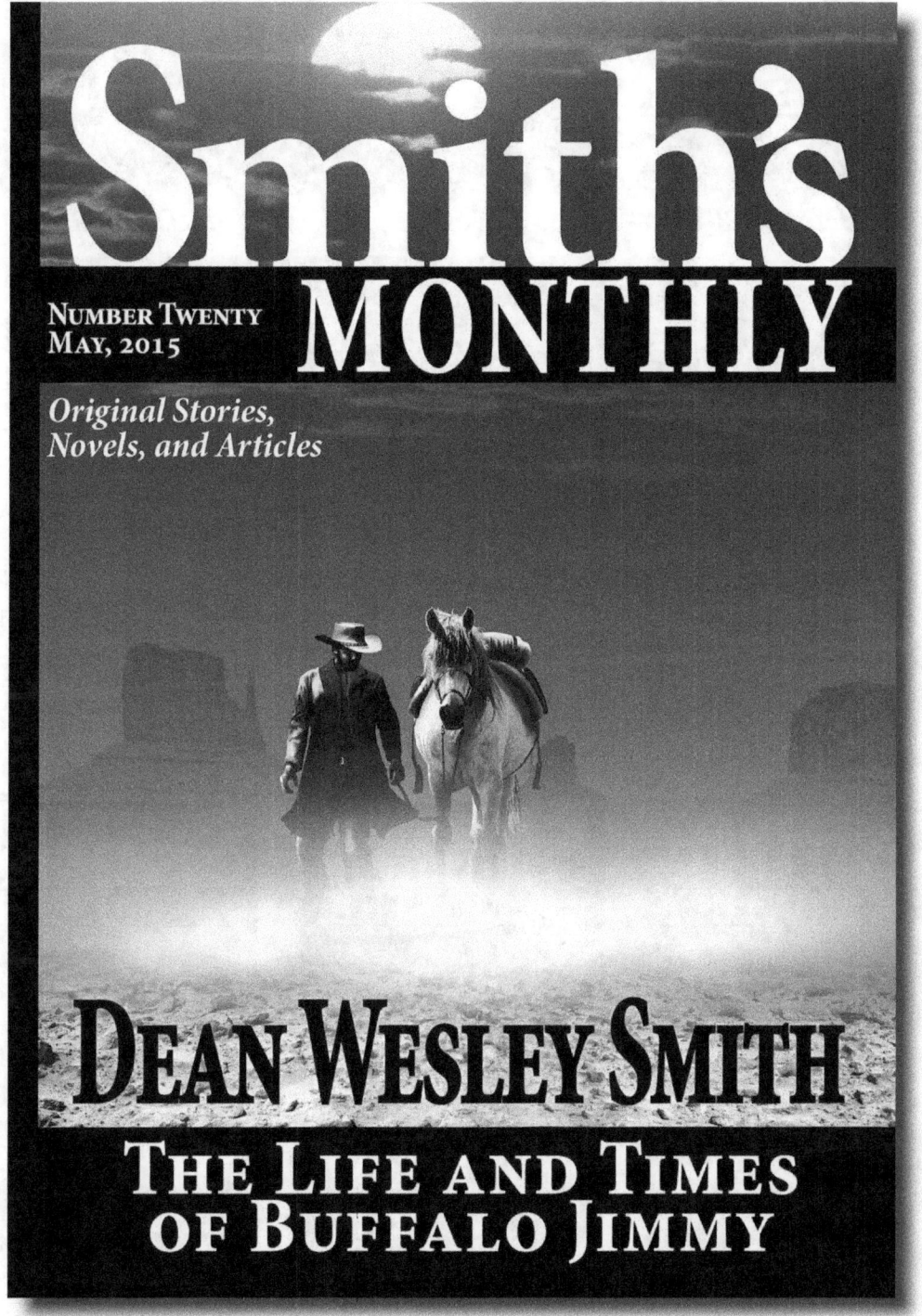

#1... October 2013

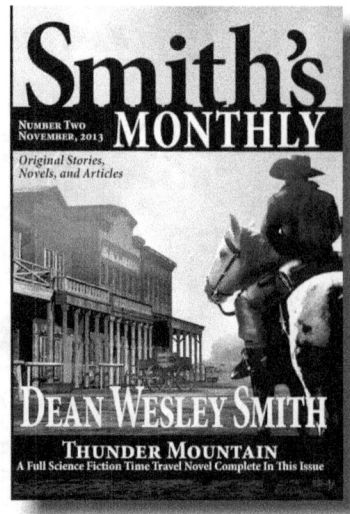

#2... November 2013

#3... December 2013

#4... January 2014

#5... February 2014

#6... March 2014

#7... April 2014

#8... May 2014

#9... June 2014

#10... July 2014

#11... August 2014

#12...September 2014

#13...October 2014

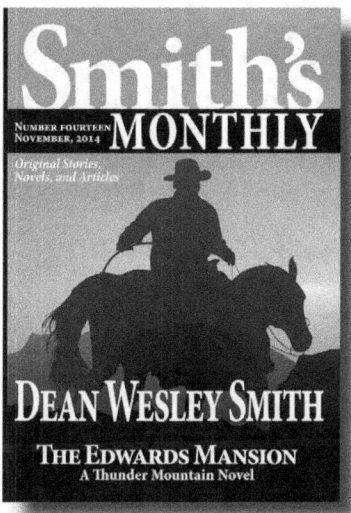

#14...November 2014

#15...December 2014

#16...January 2015

#17...February 2015

#18...March 2015

Thank You!!

Walter White Cat and I would like to thank
the following wonderful people who support my blog
and my work through Patreon.
Your support is very important to me.
Thanks!

Rob Cornell

Erick Lindman

Christopher Ridge

Miguel Angel Alonso Pulido

Nancy Hendrickson

Ryan M. Williams

Jacob Proffitt

Ryan Whiteside

Marian Goldeen

John Connelly

Gary Speer

Megan Bryce

Michelle Tatam

Ann Tucker

Kari Wolfe

Scott Gordon

Kathryn Rooney

Sherman Cox

Fen

Livia Quinn

Amri Ackers

Robin Brande

J.R. Murdock

Kathleen McClure

Michael Kelberer

Gunnar Gunderson

F.I. Goldhaber

Mary Jo Rabe

John Kilgallon

Dave Hendrickson

www.ingramcontent.com/pod-product-compliance
Lightning Source LLC
Chambersburg PA
CBHW081151170626
46813CB00009B/3149